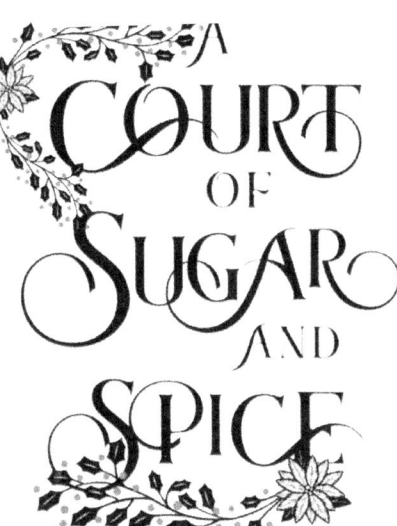

REBECCA F. KENNEY

This book is a work of fiction. Names, characters, places, and incidents are the product of the author's imagination or are used fictitiously. Any resemblance to actual events, locales, or persons, living or dead, is coincidental.

Copyright © 2022 by Rebecca F. Kenney

All rights reserved. In accordance with the U.S. Copyright Act of 1976, the scanning, uploading, and electronic sharing of any part of this book without the permission of the publisher is unlawful piracy and theft of the author's intellectual property. If you would like to use material from the book (other than for review purposes), prior written permission must be obtained by contacting the publisher at rfkenney@gmail.com. Thank you for your support of the author's rights.

First Edition: November 2022

This book is the creative work of one human author.
No generative AI was used in its development or writing.
No part or whole of this work may be used to train generative AI
in any capacity for any reason.

Kenney, Rebecca F.
A Court of Sugar and Spice / by Rebecca F. Kenney—First edition.

CONTENT GUIDANCE

Family death, violence, gore, monsters, blood, sexual threat, light bondage, light CNC, primal play, public sex

1
CLARA

The house rears up, mountainous and morose, craggy with dormer windows and crooked little slanted roofs and odd bits of towers, like pointed noses. It seems to peer down unhappily at Louisa and me, despite the fact that both of us have dressed impeccably for our arrival.

"I still say we don't need a guardian," mutters Louisa.

"Of course we don't. We're both over twenty. But we have no money, no place to go, and no useful skills."

"Your paintings—"

"Painting is not a useful skill." I taste the bitterness of Papa's frequent reminder on my tongue. Art does not pay. Not in this district. And due to the unreasonable conditions of Papa's will, I won't be able to afford to leave this district for another few years.

Louisa and I have been barred from accessing our inheritance until we turn thirty or until we marry, whichever comes first. In the meantime we are to live with a man Papa appointed as our guardian many years ago—our godfather, Uncle Drosselmeyer.

"Must we call him our uncle, though?" asks Louisa. "He isn't, not really. Just an old friend of Papa's."

"I suppose we'll call him whatever he wants to be called," I reply vaguely, occupied with counting our bags and trunks. The carriage driver doesn't wait for me to ascertain that we have everything—he merely chucks the reins and urges the horses ahead, as if he's eager to be gone from this place before nightfall. Fortunately all our luggage is accounted for.

"Come on, then. Might as well get it over with." Louisa hoists two bags over her shoulder and picks up a suitcase.

Other visitors to this house might have waited for the servants to help with the luggage, but Louisa and I are used to doing everything ourselves. Papa didn't trust servants, nor did he care to spend money on paying them when he had two perfectly good daughters to handle the chores.

"If only we could earn the money to move to Engelbourg, just the two of us. We could hire ourselves out to cook or clean." I pick up a carpetbag and drag our trunk by one handle. "Or mend. I can mend clothes."

"I doubt our guardian will take kindly to his wards scrubbing privies and floors." Louisa wrinkles her nose. "As for me, I plan to marry quickly so I can get my money."

"I'm not sure how many prospects you'll find here." With a grating lunge, I haul the trunk up the last stone step and pause, turning to survey the countryside around us—a bleak expanse of brown fields, leafless gray trees, dark distant moors, and black hills in the far distance, beneath a soggy gray sky.

"It's rutting unfair, that's what it is," moans Louisa, turning her back to the front door and following my gaze. "Not a house to be seen. Not even a barn with a strapping stable boy, or a flock of sheep with a virile young shepherd."

"Would you listen to yourself? You can't speak like that here. Uncle Drosselmeyer sounds like a very proper older gentleman. He must be, if he was Papa's dear friend."

"You're right. I can't imagine Papa having a rake of a friend with loose morals." Louisa pushes out her lower lip. "That would have been so interesting, though! I could have seduced him, and—"

"Seduced me?" says a low voice behind us. "Gracious, how shocking."

I whirl, my stomach plummeting. While we were gazing at the countryside, one of the large double doors behind us opened without so much as a squeak, and in the aperture stands a lean man in a dark suit. The suit isn't any style I've previously seen—it has multiple standup collars, their corners bent at random angles, and his entire tailcoat is slashed with pockets and rows of buttons in odd places. The cuffs splay wide, framing thin fingers laced with delicate brass rings, some featuring tiny gears or miniscule gems.

Uncle Drosselmeyer's face is narrow, with sharp triangular features and thin, compressed lips. He wears thick, brass-rimmed spectacles and sports a neat brown beard. It's difficult to tell his age.

"I'm so sorry," I gasp. "Don't mind Louisa, she—she—"

"I'm quite out of my mind," my sister says cheerfully, thrusting out her hand. "I often say the first thing that pops into my head. You must learn not to pay me any attention."

Drosselmeyer steps forward onto the snowy doorstep, taking the other handle of the trunk I'm dragging. "I make it a habit to always pay attention when a woman speaks to me. It's the ones who are out of their minds who have the most fascinating and insightful things to say."

"I like you," Louisa waggles a finger at him, smiling. "Yes, I think we'll get along just fine."

She hustles inside with her share of the baggage, and Drosselmeyer helps me with mine.

"Thank you for opening your home to us," I say. "I know it must be difficult, making space for two strangers."

"We may never have met in person, but I feel as if I know you both," he says. "Your father wrote letters about you, from the time you were very young. You might be surprised how many stories I know from your childhood."

"Oh." I can't decide if this revelation makes me feel more secure or uncomfortable.

"I'm sure Papa had plenty to say of me!" Louisa is darting from side to side of the entry hall, inspecting the giant portraits of moody ancestors. "Clara never does anything remotely rebellious. And everyone knows it's the rebels who make the best stories."

"He had plenty to say about both of you," Drosselmeyer replies. "Put your luggage on this platform here, and step back, if you please."

Once the luggage is piled onto the metal square he indicated, he opens a panel in the wall and flips a lever. With a clank and a whirr, the platform lurches into motion, lifts, and begins to glide up the staircase, following the line of the banister up to the second floor.

"Marvelous!" Louisa claps. "Papa said you were a great innovator."

"Did he?"

"Yes," I put in. "We would love to see your workshop."

"No one enters my workshop," says Drosselmeyer curtly. Then in a gentler tone he adds, "Though I could show you my exhibition room. It's where I display my inventions once they are completed. In fact, I'm hosting a dinner party tomorrow night, and many of the district's most esteemed families will be represented."

"You don't say." Louisa shoots me an excited glance. "May we attend this fine dinner?"

"Louisa," I hiss reproachfully.

But Drosselmeyer smiles. "Of course! You are part of the household now."

"Glorious!" Louisa claps her hands. "I know just what to wear."

She dances up the carpeted staircase, following the platform that carries our luggage. I follow more sedately, just behind our godfather.

"Do people buy the things you make?" I ask.

"Sometimes. Certain things I prefer to keep for myself."

"I understand that. There are some paintings I've done that I could never bear to part with."

"Yes, your father told me you were an artist. Didn't seem too pleased about it. Fritz could never see the value in beauty for beauty's sake—always thought a thing must have a purpose. But what is life without a little gratuitous beauty?"

"Exactly." Eagerness surges in my heart. Maybe here I'll have someone to speak with about art styles and different media, about perspective and color theory.

Louisa's room and mine are on the second floor, connected by a beautiful lavatory complete with a shining copper tub. The wood paneling is dark, and so is the furniture; but there are lovely porcelain vases on the heavy dressers and side tables, and each vase is filled with wintergrass, redbud branches, and fluffy white snowbloom.

Drosselmeyer helps us transfer the luggage from the stair-lift to the rooms. Before he leaves us to unpack, he says, "Dinner will be in the first-floor dining room at seven o'clock. You may go anywhere you like in the house, but the third floor is reserved for my workshop, my study, and my suite. Please respect my privacy."

Louisa is sitting on my bed, and after the door closes behind him she says, "When he puts it like *that*, it feels wrong to think about exploring the third floor. Why couldn't he have simply glowered and declared it forbidden? Then I would have no compunction about going up there. Now, if I do, I'll have *guilt*, because he framed it as a respectful request." She sighs, plucking at the corner of a crocheted blanket.

"Face it, Lou—he's neither a rake you can charm nor a monster you can hate." I throw her a satisfied smirk. "How very sad for you."

"It is. But that dinner tomorrow night—*that* has promise, provided the guests are not all stuffy old gentlemen and their wrinkled ladies."

"Age doesn't make someone uninteresting. I would argue the opposite."

"But it does make them unmarriageable." Louisa slides off my bed. "I'm off to hang up my dresses and see which ones need pressing. I suppose I'll have to press them myself, as usual—I haven't seen any servants, have you?"

"No. Perhaps Uncle Drosselmeyer shares Papa's dislike of hired help."

"Just our luck."

She disappears through the shared bathroom, and I can hear her humming and throwing things about as she unpacks.

My methods are far more effective—a simple matter of transferring my neatly folded clothes into drawers or the wardrobe, placing my painting kits on top of a bureau, and laying out my cosmetics on the dressing table. I'm rather fond of makeup; it's paint, after all, and I do love enhancing the natural beauty of a thing.

I pause to check my face in the dressing-table mirror. It's a decent mirror, though the edges are darkened and spotted with age. At least it doesn't distort my features.

My traveling dress is fine enough for dinner, so I don't bother to change. Instead I walk to the far end of my room, where the wall bellies outward into a bay window. There's a half-circle seat, thickly padded with cushions, with built-in drawers underneath. The window frames are ornately carved, arched and peaked like the windows in a chapel. The feathery curls of frost on the panes glow faintly orange with the last light of the setting sun. I press a palm to the cold glass, then think better of it and rub away my fingerprints with my sleeve.

Next I walk around the room, testing the gaslamps. They're all in fine working order except one, which tends to gutter and fade before flaring up again. I turn that one all the way down.

Louisa is still humming and thumping around in her room. Much as I love my sister, she tends to take over any excursion and dominate any room she's in. This could be my only chance to do a little exploring on my own.

Quietly I open my bedroom door and slip out into the hallway.

The beauty of the house charms me, from the coffered walls and gleaming wood floors to the ornamental ceilings and hand-carved molding. It's a lavish work of art, far different from the prosaic, plain house we had back in Lindgard. But then, Lindgard was a city of hardworking, prosaic people, intent on amassing wealth for no other reason than to possess it.

To me, wealth should be transitory. Money is simply a way to get more beauty.

I peek into several rooms on the second floor—a small library with an adjoining map room, a couple more guest rooms and bathrooms, and a large linen closet—and then I descend to the first floor. Off the main entry hall there's a parlor, then a billiard room.

A huge painting at the back of the billiard room catches my eye. It's a landscape, but like none I've ever seen—filled with oddly shaped trees, iridescent grass, and twisted figures half-hidden among leaves. The gilded frame tempts me, so I run my fingertips along it, delighting in the delicate curlicues—until my fingers encounter an odd bump, also gilded, but out of sync with the rest of the design. Puzzled, I feel around it, then press on it.

The bump gives just a little, and when I press harder, the painting pops loose and swings slightly outward.

My heartbeat speeds up as I swing the painting farther away from the wall.

Behind it is a secret door.

I should go tell Louisa what I've found. She'll be peeved if I go any farther without her.

But she always gets to discover things and do things. I'm more cautious by nature, so usually by the time I've analyzed a thing and decided in its favor, Louisa has already plunged right in.

That difference between us always confused my father. Perhaps he thought that I, as the creative type, had no right to *also* be well-organized and prudent. But artists come in all varieties. Some are impetuous, loud, and colorful, and some like to sit quietly, analyze a beautiful thing, and soak it right into their souls. Some like to keep all their paints and brushes perfectly organized.

Some like to occasionally make discoveries without the presence of their beloved but overenthusiastic sister.

I turn the knob of the secret door, and it yields easily. If Godfather Drosselmeyer didn't want anyone in here, surely he would have locked the door.

Cautiously I enter the dark space beyond. By the light leaking in from the billiard room, I locate a button on the wall. When I press it, several gaslamps ignite at once.

I step inside, pulling the painting and the secret door shut behind me.

I'm in a long, narrow room, a brilliant gallery filled with statuary, paintings, and artifacts.

A closer look at the artifacts beneath the bell jars and glass cases reveals items I can't quite identify—a cap dyed several shades of brown, a jeweled claw, a set of pearly white fangs on a gold chain, and a dagger that seems to glow faintly silver where it disappears into its sheath. Pinned to the wall there's a pair of dragonfly wings, much too large to have come from any dragonfly I've ever seen. Above them is a pair of antlers, sparkling white.

In a glass cabinet in one corner there's a tall golden staff with an amber orb at the top. And in that orb is an eyeball. I could swear when I glance away, then look back at it, the eyeball is pointing in a different direction.

The statues are strange, too. They seem to be carved of soapstone in various shades, from pale reddish-brown, to light jade, to creamy white, to soft gray. They resemble humans, but their bodies are longer, the proportions slightly different. Some of the figures' ears are like a fawn's or a calf's, while others are sleek and pointed. Their faces, too, are unexpected. Some run the normal human gamut of broad, narrow, rounded, symmetrical or lopsided. Others have distinctly bestial qualities—wolfish muzzles, bovine snouts, shrewd fox faces, insectoid jaws with mouthparts.

Did Godfather Drosselmeyer make these? I never heard Papa mention him being a sculptor.

A thump overhead startles me. Skittishly I race back to the hidden door, slip out, and push the painting back into its spot.

When I turn around, a wooden face is smiling at me with hideous cheer.

I stifle a scream with my palm.

The figure before me is life-sized—a wooden puppet dressed in a maid's black uniform, with a stiff wooden skirt and jointed wooden legs. Her wooden features have been carved and polished with such care they seem lifelike.

As I stare, thin wooden eyelids close over her eyes, then open again. Her painted mouth curves in a perpetual toothy smile, and she has glossy brown carved hair, with a round bun at the back of her neck. She's holding a feather duster.

With jerky steps, she minces past me and brushes the duster along the edges of the ornate painting. Then, with a crooked head tilt and that painted smile, she moves awkwardly sideways and begins dusting a bookshelf.

"Gracious," I breathe, backing away.

"You've never seen an automaton?" The voice from the doorway of the billiard room startles me. I jump hard, and Godfather Drosselmeyer chuckles.

"Forgive me." I press a hand to my chest. "No, I've never seen such a thing. How does it function?"

"Clockwork," he says. "You've seen the figures in music boxes or cuckoo clocks, how they move and repeat certain patterns?"

"Yes, but—"

"I've simply increased this one's size and optimized its performance for certain tasks. Nothing to it, once you understand the science."

I'm no scientist, but I've had a decent education—at home, of course, since Papa didn't trust schools. Still, I have a foundational understanding of physics and mechanics. Nothing I've learned supports the possibility of such an automaton.

But Drosselmeyer is an innovator. He deals with advanced technologies. Maybe he has unlocked some secret to self-motivated clockwork puppets.

Strange that I don't see any clockwork on the maid—just wooden joints.

"It's nearly time for dinner," says Drosselmeyer. "Go fetch your sister, if you would be so kind."

It's an obvious dismissal. He doesn't want me in this room any longer, nor is he prepared to entertain more questions about the automaton. Is it because he doesn't like explaining high-minded science to regular people? Or is there some other reason?

I hurry upstairs, dart into Louisa's room, and close the door. "I have something to tell you."

2
LOUISA

Clara's story delights me. Secret rooms? Puppet maids? Nothing this interesting ever happened at home.

I want to go see the secret room at once, but Clara makes me finish unpacking first, and by the time I'm done, we have to go down for dinner. Lucky for me, dinner is served to us by a pair of wooden automatons—both women, both wearing black uniforms. Their movements are jerky, and there's a faint creak of wood sometimes, but they're practically soundless.

"Why use these and not real people?" I ask.

"Cheaper," says Drosselmeyer. "And less annoying."

"But surely real people could accomplish a wider range of tasks," Clara puts in.

"You'd be surprised. How's your roast beef?"

"Delicious," I reply. "And on that note—what's the situation as far as 'beef' in this area? And when I say 'beef,' I mean beefy men."

"Louisa!" gasps my sister.

"They don't have to be men of means," I continue airily. "When I marry, I'll have the means."

"Indeed." Drosselmeyer cuts a piece of meat. "Perhaps you forget, however, that as your guardian, I must approve any match you desire to make."

Clara kicks me under the table, a clear sign that I must not get angry. I must not rebel too openly or protest too loudly. Loud, careless Louisa, always someone to be quieted and apologized for.

I am so damn sick of hearing her say, "Louisa!" to me in that reproachful tone.

I am so damn sick of being treated like a rebel who must be curbed, simply because I want to make my own choices and enjoy my life the way I see fit.

But for now, as much as I hate to admit it, Clara is right. I need to appear docile and obedient, at least until I figure out the character of our new guardian.

"Of course, Uncle Drosselmeyer," I say sweetly, with a huge smile. "I shall be delighted to rely on your judgment."

As we finish dinner, I watch Drosselmeyer closely. Despite the slipshod appearance of his clothing, he takes care of himself. He's lean beneath the clothes, and strong, judging from the way he handled our luggage upstairs, on the way to the rooms. His beard is perfectly trimmed.

Clara said he isn't someone I can seduce. I beg to differ. I can seduce anyone. The postman, our neighbor's gardener, the tutor Papa reluctantly hired to help Clara with math, the baker's son, the assistant at the book shop... and many more. Can I help it if men find me irresistible? Women, too. There was the neighbor girl I kissed when I was thirteen, the baker's buxom daughter, and a girl in the village choir whom I fingered to climax under her robe during a festival performance.

I prefer men, though—there's something so primal in the way they want me, the way their bodies react so boldly, prominently. I love a low, helpless male moan so much. I wonder if I could tease one out of Drosselmeyer.

But I need to be strategic about this. Seducing him probably isn't the way to get him to approve my choice of a husband, whenever I make that choice. This may call for a different kind of manipulation. And it starts with me finding out what he's hiding on the third floor.

After dinner, Drosselmeyer takes us down a long hallway toward the back of the house. He shows us the ballroom, the second dining room, the music room, and the corridor leading to the conservatory. There's another hallway that apparently leads to the kitchens and the old servants' quarters, but we continue onward, stopping before a pair of huge double doors, inlaid with chips of porcelain or glass or something—a mosaic of sorts. Clara seems very impressed by it.

Drosselmeyer throws a lever beside the doors, and I hear the faint hiss of gas through piping.

"Welcome," says Drosselmeyer, "to my showroom." And he flings open the doors.

Beyond, uplit by golden gaslight, lies an immense domed space, huge enough to swallow us up—so enormous I feel like an ant beneath a giant's bell jar. Iron beams crisscross overhead, supporting the large curved panes of glass, a frosty layer between us and the black night. To some faraway traveler, the glass dome must glow like an amber beacon amid the stretches of bleak countryside.

In the center of the sprawling tiled floor is a giant round platform with circular tiers of shelves. On the shelves repose various mechanical contraptions, mostly of the clockwork variety. Other knickknacks, bits, and bobs are tucked away on the rows of shelving that line the left-hand wall, and I catch a glimpse of more items secreted in glass cabinets to my right.

Amid the bronze gleam and the brassy glitter, Clara seems utterly overcome. "My god," she breathes, then covers her mouth. "I'm sorry for using strong language, but—it's so incredibly beautiful."

Beneath his neatly pointed beard, Drosselmeyer's mouth parts in a smile. He steps over to a crank on the wall and begins to work it, and as he does, the circular platform starts to revolve slowly. Once it picks up speed, he lets it go, and it continues turning without further interference.

"These are primarily items for household and business use," he says. "But there's something back here I think you'll appreciate a good deal more."

He leads us around the revolving platform, into the rear half of the room—and this time I gasp in tandem with Clara.

The entire back section of the space is occupied by an enormous dollhouse, built right out of the wall, with its first floor about knee-high. Tiny gaslamps gleam in its windows, illuminating parlors, hallways, bedrooms, a kitchen, a dining space, even an attic.

"Watch." Drosselmeyer opens a panel nearby and pushes a few buttons. With a soft whirr, figures begin to move through the interior spaces of the dollhouse, gliding along prescribed paths.

The whole thing is as strange as it is fantastic. First of all there's the unusual size of the dolls—they're each about the length of my forearm, from elbow to middle finger—which makes the house itself simply enormous as a plaything. But it's not a plaything, of course, because it belongs to a grown man, an inventor who for some reason has spent his time outfitting the entire thing with miniature furniture.

I suppose when you build practical things to sell, you must sometimes indulge in a passion project on the side. But it seems an odd choice for a man like him—carving these wooden dolls or puppets and setting them into a furnished house.

"Can they come out of the doors? Or look out the windows?" I ask.

"No, they do precisely what they are made to do, and no more," replies Drosselmeyer.

"Hm." I walk along the front of the house, peering inside. The dolls inside look a little off to me—strangely proportioned, somehow. They have fierce eyes and grimly painted smiles. Some have sharp teeth and pointed ears. Others have tiny wooden claws.

"May I touch one?" Clara asks. No wonder she wants to look more closely; every doll's outfit is painted onto their body in exquisite detail. Some even have tiny cloaks of real satin.

"This is my newest addition." Drosselmeyer reaches toward the front door of the dollhouse, where stands a male doll with handsome carven features and a scarlet uniform, like a soldier's. "This one is a bit of an experiment. He isn't just a doll, see?" He tweaks something on the doll's back, and its mouth opens wide. "You can place a nut just here, and crack the shell between his jaws."

"Oh, I want to try!" I exclaim. "Where are the nuts?"

Clara frowns, but Drosselmeyer chuckles. "In the kitchen. There's a row of canisters, all labeled."

try to be careful, but sometimes my limbs end up in different places than I expect them to. Sometimes my arms swing wider or my legs step farther than I anticipate. I'm naturally clumsy, I suppose.

I hate that I ruined Drosselmeyer's newest piece of craftsmanship on my first night in his house. Perhaps, if I can fix it well enough, he'll never notice what happened.

On a nearby wheeled cart there are a few tools—among them a small tub of paste. But I don't have time to glue the bit of wood back into place now. Maybe I can do it tonight, when I plan to be out and about, exploring.

I slip the bit of wood into my pocket and rejoin the others.

When I'm finally back in my room, I take turns with Clara in the bathroom and then crawl into bed, yawning and exclaiming about how tired I am. She seems surprised that I don't want to sit up and talk about our new home. I do, eventually, but that can wait. Right now all I can think about is repairing the Nutcracker and then going to the third floor.

Back home, the neighbors called me flighty. Distractable. Prone to flit from one point of interest to the next. All that is true, but sometimes I fixate on a thing, and I simply cannot think of anything else until I've done it.

I wait until I'm sure everyone is asleep. Then I wrap a soft robe around myself and transfer the Nutcracker's sliver of wood from the pocket of my dress to the pocket of my robe. I ease my bedroom door open and tiptoe out.

I should have taken a candle. The gaslamps are all turned down, and the hall is nearly pitch black. Somehow I manage to feel my way forward until my foot, probing ahead, encounters empty air. The staircase.

Step by step I move down it. The uncurtained foyer windows admit some moonlight, so I'm able to locate a candle and matches on a side table near the parlor doors. As I shake out the match after lighting the wick, I notice chains drawn across the front doors, secured with heavy locks. There are iron locks on the windows too. Strange. But the house is filled with one-of-a-kind inventions—I suppose Drosselmeyer must take precautions against thieves.

Candle in hand, my nightgown whispering against the carpet, I glide down the long hallway to the back of the house. The darkly paneled walls reflect a hazy golden blur as the candle flame passes. I trail my free hand along the panels, counting them idly, until my hand brushes over something that isn't a wall panel.

I turn—

And there's a face leering at me.

Shock roars through my body, and I yelp, leaping back.

When nothing happens, I lean forward cautiously, holding out the candle.

It's one of Drosselmeyer's automatons, standing motionless in an alcove, grinning.

"You're fucking creepy, you know that?" I whisper to it. "But I suppose it's not your fault."

The thing doesn't move. Not a twitch.

"Right. Carry on." I give it a two-fingered salute and continue down the corridor.

Once I reach the showroom, I flip the lever for the gaslight and struggle with the doors. They're heavy, but with a defiant shove, I manage to push one door partway open and squeeze through the aperture. I'm thicker-bodied than my sister, mostly because she forgets to eat when she's painting. In fact, when she's deep in a creative spell, she usually lives off whatever sweets we happen to have around—cookies, sugarplums, toffee, peppermint sticks. Not that Papa ever permitted many of those, either, but I managed to smuggle them in thanks to our obliging young postman. If there's one thing my sister and I share, it's a love of sweets.

I can't stay in the showroom long, not with the whole place lit up to high heaven. I have no idea if Drosselmeyer's bedroom windows face this way; it's more likely they'd face the front of the house. But on the off chance he might notice his showroom shining through the night like an earthbound star, I'd better hurry.

After unsealing the tub of paste on the work cart, I reach into my pocket to get the splinter, only to slice my finger on the sharp edge.

"Ow, damn it!" I inspect the damage to my fingertip. A small cut, but it seems eager to bleed everywhere and make my night more difficult. Lovely.

More swears spill from my lips as I daub paste onto the sliver of wood. The pale glue turns pink with my blood, but it should work just as well.

I pick up the Nutcracker and settle the splinter into the crevice along his arm. I press it tight for a few seconds, waiting for the glue to set. Blood from my finger is getting on his shoulder, too. I'll have to wipe that off before I leave.

Suddenly the Nutcracker vibrates in my hands. I nearly drop him. "Shit," I hiss. "What the hell?"

My naughty tongue is courtesy of Clara's math tutor. He taught me all kinds of words I could say while I came on his dick. I was sorry to see him go when his sessions with my sister came to an end. He had very fine equipment.

The Nutcracker remains inert, so I decide I imagined the vibration. Firmly I press on the splinter again. Just a moment more, and then I can leave this place and go up to the third floor.

A shudder runs through the Nutcracker, energy traveling from him into my hands—or is it the other way around?

I stare at him, at the pink circles on his cheeks, the sharp angles of his eyebrows, the crisp line of his jutting jaw, and the faint pattern of the wood grain, visible through the glossy paint on his face.

According to Drosselmeyer, he creates most of his puppets with specific movements and tasks. Maybe this one moves, too, and he didn't tell us about it.

Again the doll spasms in my hands—and I could swear he grows a fraction larger.

"Something is very wrong with you," I whisper. "I think I'm done fixing you now. You can go back to guarding the dollhouse."

I reach out to put him back on the doorstep, but his jointed body bucks, extends, explodes to five, six—no, ten times his size—he's out of my hands, poised stiffly on one knee on the tiled floor, while ripples of green light roll over his wooden body. I recoil as he shudders, flares brighter for a moment, and then goes still.

He looks different. Still stiff and jointed like a puppet, but life-size now, and a bit less—wooden. And the nut-cracking lever on his back has disappeared.

He's staring down at the floor, his black hat firmly in place, one fist planted on the tile.

Then his head jerks up, and he's staring at me.

He's alive.

Incomprehensibly, undeniably alive.

His red mouth works as if it's difficult for him to move it, and his cheeks look stiff as boards. The corners of his jaw unhinge a bit as he opens his mouth. I shudder at the sight.

"Mortal girl," he croaks. "You will assist me."

"Excuse me—that's mortal *woman* to you," I say, breathless.

"Help me up."

Something in his manner irritates me. Besides which, he's a damn puppet come to life, and I'm honestly reluctant to touch him.

Maybe I'm dreaming. I slap my own cheek hard to be sure. It stings, so I must be awake.

The Nutcracker stares at me. "What is that? Some type of human greeting?"

"Yes, that's a human greeting." Sarcasm feels good. It steadies me. "Why do you keep saying 'mortal' and 'human' that way? What are you?"

He places jointed fingers against the base of the dollhouse, rising with several creaks and grunts of effort. "I was—I am—a prince of Faerie."

I stare. "Indeed. And I am the Queen of this land."

"Really?" He looks me up and down doubtfully. "You don't look it. I thought you were simply a guest of that horrible hunter."

"Hunter?"

"The man who brought you in here to stare at me—at us. Drosselmeyer."

Curious as I am about the mysteries underlying his words, we can't discuss them here, with the lights blazing.

"Can you walk?" I ask.

He crooks one of his legs and slides it forward awkwardly. When he tries to take another step, he wobbles and almost crashes to the floor. I catch him, nearly screaming at the strange feel of his body. It's like—living wood. Slightly pliant, like a sapling, but with a polished, unyielding texture.

"You're going to tell me everything," I say. "But first we have to get out of this room, and I have to go get my sister. I know somewhere safe I can put you in the meantime."

"I'm not an object to be stowed away," he grunts as we hobble across the showroom. "I am—"

"A Fae Prince, yes, yes. We'll get to that. For now, do shut up."

"You know," he says airily. "I don't think I like you much, human."

"The feeling is increasingly mutual."

Thank the stars he doesn't talk any more until I get him safely into the secret gallery Clara told me about. Bless my sister for her need to tell me every little thing, including how to open the painting that conceals the door. Goodness knows we have our differences, but she and I always talk to each other, about everything. It's the only way we survived our restrictive upbringing.

"Stay," I tell the Nutcracker.

The pink circles on his cheeks seem to darken. "The insolence of you mortals. It's not to be borne."

"You'll have to bear it, since it seems you're in some kind of trouble and I'm your only hope." I smile sweetly at him. "You might want to lean against something before you fall over."

3
CLARA

"Wake up, Clara. Wake up!"

I blink, dazed by the sudden light of a candle. "Louisa?"

"There's something I must show you, right now! Come!" My sister's eyes are wild, her fingers tight on my arm.

"Why? What did you—oh heavens, did you go up to the third floor?"

"Of course not. Come with me."

Snatching a robe, I follow her downstairs, then through the concealed door behind the painting. "I already know about this room, Louisa," I grumble. "What do you think—oh! Oh my god—what is *that*?"

"That," says Louisa triumphantly, "is the Nutcracker."

"I am not a Nutcracker," says the tall figure. "I am a prince of Faerie. King of the Court of Delight, actually, or I would be by now, if that Fae hunter Drosselmeyer had not captured and cursed me."

"Right. I'm going back to bed." I turn my back on both of them.

But Louisa snatches my wrist, pulls up my sleeve, and pinches my arm, hard.

"Ow!" I jerk away from her.

"You're not dreaming." She seizes my shoulders. "I thought I was, too, but this is real. *He's* real."

"I can explain all this in very simple words—so simple even mortals can understand," offers the Prince.

I peer around my sister, frowning at him.

She sighs. "Yes, he talks like that. Has a very poor view of humans, apparently, even though one was clever enough to 'capture and curse' him, so he says."

"Drosselmeyer is not just any human." The Nutcracker takes an awkward step nearer to us, holding onto the wall. "He is far more intelligent than most of your kind, and he's been hunting my race since he was quite young. He has studied us for decades—learned our weakness, developed poisons, traps, and weapons to subdue us. And he's a sorcerer, specifically gifted with the ability to cast terrible curses. Most of the dolls, puppets, or automatons you see in this house are cursed Fae, trapped here and forced to do his bidding."

"I *knew* those automatons weren't scientifically possible," I exclaim. "So why are you moving and talking and—life-sized?"

"My blood had something to do with it," says Louisa slowly. "I broke a little piece off the Nutcracker when I dropped him, and when I tried to glue it back on tonight, I cut my finger. My blood got on him—in him, I suppose." She points to the Nutcracker's arm, where a long sliver of the wood has been clumsily replaced.

"Yes, your mortal blood interfered with the spell temporarily," says the Nutcracker. "But I fear the effect won't last much longer. To be permanently freed from the curse, I must return home to Faerie and immerse myself in the Unending Pool. Only then will I regain my true form and my powers."

I can hardly grasp what he's saying—it seems so foolishly fantastical, like something out of a child's storybook. What if he's actually some local farmer's son whom Louisa convinced to dress up like a Nutcracker and trick me? Though when would she have had time to make such a costume, or consort with any locals?

Frowning, I approach the Nutcracker and tug at his arm. He still feels wooden, though more malleable than before.

"What about everyone else who is trapped here?" I ask. "Don't you care about them? Aren't they your people, too?"

"Of course I care." He looks down his neatly carved nose at me. "But if I don't return quickly and reclaim my throne in Faerie, the Court of Dread will take over my kingdom. Their king may have already invaded our lands. My priority must be re-establishing my rule and protecting everyone else in the kingdom. After that, perhaps I can find a way to free the others who are trapped here."

"I can dribble more blood on them," Louisa offers.

"I'm afraid it would require too much of your blood," the Nutcracker says. "My curse is new, but many of them have been cursed for years. The amount of human blood it would take to enliven them, to keep them mobile long enough to get them through the portal to Faerie—it would kill both of you. I suspect you wouldn't like that plan."

"Not much," Louisa says dryly.

"If you knew what Drosselmeyer was doing, why haven't you tried to help the others he's captured?" I ask the Prince.

"The portal he uses opens in a different part of Faerie every time—it's impossible to predict where or when it will appear. Drosselmeyer has cursed the portal so no Fae may pass from our realm to his, unless he wishes it. We have other doorways to the human world, but the few who use them haven't been able to find Drosselmeyer's house."

"But why would Drosselmeyer do this?" I ask. "There must be a reason."

"Why do humans hunt anything? For hunger, or for sport." The Nutcracker looks at me, a desperate sadness brimming in his green eyes. "Please, you have to help me get home. Please help me save my people."

Louisa snorts. "*Now* you have nice manners?" She tugs on my arm, pulling me aside and muttering, "What if this one and his people are evil? What if Drosselmeyer is protecting the human world from their kind? We shouldn't interfere."

She has a point. In most of the legends I've read, the Fae are wicked creatures, prone to torturing hapless humans, replacing children with changelings, and encouraging all sorts of debauchery. We had a huge old book about faeries—there were sketches in it that Papa would have ripped out if he'd known they were there. Sketches of naked Fae coupling in every conceivable position.

Biting my lip, I eye the Nutcracker's tall form. His uniform is stiff, like very heavy parchment or hard leather, and the hem of his jacket falls to his thigh, so I can't tell if he has genitals of any kind. What does he look like in his true form? And has he participated in any debauched revels?

Goodness, I'm thinking like Louisa. I must stop it.

"Even if we wanted to help you, we have no idea how to get you to Faerie," I tell him.

"The portal Drosselmeyer uses is in this house. It must be," says the Nutcracker desperately. "Listen, I can feel myself hardening again—"

Louisa snorts, a sharp burst of hysterical laughter, and nearly drops her candle.

The Nutcracker quirks an eyebrow at her.

"Never mind," she chokes. "What were you saying about getting hard?"

The circles on his cheeks turn a deeper shade of pink. "Ah, I see the joke now. How delightful that you can indulge in carnal mockery while I'm suffering."

Louisa is still giggling, trying to muffle the sounds. When she's overtired, she sometimes goes into fits of laughter she can't control.

"It's not you," I assure the Nutcracker. "She's tired. We'll look around for this portal, and when we find it we'll use blood to wake you up again. What exactly should we look for?"

The Nutcracker's features are visibly stiffening. Words leak between his teeth as his lower jaw locks back into place. "A door—to nowhere."

His body tightens, shrinking smaller and smaller until he's lying on the floor, a wooden soldier doll with jointed limbs and black boots. Completely inanimate, though I suspect he can still see and hear in this state.

I pick him up carefully. "Louisa, would you *try* to stop laughing? We need to put him back where he was. And then you need to get some sleep."

"What about looking for the Faerie portal?" She bursts into more giggles. "I hear myself saying it, and it's just—it's ridiculous. This is all ridiculous."

"We can't search for it tonight. We need rest. Perhaps tomorrow, during Drosselmeyer's party, we'll have a chance to sneak up to the third floor and look around."

The next evening, Louisa and I dress in our finest clothes, and she lets me do her makeup, which is unusual. She typically goes to parties with barely a brush of powder on her face. She's pretty enough without it, of course. Hers is that sharp, bright-eyed, vivacious prettiness that never fails to catch men's attention. Not many women are immune to her, either.

As for me—well, an elderly great-aunt once told Papa that I had "a quiet kind of loveliness." Which is true. But I'd be lying if I said I hadn't wished for Louisa's impetuous brilliance, more than once in my life.

She's wearing a gown of rich rose that perfectly complements her golden hair. I'm wearing one of deep green, just right for my coloring and my auburn locks. We haven't been girls in a few years, and propriety dictates we pin our hair up for a formal party such as this, but both of us have left as many curls down as we dare.

Louisa and I spent most of the day wandering the gardens or browsing the library shelves. I knew if we spent too much time around Drosselmeyer, my sister would be tempted to ask him questions, and we can't afford to raise his suspicions—not if we're going to discover the truth of all this.

Fortunately, after breakfast, Drosselmeyer went up to his workshop on the third floor. We haven't seen him since then—except once, when he came down to let in some florists, workers, and serving girls, all hired for tonight's party. They've been working alongside the automatons to prepare the house, and none of them seem to think anything strange about the moving puppets. I suppose Drosselmeyer's reputation as an inventor has spread throughout the countryside, and that's as much as most people care to know.

It's strange to me how many people can see the wonder of a thing and simply accept it, without inquiring why it was made or how it works. Yet as Louisa and I stand near the staircase, beside an urn overflowing with scarlet poinsettias, wintergrass, and snowbloom, I see it over and over—people gliding into the house, exclaiming delightedly over the automatons and taking drinks from the trays they hold, without questioning the puppets' presence at all.

In fairness, I did nearly the same thing. I questioned the puppets' existence internally, but then I let it go. I won't make that mistake again.

"This party is so fabulous, isn't it, Clara?" Louisa whispers. Once several guests have arrived, she dances off to mingle with them, chattering merrily to perfect strangers as if she has known them all her life.

If only I had such a gift.

The new arrivals greet Drosselmeyer at the door, pausing briefly while he gestures politely to me and says, "Allow me to introduce my ward, Clara."

I smile and give a little curtsy, and the guests acknowledge me with a nod, a bob, or a bow of their own. Beyond that, I don't attempt conversation, so they pass on, taking their drinks from the automatons and moving into the other rooms of the house, which are all open and brightly lit, smelling of cinnamon, apples, and spiced punch. We are nearing the midwinter holidays, and signs of the season are everywhere.

I gaze around the foyer, wishing I could depict all of this in my own style. I'd do a panoramic painting of the entire scene on huge canvases, and then I'd create smaller still-life vignettes, focusing in on the exquisite details—the drape of evergreen boughs, the glow of ruby-red berries, the hazy gaslight on the edges of gilt frames. An elegant beringed hand sliding down the banister. The curl of a man's hair against his collar.

I don't dare bring my sketchbook and pencils downstairs. But in my mind, I try to capture each image and save it for later.

Once everyone has arrived, we transition to the dining room, where we're served a delicate soup of winter squash, tiny potatoes drenched in butter and sprinkled with herbs, succulent slices of duck breast, garlic-buttered mushrooms, glazed carrots, soft bread rolls, and rich cakes topped with syrupy nuts and fruit. It's all delicious, but I can barely enjoy the food, because I'm too busy sneaking glances at Godfather Drosselmeyer.

He certainly doesn't look like an infamous Fae hunter, in his slightly untidy suit and shiny spectacles. He looks like a reclusive yet modestly charming inventor—affable, humble, and likable. Not the type of man who would turn living beings into his slaves.

But the objects in the hidden gallery certainly looked rather otherworldly, even Fae. And unless Louisa and I were the victims of a strange shared dream, complete with tactile sensation, the Nutcracker actually came to life last night and told us he was a Fae Prince.

Louisa doesn't seem bothered at all by the possibility that a Fae realm might exist. She's happily ensconced between a rotund, pleasant-looking gentleman in his thirties and a pimply young man with bulging eyes. Both seem very eager to monopolize her attention.

Finally, Drosselmeyer signals the end of the interminable dinner by rising, laying down his napkin, and saying, "Ladies and gentlemen, I know you're all eager to see what I've been working on this year. We'll go and observe my creations now, and I'll demonstrate some of them as well. There will be a silent auction for these pieces, but remember you can also place orders with my factory across the river in Surrach."

Everyone rises from the table, chattering excitedly. They pour out of the dining room and down the hall in Drosselmeyer's wake.

Louisa appears at my elbow. Somehow she divested herself of her two admirers. "We'll wait until they're all fascinated by something he's showing them," she murmurs. "Something flashy. While they're occupied, I'll get the Nutcracker. If anyone notices me taking it, you create a distraction."

"What sort of distraction?"

"God, darling, I can't plan everything myself, can I? You'll think of something."

She dances off again. Apprehension tightens my stomach, but I try to look pleasant and enthusiastic as I move with the guests into the showroom.

Here too, are the signs of holiday festivities. Garlands and red ribbons swoop at intervals from the domed ceiling. Tiny brass stars on strings dangle above, twinkling and flashing. There's an aroma of vanilla and cinnamon, along with the faint scent of metal and grease.

I sidle along the edge of the room until I'm near the giant dollhouse. A few guests gather near it, exclaiming over the "new" characters which have been added since they were last here. One man in a bulging waistcoat picks up the

Nutcracker, ogling the wooden soldier through his monocle.

"Look at this, Herb," he says to the man beside him, and he waggles the Nutcracker's jaw. "Think we can convince Drosselmeyer to alter this one into a doll who sucks cock?"

He's speaking low, but I can hear every word, and I'm deeply shocked. I've never heard anyone speak like that in polite company.

The monocled man turns the Nutcracker upside down, peering between his legs.

"Lord Banquist." Louisa's bright tone distracts him, and he sets the Nutcracker down.

"Why, yes, my dear, what can I do for you?" His tone is thick, oily, ingratiating. I don't like the way he looks at my sister. But she bends at the waist slightly, bowing her shoulders forward so her cleavage is even more dramatic, while she twirls her fan.

"Would you be a darling and find one of those funny automatons with drinks?" she says. "I haven't had nearly enough wine, and I want to be just a little—bit—naughty." With each word, she walks her fingers farther up the monocled man's shoulder.

"Of course, my dear." He hurries off, accompanied by his friend.

"Did you see the way he looked at you?" I murmur. "You shouldn't encourage it, Lou."

"The crawling eyes of men aren't something I fear," she says. "They can do nothing to me here, except what I allow. Why shouldn't I use their cravings to my benefit?"

"Being looked at that way would make me feel so cheap, though. Cheap and dirty."

"Poor Clara." She circles my shoulders with her arm and squeezes. "Men are going to look at you that way whether you like it or not. You can fret and stew about it, or you can turn it into power."

"But they *shouldn't*," I say stoutly. "The world needs to change."

"Maybe it will. But until it does, I choose to manipulate what *is* to my advantage, rather than pining after what should be. Ah, look there! Our two-faced godfather is beginning to show off his wares."

First Drosselmeyer demonstrates a clockwork device that can fly, transporting small objects through the air. He marks a target location with a projected dot of light, and the clockwork flier carries a rose from his hand to the lady he indicated. A storm of clapping ensues.

"Now?" I whisper to Louisa.

"Not yet."

The crowd demands a second demonstration of the flier, and this time Drosselmeyer marks a spot high up in the dome—a tiny ledge near its apex. Everyone cranes their necks to watch, even the monocled gentleman and his friend, who are returning with the wine Louisa requested.

"Now!" I hiss, and Louisa nods. She picks up the Nutcracker, holding it among the folds of her skirts as she makes her way through the crowd. I circle the room on the opposite side, scanning the crowd for anyone who might notice our exit. All are distracted, watching the flier's progress toward the arched ceiling.

Louisa is safely out of the room, and I'm about to follow when I happen to glance at Drosselmeyer's face. At the same moment, his attention veers from the flier and he meets my eyes.

A current of awareness passes between us. His expression changes as our gazes lock, and I can see it in his face—a wordless realization that I *know*.

His eyes flare slightly wider.

And in that moment I believe everything the Nutcracker said.

I hold Drosselmeyer's gaze a second longer. Then I duck out of the showroom and follow Louisa.

4
LOUISA

When Clara catches up to me, she's breathless and flushed.

"He knows we know," she gasps.

"What? Who?"

"Drosselmeyer. He looked at me, and I looked at him, and I just—somehow he understood that I know his secret."

"You're not making sense."

"He can't leave his guests, not right now, but he'll make excuses to get away as soon as he can. We have to hurry."

"Right." I tuck the Nutcracker under my arm and gather my skirts so I can take the stairs faster.

We mount quickly to the second floor, then follow the hall to the end, where the third-floor staircase is.

But when we reach the landing at the top of the third-floor steps, there's a door barring our way. And it's locked.

"Of course he would lock it," I pant. "He's too smart to leave his private space open with so many people in the house. Fuck."

"Don't say that," Clara exclaims. She peers more closely at the lock. "This isn't like any lock I've ever seen. There's no keyhole."

"Maybe it's a magical lock. Perhaps the Nutcracker knows something about it. I'll wake him up." I peel the bit of sticking plaster off the cut on my finger. Then I bite it until the blood wells out again, and I daub the Nutcracker's chest generously with the blood.

"Ugh, don't paint him with it," says Clara.

"I want to be sure he stays full-sized long enough this time," I tell her, slathering on more blood. The wooden figure begins to shake in my hands, and a moment later the Nutcracker explodes to his full size. He stares down at his bloodstained jacket, then throws an annoyed glance at me.

I give him a merry smile. "Such a joy to see your frowning face again, Your Irritableness."

"You'd be irritable too if you were stuck under a curse," Clara says. "We need to get through this door, Nutcracker, but there's a strange lock."

Stiffly he leans toward it, narrowing his eyes. "An iron lock, so Fae can't touch it. It can only be opened by the application of mortal blood. And it might be spelled to work with Drosselmeyer's blood specifically."

"Let's hope not." I squeeze my finger harder, forcing more red drops to well out through the slit in the skin. "Why is there so much blood involved with magic?"

"Blood is life," says the Nutcracker simply. "And it contains salt, as well as trace amounts of iron—not in a form that can harm a Fae, but potent enough to serve as a catalyst for spellwork or a disrupter for curses."

"So the more of my blood I splatter on you, the more Fae you'd become?" I dab several drops onto the iron lock.

"My physical body would be increasingly restored, yes, but the effect would not be permanent, nor would I regain my powers," says the Nutcracker. "That can only happen when I bathe in the Unending Pool, the original source of Fae magic and the only place where the most powerful curses can be dispelled."

"What if you *drank* my blood?"

"Ugh, Louisa." Clara winces.

"Just a question." I smear more crimson onto the lock, and it responds by vibrating abruptly. Gears whirr inside, and something clicks. When I try the door handle, it moves, and the door swings open.

"You can answer that question later," I tell the Nutcracker. "Right now we need to hurry. Drosselmeyer suspects that we're up to something. He had a sort of eye-to-eye conversation with my sister."

The Nutcracker glances at Clara.

"There were no actual words," she says apologetically. "I just got this feeling, like an understanding passed between us."

"Hm." He keeps looking down at her as we move down the third-floor hall. He seems better able to walk this time, perhaps because of the extra blood I gave him. "Your name is Clara?"

"Yes."

Something in the way he says her name, and the soft tone of her response, and the way they're looking at each other with such interest—it irks me. I push between them, forging ahead.

"I seem to remember saying we need to hurry," I say brightly. "Let's hunt for this portal to Faerie. What does it look like?"

"As I told your sister, it looks like a door to nowhere," says the Nutcracker.

"That's so helpful. Could you be a bit more specific?"

"You'll know it when you see it."

I round on him, incensed. "We're trying to help you."

"And I—" His wooden face flinches as if he smells something rancid. "I am—grateful. Thank you."

"That looked like it hurt. Not used to expressing gratitude, are we?"

"Not used to needing anyone's help," he says, low.

"I'm sure you had guards and servants and advisors helping you all the time. You probably never noticed. Typical for a careless, spoiled prince."

"Louisa!" Clara catches my arm and pulls me ahead, dropping her voice. "Why are you being so mean to him?"

"He annoys me. A stuck-up royal expecting us to be grateful that we get to put our home and our future at risk to help him." I snort and jerk away from her. "Oh, look—more doors. Perhaps His Monarchial Goodliness can help us open a few and look for this mysterious portal."

But the instant the Nutcracker touches a door handle, he gasps and recoils. "More iron. Drosselmeyer must have been afraid one of the cursed automatons would regain their faculties and find a way up here. He doesn't want any of his trophies escaping."

"Fine, we'll do it ourselves." I sigh. "Clara, you take the doors on the right. I'll check the ones on the left."

A couple of the doors are locked— prosaically so, no blood required. But halfway down the corridor we encounter two doors facing each other, each with iron locks like the one at the top of the stairs. I bite my finger again and paint each lock with my blood, and they both unlatch with a grating rasp.

I open the door on the left, while Clara ventures into the room on the right.

The space I enter is dark, but when I fumble along the wall by the door, I locate a thin gas line, which I follow up to a lamp. When I turn the switch, a long room comes into view, lined with heavy cabinets, drawers, and shelves. Green and amber bottles glimmer in the gaslight, each glass surface bearing a pasted label in swirling script. The drawers are labeled too, but I don't take time to read the words.

My gaze sweeps over a broad worktable, covered with wooden trays. The bottom and sides of some trays bear dark splotches, as if old blood has saturated the wood so many times it can't be scrubbed out.

Between the trays are small brackets containing tiny glass tubes, scalpels, pens, and other items I can't identify.

There's another table at the far end of the room, big enough for a very tall, very broad man to lie on it. Unlit gaslamps branch over it, and hanging from the table's edges are manacles and shackles that look to be made of iron, though I can't see them clearly in the gloom.

But the main feature of the room stands to my right. An upright circular frame, taller than I am, woven of leafless branches and coiling roots. It seems to have grown right out of the floorboards.

There's nothing inside it, nothing beyond it. It is simply a round doorway—to nowhere.

"My god," I say faintly. "I think I found it."

"Louisa!" Clara calls from another room. "You need to see this."

I'm tempted to stay where I am. When I look at the woven circle, something tugs deep in my heart—pulls me toward it. But Clara calls for me again, so I turn away and hurry into the room she opened.

And my jaw drops.

The room is filled with weapons and traps. Nearly-invisible nets that glimmer faintly in the light, spiked maces, slim swords, ropes studded with iron shards.

The Nutcracker stalks creakily into the room. "Some of these are the hunter's weapons and traps," he says. "The others are the weapons of my people, stolen from them when they were captured and cursed."

He points to an ax whose wedge-shaped head looks to be carved from ice, or from crystal. Its handle is beautifully woven of interlacing vines, knotted and hardened to form a solid grip.

"That was my friend Andil's weapon," he says. "She is one of the automatons who serves in the hunter's kitchen. I never knew what had happened to her until I was captured myself and saw her in her cursed form. Even before that, I suspected Drosselmeyer had taken her, but he has grown very sly in his work. He's skilled at entering our realm unseen. He used to capture only the unwary, the over-confident—but for the past two years he's been hunting seasoned warriors."

"And how did he capture you?" I ask.

He meets my eyes for the first time tonight, and his gaze is like a lightning bolt, piercing mine with a pain so fierce I can almost feel it in my own heart.

"I do not know," he replies. "I cannot remember the events of my capture, only that I woke up in a room of this house, bound to a table with iron shackles. There Drosselmeyer performed the curse that stripped me of my powers and turned me into this—this *thing*. He took me away at a most volatile time for my court, and left my people vulnerable to the invasion of the Rat King."

"The Rat King?" Clara's eyes widen.

"King of the Unseelie, Lord of the Court of Dread," says the Nutcracker. "I will take a weapon, and then we must find the portal with all haste."

"I found it," I say. "It's right across the hall, in some sort of study or laboratory. There's a table with chains and shackles there as well—probably the one you were bound to when you first arrived."

Clara meets my gaze, a faint triumph in her eyes, and I nod resignedly. No doubt about it now—Godfather Drosselmeyer is a Fae hunter.

Usually I have a more fluid notion of good and evil than Clara does, but she seems to deem the Prince worthy of our help, while I can't help wondering if there's something sinister about the Fae—some reason Drosselmeyer believes it's right to capture and confine them. How are Clara and I to know the true character of this Nutcracker prince? Should we really let him leave? What if he has done something inexpressibly wicked, and releasing him will only prompt him to do more evil?

"Can you lie?" I ask him abruptly.

The Nutcracker has picked up a Fae sword, rapier-thin and glittering like frost. He looks up from the blade at me.

"What is the point of that question?" he says quietly. "If I say 'no,' I could still be lying."

"I'm not sure we should let you leave." My fingers inch toward a weapon on a table nearby—a knife with a slight S-curve to its ice-blue blade. "What if you're actually some wicked monster whom our godfather removed from the world for a good reason?"

"He's not," protests Clara. "Louisa, I can feel that he's not."

My hand closes on the cool, pearly hilt of the dagger. "I'm not so sure. Why would a good friend of our father's—one to whom he entrusted us and our fortunes—why would he do something so wicked as to enslave creatures who are perfectly harmless?"

"I never said the Fae are perfectly harmless," replies the Nutcracker, holding my gaze. "Far from it. But those of Seelie-kind are more high-minded, just, and intelligent than humans. We live long and wisely. When we err, we learn from our mistakes and do not repeat them. Can you say the same of your race?"

"Not all humans are the same." I move toward him, knife in hand. "You despise us, yet you ask us to trust you over our father's dear friend. The arrogance of it." I laugh lightly, a nervous excitement flooding my body. I've never held a weapon like this, and it sends a thrill of power along my arm, through my heart.

The Nutcracker looks more human tonight than he did last time—his emerald-green eyes are less painted, more liquid—his limbs are less stiff, and his mouth is broader, softer. His square, jutting jaw is set, and his fierce gaze blends dark anguish and haughty courage.

"What would happen if I cut you with this, I wonder?" I tuck the tip of the dagger under his chin, tilting it up. "Would you bleed?"

"Louisa, what is wrong with you?" Clara gasps. "Stop this. I don't think he's tricking us."

"You've read the same stories I have," I throw at her. "The Fae are tricksters by nature."

"Now who's assuming that the members of a particular race are all the same?" says the Nutcracker dryly. The sword hangs from his hand, but he doesn't lift it or threaten me with it.

I let the blade trail down the carved lines of his throat, right to the edge of his collar. The material isn't painted on anymore—it has separated from his skin.

"We'll let you pass through into Faerie," I say. "But not alone. I'm going with you. We'll see if what you say is true."

I look up at Clara, expecting her to protest. But her eyes are alight with a craving that surprises me.

She's an artist, a lover of the beautiful and the wondrous. It shouldn't shock me that she wants to have a look at the Faerie realm. Cautious though she is in most areas of life, she occasionally makes a leap with me—like when our postman brought his good-looking cousin around one night. Clara and I crept out the back kitchen window and spent two hours with the boys in the garden shed. Later she told me she gave up her virginity there, in the dark, among the clay pots and the bags of seed.

Her tryst with the postman's cousin came after months of her expressing dissatisfaction that she was still sexually inexperienced. She made a careful choice to leave childhood behind that night.

Yes, she has moments of rebellion, but hers is a calculated recklessness, always with a reason. I do love that about her. And I love that she's not fighting me on this.

But the Nutcracker has other ideas.

"No," he says sternly. "You can't come to Faerie. Without me on the throne, the entire Seelie kingdom may be at war—or they may have already fallen to the Rat King and his armies."

"Wouldn't someone else have taken your place? Surely there's a line of succession," Clara says.

"It's not the same in Faerie as it is in human kingdoms. Our monarchs are magically bound to the realm they govern. The throne and the crown do not yield power until the former monarch dies or relinquishes the role willingly. I didn't die, so there could be no true succession. I've been alive, but trapped in another form, so I couldn't yield my rights to the next ruler. Which means the throne has been sitting empty, the crown untouched."

My mind churns through the logic of it. "Then the Rat King can't truly conquer your realm unless you yield it to him."

"He can't take my inherited power, no. But he can conquer in every other way that matters. He's already a king of Faerie—he can extend his own power into my territory and begin to corrupt my people and their lands. I need to get back now, and I don't want a couple of mortal girls in voluminous skirts slowing me down."

He moves past me, holding the Fae sword, wobbling on his stiff legs.

"Slowing you down, eh?" I scoff. "You seem a little slow on your own. What about when my blood wears off, and you turn back into a Nutcracker doll? How will you reclaim your throne and your power then?"

Slowly he turns, a reluctant dread on his face.

"Go on," I say sweetly. "You can do it. Admit that I'm right. You need us. You can't make it to the Forever Pond without our help."

"The Unending Pool," he grits out. "Fine. You may accompany me. But only until I can secure other aid. Then you must return immediately to your own world."

I squeal, almost clapping my hands until I remember I'm still holding the dagger. I very narrowly escape slicing my own palm. The Nutcracker Prince notices and rolls his eyes.

"Let's go." He stalks across the hall to the study.

Before I follow him, I snatch the belt and sheath that go with my dagger, buckling them around my waist. Then I grab a bag from the floor beneath one of the tables, and I shove a few interesting objects inside. Clara takes a pair of carved, bone-white knives with her as well.

Then we dash across the hall into the study, where the Nutcracker stands before the ring of branches, staring into it.

"You said the portal moves, that it opens in a different place in Faerie every time," Clara says. "What if it moves while we're in Faerie? How will we know where it's going to open next, so we can get back?"

"It's likely that Drosselmeyer moves it himself," the Nutcracker replies. "Without him along to alter its position, it will probably remain active and open in the same spot until your return."

"But what if—"

"Stop, Clara." I elbow her lightly. "Too many questions. Let's jump, and see what happens. It's an adventure, like the ones we used to dream of as girls."

She nods, chewing her lip, and her brow furrows with determined anxiety.

"What are you waiting for?" I ask the Nutcracker. "Do you need to activate it somehow?"

"No, it's active," he mutters. "I can feel it. But I was hoping to find some way to control what part of Faerie we enter. We can simply step through, but I hesitate to do so without being sure where we'll end up. We might tumble into a depthless bog or topple off the edge of a cliff, or—"

A door bangs somewhere far away. I think it was the door at the top of the staircase, and I'm almost sure I hear footsteps approaching rapidly.

"We're out of time," I hiss, and I shove both Clara and the Nutcracker through the ring, leaping after them myself.

How funny it would be if we simply stumbled through and nothing happened—if we stayed in the same room.

But we don't.

One step, and everything changes.

5
CLARA

Color blasts into my mind.

Radiant, vivid, overwhelming color, a dazzling cataclysm.

I can't speak. I can't breathe. I can only stay, where I've fallen on my knees, and stare.

"Up," says a voice. "Up, both of you. Drosselmeyer will come through after us—he'll find us. You have to get up."

Somewhere near me Louisa is panting, fast and frantic. She's in pain, in danger, or maybe in ecstasy.

My eyes are open as wide as I can make them go, trying to encompass the sheer glorious beauty, trying to make sense of the shapes, the colors.

Trunks, tall and golden, but also lithe and lavender. Trees, but they grow together into arches, pointed windows, and long colonnades like no trees would in our world. A bluish-lavender mist blurs the distance, highlighted with soft pink spots like dim rosy fireflies.

And the ground—chunks of amethyst and topaz, pebbles of translucent amber, ivory-white roots snaking through it all, joining and branching and uncoupling and melting together again.

There are holes in some of the trees—orifices bulging with pulpy glowing cells, like the fruity insides of a blood-orange, and those cells are studded with tiny sky-blue crystals or threaded with purple veins.

I can't make sense of it. I don't understand it, yet I want to worship it all.

"I should have warned you." It's the Nutcracker again, reaching down, gripping my shoulder. He squeezes hard, and the pain is welcome—it's clarifying. "The first sight of Faerie can make some human minds collapse. It's usually temporary."

"Usually?" Louisa's voice is shrill with laughing panic. "Yes, you should have warned us."

"I told you not to come. But you made such an excellent argument as to why you should accompany me. Close your eyes, both of you."

"I don't want to," I whimper, but I manage it. With my eyes shut, I can still see a hazy echo of the Fae world, but it's not all-consuming. I can breathe. I can think.

Scent drifts into the colored darkness—delicate florals, fruity richness—and then a sweetness beyond anything I've smelled before—faint, distant, and enticing. I feel the softness of a breeze meandering through the trees, wandering over my cheeks. I can hear sounds, too—the coo of unfamiliar birds, the rustle of foliage somewhere high overhead.

And I can hear Louisa, louder as the Nutcracker tries to cajole her into closing her eyes.

"I won't," says Louisa defiantly. "I'm stronger than you think. I can handle it. I can—oh god—" She's still panting, faster than ever.

"Hush now." The Nutcracker's fingers leave my shoulder, and his voice moves away, toward my sister. "Close your eyes. Here, take my hand. You won't be alone here. I will guide you. Try to slow your breathing, mortal."

"Don't—call me—mortal," Louisa gasps.

"Louisa, then." His voice is a velvet curtain swept over her name. It reminds me of how he said my name in the hallway—only then, his voice was merely gentle and friendly. This time there's a richness, a purple depth to his tone.

Louisa exhales, and her breathing slows.

"Good girl," says the Prince. "Keep holding my hand, Louisa. I'll take your hand as well, Clara. There now. You two help me walk on these curse-addled legs of mine, and I'll guide you."

Slowly we begin to move. My shoes are low-heeled, thank goodness, but it's still difficult to walk across such ground—chunky gemstones and intertwined roots. I nearly turn my ankle a few times.

"Quickly now. As quickly as you can." The Nutcracker's voice is taut with concern. "The hunter will soon figure out that we went through the portal. He'll be after us before we—"

"Clara! Louisa!" A commanding shout from behind us. "Don't go with him. He's not what he seems. You don't know who they are, what they do—"

"Open your eyes," urges the Nutcracker. "We must run!"

I open them, just a little. Just enough to see what's in front of me. But my heart is pounding, because our guardian voiced the very doubts Louisa mentioned back in the weapons room.

We're running now, as best we can, hobbling and hopping away from the portal. I risk a glance backward, and there's Godfather Drosselmeyer. He lifts something—a kind of clockwork crossbow—and aims it at the Nutcracker.

"Down!" I scream, flinging myself flat and dragging the Nutcracker with me. The missile whines right over his head, knocking his hat askew.

"Stop!" shouts Drosselmeyer. "Stop, you idiot girls! You'll ruin everything!"

A moment ago I might have considered going back, at least to talk. But I don't fancy being called "idiot girl" and having someone shoot so close to me.

Louisa must be thinking the same thing— she's on her feet again, helping me get the Nutcracker to his feet. "Faster!" she cries, but I see her look up, eyes wide—and I look, too. I let the glory of Faerie back in.

Its radiance is dizzying. I try to run, but all I want to do is stand still and absorb the countless textures, multihued shadows, and astonishing patterns. Everything is painfully sharp, agonizingly detailed.

Another bolt whizzes by, between the Nutcracker's head and Louisa's. Dimly I hear Drosselmeyer shouting curses, or words in another language, perhaps. The words of a spell.

"Shut your eyes," begs the Nutcracker. His words register slowly, like molasses dripping into my brain.

I think I should obey.

But before I can, eight tall figures in dark robes emerge from between the lavender and gold trunks of the trees.

The sight of them is as incongruous as it is startling. They're so brutally hideous in contrast to everything else that my mind snaps into balance at once.

They're tall and slim, like the Nutcracker. But they wear long black robes, spiked pauldrons crafted from some unfamiliar metal, and collars of coarse fur. Some carry swords, others thorny-looking clubs. But the thing they all have in common, the thing that makes my palms sweat and my spine tingle with horror—each of them has the head of an enormous white rat. Their beady black eyes gleam with maleficence, and each rat's head wears a wide smile laced with rows and rows of serrated black teeth. A miasma of rank shadows seems to form around them, dulling the color of the world and fouling the air.

I scream.

"Fuck," whispers the Nutcracker.

Louisa draws her dagger, the one she used to threaten the Prince. She braces herself, legs apart.

Frantically I follow her example, dragging my bone-knives out of their small sheaths. When I buckled them around my waist before entering the study, they seemed over-large and unwieldy. Now they look much too small in my hands. Too small to protect me, or my sister, or anyone else.

With an awkward, wooden jerk, the Nutcracker draws his sword too.

The rat-headed soldiers approach us, brandishing their own swords and clubs.

I look over my shoulder, back to where Godfather Drosselmeyer stands aghast, staring at the oncoming monsters.

"Help us!" I scream.

He grips his crossbow. Takes a step forward.

The rats snarl in anticipation, a guttural, unearthly hiss.

Drosselmeyer turns and charges back through the ring of woven branches. He disappears.

And the next second, the portal does too.

He shut it down, or moved it somewhere…

Whatever he did, it means there's no chance of retreat.

No way back.

"Stay behind me," says the Nutcracker breathlessly. "I will protect you."

"You can't, fool," snaps Louisa. "You can barely manage that sword." She casts me a fiery look. "Clara, help him hold them off for a moment, while I see what I've got in this bag."

"Hold them off?" My voice shrills, and the rat-headed monsters snicker. They don't seem to be in a hurry—they keep pacing slowly toward us, savoring our fear. They've split into three groups. Two advance from the front, while three circle around to the left and three to the right. They plan to come at us from all sides, so we can't run.

"I don't know what these are," says Louisa cheerfully. "But they can't hurt."

She holds up a ridged ball and presses the button on its side with her thumb. The ball begins to hum, louder and louder.

"Throw it!" I shout.

Louisa flings the ball toward the two oncoming rats. One catches it, vents a derisive snort, and starts to toss it behind them.

The ball explodes in midair, a concussive burst of hot fire and bits of metal. All three of us hit the ground, and Louisa throws herself on top of the Nutcracker. I'm not sure why, until a shard of hot metal lands near me with a glowing hiss.

Iron. This was a bomb specifically designed to harm the Fae.

The two rats in front of us have been reduced to scattered, steaming chunks. The reek of burnt flesh rises into the air. One of the rat's heads was only partly destroyed, and underneath the scorched white fur I see a face—not a rat at all, but something else. Not human, but wickedly, beautifully Fae. The eye is open, its slit pupil fixed vacantly on the roiling smoke.

The Nutcracker climbs to his feet, staring at Louisa. But the remaining six soldiers rush at us with screeches of anger.

"Throw another of those things!" I yell to my sister.

"I have one more," she shouts. "There were only two in the weapons room!"

"Now!" I scream.

She seizes the second bomb, presses the button, and flings it toward the group of three on our left. But they're much closer to us than the other two were.

"Run!" shouts the Nutcracker, and he shoves us both toward the trio of rats on our right. We're practically racing into their arms when the bomb explodes behind us.

6
LOUISA

The shockwave flings me forward, and I crash onto gem-studded, root-laced ground. Every muscle and bone in my body screams from the impact. Even if by some miracle I didn't break a rib, I will have bruises for days.

I've lost my dagger. I scrabble around for it, hunting desperately—until my fingers graze a spiked black boot. The rancid smell and the black hem of a robe tell me it's a rat soldier. Standing right over me.

I look up.

Grinning, he lifts his thorny club.

A twinkle of light on silver metal, and the slim blade of the Nutcracker's rapier slides into the rat's leg, piercing it through and through.

Enraged, the creature squeals and swings the club at him instead. It bounces off his arm, stripping away a few splinters.

If he takes many more of those blows, his arm might break right off. And I don't know what that would mean for his real body, once the curse is dispelled.

My fingers close on the dagger hilt, and I scramble to my feet. Clara is already up and fighting one of the rats—if shrieking like a banshee and slashing wildly with her knives can be called fighting. It seems to be doing the trick, for now. The rat is circling her warily, keeping his distance.

The other two rats close in on the Nutcracker and me.

"Get up." I kick the Nutcracker's ribs. "Time to fight alongside a puny mortal, oh great and powerful prince."

He groans, his jointed limbs creaking as he gets onto his knees. Then he leans toward me and clamps a hand onto my shoulder, using me to pull himself up.

"I'd give anything to have my real body," he grits out.

"I'd be glad to have your real body right now, too," I say. "No such luck. We must make do with what we're given. Back to back is the best course, I think."

He throws me a surprised look and moves into place. "Indeed. We take these two, and then we help your sister."

Clara is darting around trees now, keeping the trunks between her and the third rat soldier. She's quick. She'll be all right for a few minutes.

One of the rats charges me, and I slash at him, yelling. He snickers and swings his blade, a blow I almost don't block in time. He rains more blows down on me, until I'm caught in a desperate dance, in which every move of mine must accurately deflect the oncoming blade or I will die.

My brain's tendency to switch focus to the newest shiny thing works to my advantage here. My attention dances forward, backward, and side-to-side along with the rat soldier's blade, jumping to each incoming blow just in time for me to block it.

When I'm frightened, I talk. For some reason it helps me.

"Still alive, Your Nobleness?" I throw over my shoulder.

"Barely," he replies. "The iron shards from the bomb—you protected me."

"You're welcome."

"And here I thought you disliked me."

"I do. I'm fairly sure the feeling is mutual."

"Indeed. Duck!"

We both bend, narrowly avoiding a swipe of a rat's blade. I block the next blow with my dagger. Thank goodness it's a longish blade, more like a short sword, not like the tiny knives Clara picked. Still, I'm a breath away from getting my throat slit or my arm sliced open. My muscles are beginning to ache, unused to such strenuous labor.

"You heard my godfather's warning, that you're not to be trusted," I say. "That you're not what you seem."

"Not what I seem? No, I'm not usually a wooden doll, in point of fact." He staggers, crashing against my back for a second, and I try to brace him up while holding off my opponent's sword. The rat leans in, grinding his blade against mine.

"Give up, mortal." The rat soldier's voice skitters through rows of sharp black teeth. "Yield to me, and I promise to fuck you before I kill you."

"How is that a bargain?" I gasp. "I've slept with all sorts of people—I'm not picky—but I draw the line at a foul rat-bastard."

"I'll make you scream for mercy." The rat gnashes his teeth, still exerting pressure on my dagger.

I can't hold him back any longer. I've got the hilt gripped in both hands, but my arms are shaking.

The rat soldier catches my wrist in his other hand and twists. I scream at the sudden flare of pain, my fingers unlatching from the dagger hilt, letting it fall.

The rat seizes my throat. His fingers are gloved, leathery, unyielding—slowly compressing my airway. He's inhumanly strong, and I realize he's been holding back the entire time. Toying with me.

He picks me up by my neck and slams me onto the ground.

My party dress is ruined already—smudged, torn, and singed. The rat seizes my skirts, but I kick him in the face and flip over, crawling away on my belly.

A mistake, because face-down I can't defend myself as well. His weight crashes onto me.

I don't have anything left. No dagger, no bag of weapons, no Nutcracker prince at my back. Only myself.

I twist, shrieking my rage, trying to claw him off my back, but the rat delivers a blow to my face. Pain blasts through my cheekbone and jaw. My arms go limp; I'm too dazed to move.

He's fumbling with my dress, pushing it up my legs.

Then a storm of rustling skirts and wild fury hits the rat, and I feel him roll off me.

"Get away from her!" screams Clara.

Never in my life have I heard my sister use that tone, not even during one of our many fights.

There's a repeated, squelching rasp—I think it's a blade jabbing through flesh, over and over.

Groggily, clutching my bruised face, I manage to sit up.

Clara, my cautious, sober Clara—my quiet, artistic sister—she's plunging a knife into the body of the rat, again and again. Tears glitter on her cheeks, and her hair has completely fallen out of its updo.

I crawl over to her and touch her shoulder. "He's dead, Clara. You can stop."

She pulls her knife out. Throws it aside. Then she turns into me and collapses against my shoulder, sobbing.

Patting her back, I glance to my left, where the Nutcracker has just succeeded in running his opponent through the chest. Some distance beyond, the third rat is snarling, his hand pinned to a tree by Clara's other knife. Wearily the Nutcracker stalks over and stabs him through the heart as well.

The beautiful forest is quiet, except for Clara's hitching breaths and a trickle of birdsong.

The Nutcracker limps toward us, blood dripping down his blade. "We were lucky they had aura magic, not focused magic."

"What do you mean?"

"They were using their Unseelie magic in aura form, to spoil the air and befoul the earth. Had they been using it in focused form, they would have overcome us much more quickly. My magic is still inaccessible to me, and daggers are of no use against spells."

"You're also fortunate we decided to come with you," I tell him. "Otherwise you'd be dead."

"Yes, most likely my head would be on its way to the Rat King. Are you all right? Your face—" He bends stiffly, reaching toward my bruised cheek.

I pull back. "I'll be fine."

"That soldier… that is, I should have gotten to you sooner. I was trying..." He looks pained. "I wouldn't have let him—I—"

"It's all right. Clara got to me first."

My sister pulls back, wiping her eyes. "I should be comforting *you*, Louisa. I'm sorry. I'm all right now."

She's used to apologizing for tears. So am I. Our father despised crying—said that tears were a woman's tool to manipulate men. Clara and I learned long ago that we should only shed them in secret.

"Don't apologize," I tell her. "Papa isn't here to fuss at you."

"No. He's not here. And our godfather, our guardian—he left us." She looks at me, her lashes still wet. "Drosselmeyer left us to die."

I nod. "He's a cowardly asshole."

"Louisa, we can't go back now. The portal is gone, and Drosselmeyer—who knows what he would do to us, for helping the Nutcracker escape? And that means we—we're stuck—"

"Don't," I say, frantic, gripping her arm. "Don't say it. Not yet. We only have to think about the next step, no farther."

I can't bear to think what it means that the portal is gone, that we've burned the bridge with our guardian. I can't face that reality yet.

I climb to my feet and help Clara up, too.

"I think we can safely assume that the Unseelie have overtaken your realm," I say to the Nutcracker. "Those were Unseelie Fae, yes?"

"Servants of the Rat King." He gives me a dejected nod. "It is as I feared. And those eight were merely a scouting party. There will be more, many more. We cannot stay here, and we cannot fight another group like that by ourselves. We need help."

"Surely you have servants, soldiers, allies?" suggests Clara.

"My soldiers will be dead, imprisoned, or defending the last bastions of this realm," says the Nutcracker. "And my servants were all in the royal city. As for allies—if I'm right about what part of the kingdom we're in, there is someone close by who may be able to help us."

"A friend of yours?" asks Clara.

The Nutcracker inspects his damaged arm, then works the joint, wincing. "No, I wouldn't call him a friend—it's much worse than that. He's family."

7
CLARA

I never thought I had it in me to kill a living thing.

But the black blood of the rat soldier, sprinkled all over my dress, says otherwise.

And I didn't just kill him. I demolished him. I'm not even sure how many times I stabbed him.

I hang back, behind the Nutcracker and Louisa, trying to cope with what happened. My hands and legs are a little shaky, but inside I feel calmer than I have any right to be, considering what I've done. It's as if some poisonous knot in the pit of my chest has been unwound.

I think I have been murderously angry for a long time, and I didn't know it. I'm certainly better at fighting and killing than I ever suspected. That should scare me, but in a place like this, it could be an advantage.

Unless this fight was simply beginner's luck, and next time I'll fail miserably and die.

Not a bad place to die, this.

Now that we've passed beyond the murky, foul influence of the rats, the mind-glazing beauty of Faerie floods my mind again, but its radiance and its excruciating level of sharp detail aren't quite as overwhelming this time. I'm entranced and astonished, but not overcome. And if I start to feel light-headed, I simply look down at the dark blood on my dress, and I think of how the first rat screamed when I pinned his hand to a tree with my knife.

We've passed through the belt of jeweled forest, and the landscape around us has changed. We're climbing up steps formed of twisted roots and crooked stone, through a veritable cathedral of green-tinged tree trunks that form countless natural archways. Sunlight pours down through emerald-and-yellow leaves, bathing the interior of the forest in limpid gold.

My thigh muscles ache from climbing, and there's a pinching pain in my side. I have bruises everywhere, and I'm fairly sure Louisa does, too—she's limping as we go.

At last we break out onto a ledge washed in sunlight.

"It looks like the same sun from our world," I say.

"It is," replies the Nutcracker. "The mortal world and the Fae realm are but two sides of the same coin. We've not far to go now—the valley just below this ridge is where my cousin lives. He's a bit of an ass, but he's also a powerful warrior and spellcrafter. He likes to wander, so it may take us a while to find him."

He leans against a tree, his breath shallow. Is it my imagination, or do his limbs seem to be stiffening?

"It's happening again, isn't it?" I say. "You're reverting to your nutcracker form."

"The effect of Louisa's blood lasted a bit longer here, in my native realm," he grits out. "But I fear it has finally worn off."

Louisa drops her weapons bag, takes her dagger from its sheath, and cuts her sleeve, ripping back the fabric to reveal her forearm. Shallowly she slices the top of her arm, swipes two fingers in the blood, and swabs some on the Nutcracker's chest.

"You didn't answer me before," she says. "What if you drank my blood? Would an internal application help more than a surface one?"

"I'm not sure."

"Here." She holds her bleeding arm up to his mouth. "Drink."

He's taller than she is, but since he's leaning against the tree, they're practically eye to eye. I wish I could paint them like this—the Fae prince with his stiff limbs, his scarlet uniform, and his handsome, rigid profile. His lower jaw hangs slightly open as he stares at my sister.

She's a glorious mess, her rose-colored gown dirty and torn, blood dripping from her arm, an ice-blue dagger clutched in her other hand. Like me, she has lost nearly all the pins holding her hair in place, and it tumbles down her back, brightly golden as the sun.

Beyond them is the yellow sunset sky and the colorful landscape of Faerie—a wilderness of tall bluffs veiled in waterfalls, slim peaks linked by narrow bridges, multihued forests and countless silver streams.

"Drink," says Louisa. "Unless my dirty mortal blood is beneath you."

"Only the Unseelie consume blood." The Prince turns his face away.

"But this could help you, yes? You said there are more of those rat-things out there. If they attack us, we'll need you in the best possible form."

"In my true form, with my usual powers, I would have demolished all eight in a moment," he says, lifting his chin.

"Yes, yes. Perhaps don't oversell your 'true form' too much, Your Illustriousness," Louisa says dryly. "Else we may be disappointed when we finally see it. Now drink."

She lifts her arm higher. Reluctantly he tips his face forward until his mouth contacts her bleeding flesh.

He drinks. And he looks at her… and suddenly I feel as if I'm observing a delicately intimate moment.

"I can see a stream down there, and I'm parched. I'm going to get a drink of water," I say.

Neither Louisa nor the Nutcracker respond, so I move down the hill, following a barely visible track through the bushes. It's a steep slope, and halfway down I begin to skid uncontrollably. My skirts catch on a sharp broken branch, halting my dangerous slide—but then, with a horrible ripping sound, half my dress tears away and I continue down the slope, tumbling into a patch of thorny bushes at the bottom.

Angrily I fight my way upright, ripping away more of the gown's fabric in the process. My shoes are scuffed beyond repair, my stockings are in shreds, and the remnants of my skirt and petticoat barely cover my upper thighs. Beyond my short puffed sleeves, my arms are covered in bruises and scratches. I should have worn a long-sleeved gown to dinner, like Louisa did. I even have scratches across the tops of my breasts, thanks to the dress's low neckline.

If Papa could see me now, looking like a derelict doll someone dragged out of the refuse bin, he would have an apoplectic fit. I must make a dreadful contrast to the Fae beauty all around me.

I struggle through the undergrowth until I reach the stream. Its sparkling waters look normal enough—clean and clear. I scoop a double palmful of the liquid and take a sip.

It's sweet. Really and truly sweet, as if someone sprinkled sugar at the source of the spring. I drink again, more deeply.

Delicious. I do believe I could drink this water forever.

A guttural sound from the shadow of a tree catches my attention. I startle back, my hands finding the blades at my waist.

The tree in question is directly across the stream from me. It's some type of willow, but enormous—three times my height, with papery blue leaves and long dragging limbs bearing small pink and purple fruits.

A figure devolves from the dappled shade under the boughs. It's another rat—not a soldier this time, not lean and trim and male in form. This one is a bear-like, hulking monstrosity, even more terrifying when it rises on its rear paws. The stream flows between us, but it's not much of a barrier if the thing decides to attack. Which it seems to be preparing to do.

I inhale, planning to scream.

The rat-bear lunges across the water and bowls me over. My spine hits the ground and all the air rushes out of my lungs.

The monster waddles over me, settling its heavy bulk against my body, sniffing at my face with its hairy, oozing nose. Its mouth hangs open, gusting noxious hot breath onto my neck.

I can't breathe.

Something heavy and bristly is coiled around my leg—its tail.

I turn my face aside and draw in a desperate breath. My body revolts immediately, and I gag.

The rat's lips wrinkle back, exposing narrow yellow teeth.

A soft whirr. Something shears through the air and sinks into the rat's eye with a gelatinous thump.

I vent a tiny, hoarse scream that's lost in the creature's agonized bellow. It recoils, moving backward, partway off me. The thing sticking out of its eye is striped red and white—like a peppermint stick, but clearly sharp as an arrow.

The rat's eye is leaking dark fluid, but the monster doesn't seem entirely dissuaded from its interest in me. It pauses to sniff my chest, then my belly, and then it snuffles toward the space between my legs.

I reach for my knives, but before I can draw one, another striped dart sails through the air. This time it pierces the rat's quivering nose.

With a scream of pain, the rat lumbers off me entirely, then rears up on its hind legs and peers around, as if it's searching for the source of the attack.

Drawing my knives, I sit upright and plunge both of them into the monster's underbelly. The hair is so coarse and thick I can't shove them in very far, not with my limited strength.

The creature roars, lifting a paw rimmed with sharp claws while I scramble backward. The heavy paw swipes toward me, each claw the length of my knife—it's going to tear me apart—

A rainbow blur passes between me and the monster. Gauzy blue wings, moving almost faster than sight. A slim, graceful figure, a trickle of light laughter.

A faerie. And not a cursed faerie, or an Unseelie—this is a Fae in their true form. *His* true form, because the laughter rippling through the air is young and male. The sound of that cocky, masculine laugh sends tiny, naughty thrills racing through my body despite my terror.

The faerie jerks the sharp peppermint stick out of the rat's nose and whizzes past its snout, dodging a clumsy blow from a paw. He jams the striped dart into the beast's other eye, does a somersault in midair, and flies down to me, while the rat-beast bellows and claws at its own face, trying to dislodge the darts.

The faerie hovers near me, the toes of his boots brushing the grass.

Eager eyes, black-lined and golden as the sun. A dazzling row of sharp white teeth. A cloud of pink hair.

That's all I get to see before he bends down, picks me up, and flies off with me.

"What are you doing?" I gasp, pushing against his hard chest.

"Saving your life, sugar." He flies higher, well out of range of the beast, and then he zooms between trees, carrying me frighteningly fast away from the hill where Louisa and the Nutcracker are.

"Stop!" I struggle in his arms. "Put me down this minute!"

Immediately he whirs into a clearing and drops me into a bed of soft, bluish grass that looks frosty, as if someone sprinkled it with sugar. He lands nearby.

I get to my feet, hot with anger and panic.

The faerie stands by, arms folded. His grin shows every one of his wicked triangular teeth.

The way he's staring makes me suddenly conscious of how little clothing I'm wearing. Never before have I let a man see me in such an immodest state. My one tryst with a boy was in a dark garden shed, so I wouldn't have to see anything and he couldn't see me.

And now a faerie male is eyeing me with a telltale smirk and lustful heat in his golden eyes.

He's much taller than I thought, flamboyantly dressed in short purple trousers and a matching vest with a blousy, gauzy iridescent shirt beneath. A snowflake hangs from the black choker around his neck. Tiny lollipops dangle from the lobes of his pointed ears. He's wearing a gauzy sort of cape, too, pinned to his shoulders with pale-blue feathers. It's such a perfect match for his wings I can barely tell where the wings end and the cape begins.

"You have to take me back," I exclaim.

He taps his chin with long, pointy black nails. "Someone as delicious as you shouldn't have a death wish."

"Not back to the *monster*—back to my friends! They'll be coming down that hill any moment, looking for me."

"Of course you have friends. I didn't think a tasty little mortal confection like yourself would be out here all alone." He prowls nearer, stalking a circle around me and inhaling deeply through his nose. "I can see why the rat went after you. You smell absolutely scrumptious."

A shudder runs through me, and my fingers travel to the belt at my waist. But I left my knives in the stomach of the rat-beast.

"Oh, you don't need that anymore, sweet thing," croons the faerie, leaning in from behind me. Deftly he unbuckles my belt, pulls it off, and flings it aside. His nails graze along my waist. "Who are these friends of yours, pray tell? Not that dreadful sorcerer Drosselmeyer, I hope, or I'm afraid I shall have to kill you. And don't lie to me, darling. I have ways of discerning the truth."

"Drosselmeyer is my godfather, but I'm no friend to him," I say. "My sister and I are trying to assist one of the cursed Fae he captured—a prince of this realm. We made it through the portal, but we were attacked by rat soldiers, and now we're trying to find the prince's cousin. He lives somewhere nearby. He's a great warrior who can help us."

"A great warrior?" The faerie laughs and drags his claws through my hair, seemingly unbothered by the tangles he encounters. "I know of no great warriors living nearby. This prince, what is his name?"

"I don't know."

"Of course not, because faeries only give their names to those they trust. You haven't yet won that privilege from your Fae companion, which means I shouldn't trust you either, should I?"

I pull away, despite the painful tug as my hair disengages from his claws. "Nor should I trust you."

"Really?" His eyebrows rise. "But I'm so pretty. And I did save your life."

I take in his lithe, long-legged form, his trim waist, the lean chest showing between the laces of his shirt. His wings are draped at his back like a cloak, and they flutter intermittently.

He *is* pretty. His face is boyish, sprinkled with freckles, sharp-jawed and wickedly charming. It's the teeth that make him slightly terrifying—all pointed, not a smooth edge among them.

"Will you return me to my friends or not?" I ask, with a defiant tilt of my head.

His smile widens. "That depends. You owe me a life debt, and now you ask a favor as well? What will you give me in return?"

I look down at my bruised legs and arms, the scanty remnants of my green dress, the tangle of auburn waves over my shoulder. Then I lift my eyes to his. "I don't have anything of value."

"That may be true in the human realm, but not here. In Faerie, mortals have much to offer. Blood, tears, dreams, bones, memories, ears—oh yes, I have several friends who collect human ears. And I know what you're thinking—no, they're not *all* Unseelie."

"I—I wasn't thinking that," I breathe. "You have Unseelie friends? So you're in league with the Rat King then?"

"What a reductive statement! A prejudiced assumption. You really shouldn't judge a Fae by their kingdom, darling." His wings expand suddenly—filmy delicate things with a bluish tint. They're so beautiful I catch my breath.

But he didn't deny owing allegiance to the Rat King. I back away from him, angry at myself for how much I want to paint him like this, with his arms crossed and his wings flared. Too bad I have to run from him.

I turn and dash into the trees, but with a whirr and a rush, he's in front of me again. I swerve, but he slams a palm against a tree, his arm blocking my path. "You won't last long in this forest by yourself, sugar. It's a risky place at the best of times—downright dangerous now, with the Rat King's folk lurking about."

"So you're not on the Rat King's side then?"

"Fuck no. He has no sense of style, for one thing. And for another… No, that's it. That's my only reason."

At my startled expression, he laughs, leaning in closer. His pink hair feathers around his ears and along his neck. It looks beautifully soft, like spun sugar. His lips are a glossy pink. They look as if they would taste delicious. The fragrance of him swirls around me—rich and sweet, like chocolate and peppermint and the scent of the air before snowfall.

"You're so cute when you're affronted and shocked." He bites his lip with his sharp teeth. "Oh, I haven't played with a human in the longest time. I forgot how fun you can be, especially the young, naïve ones. You're a virgin, yes?"

My body is already reacting to him, with a slick heated flush in places I'd rather not think about at the moment. And his casual inquiry about my virginity makes my ill-timed arousal so much worse.

"That is a very inappropriate question," I say haughtily. And then, for some reason I can't explain, I add, "And no, I'm not."

"A pity. The virgin blood of a human girl fetches a high price in this realm. You could have given me some blood in exchange for passage back to your friends. Ah well. I suppose we'll have to figure out something else."

My face is flaming; my cheeks must be the color of his hair. Every curve of my skin is tingling at his nearness.

"I'm not pleasuring you," I say. "I can find my own way back to my friends."

He rolls his eyes. "I asked for no such thing."

"Then I don't know what you want!"

It's a mark of my artistic strangeness that in this moment of anxiety and arousal, I'm mentally plotting which of my paints I'd need to combine to match the exact color of his lips. And that thought yields an idea.

"I could paint you," I say suddenly.

His golden eyes widen. "Paint me?"

"I'm an artist. I'll paint your portrait, in exchange for an escort back to my sister and our companion."

He nods, shifting back a step. "I would like that. With one small adjustment. I can see myself in a mirror any day. So instead of a portrait, you'll make me a painting of anything I choose. And you'll come to my home to create this masterpiece before you continue with your quest to break the prince's curse. Agreed?"

"Agreed." I hold out my hand, but he smirks.

"In Faerie we seal bargains differently. A kiss will do."

"Very well." I bounce up on my tiptoes and peck his smooth cheek.

He looks disappointed, but he leans down and kisses my cheek in return. His lips are slightly sticky, and his breath as he pulls away is temptingly sweet.

"I'm Clara," I tell him.

Another grin, and a shake of his head. "So free with your names, you humans. I won't be telling you mine, sugar. Not yet. Now come along, and we'll go find your friends."

8
LOUISA

When the Nutcracker lowers his mouth to my bleeding arm, I suck in a breath and hold it. I'm not fearful of blood, but it's strange, letting him consume part of me like this.

As he's drinking, he looks up at me.

His eyes are more human—well, more Fae—than ever, thanks to the blood I applied to his chest and the blood he's drinking now. They're a deep emerald green, striated with little jets and bursts of gold around the pupils. He has lashes now, too—not painted ones, but real, thick, sooty eyelashes.

He doesn't look away as he drinks deeply from my arm. Dimly I hear Clara say something about a stream and going for a drink. I should tell her to wait, but it sounds as if she can see the stream from here. We'll be able to keep an eye on her.

I count to a hundred while the Nutcracker swallows mouthful after mouthful of my blood. He's changing before my very eyes—becoming more lithe and pliant, less wood and more flesh. His stiff clothing relaxes into soft fabric, and his black hair bounces up from his head, still pinned beneath his hat, but no longer carved and painted. He seems to be growing taller, too.

"Enough," I whisper at last.

Instantly he lets me go, his full lips wet and crimson with my blood. The line marking his detachable nutcracker's jaw is all but gone now.

He straightens—and yes, he is definitely taller.

"Let's hope I won't have to do that again." He licks his lips, pulling a slight frown.

"Did I taste that bad?"

He doesn't look at me. "Let me bind this wound for you."

"Just use a strip of my sleeve. It's ruined anyway."

Swiftly he wraps the cloth around my forearm and ties it in place. "Where's your sister?"

"She went to get a drink. We need to—"

The Prince's eyes go wide and his palm slams across my mouth. He pulls me against his chest and backs up into the undergrowth, dragging me with him.

"Hush," he hisses in my ear when I voice a muffled protest. "For the love of your life, shut up, and be still."

I squeal against his palm, and he brings his other hand around to clasp my throat, cutting off my air as well as my voice.

"Shut up, or we both die," he whispers.

I go still, nodding as best I can. He eases his grip on my neck, though he leaves his fingers against my skin. Removing his other hand from my mouth, he points to the ledge where we were standing.

The ground is more familiar here, with actual grass instead of gems and roots, even though the grass has a distinctly bluish tint. But it's... *moving*. The grass is swaying more violently than the light breeze warrants.

The earth itself begins to heave upward, bulging, breaking, cracking open like a blister.

The sun is sinking, no longer bathing the ledge, but there's still plenty of light by which to see the creature that emerges.

A blunt, wrinkled head, all sneering snout, with two pinprick eyes and a huge pair of long, narrow, tusklike teeth.

The Nutcracker's breath tickles my ear. "Mole-rat."

I could have guessed as much. Except this mole-rat is gigantic, with a head larger than mine and a neck just as thick as its head. The skin covering its long, round body is a sickly pale pink, thin and wrinkled.

A naughty impulse seizes me, and I turn my head, feeling the slide of the Nutcracker's fingers against my throat. I tilt my face up and breathe words toward his ear. "It looks like a dick."

His whole form stiffens. I can practically feel the shock vibrating from him. I start to snicker, and he clamps his hand over my mouth again. I smile silently against his palm.

More and more of the mole-rat's long, flaccid body keeps sliding out of the hole—so much that the creature begins to coil itself like a snake.

A bird flies by, swooping low over the grassy ledge, oblivious to the coiled creature.

One moment the bird is winging along, twittering merrily. The next second, the mole-rat's dull, rounded snout erupts into a wide maw, ringed with rows of fangs. Its gullet is huge, capable of swallowing a man whole. Half a dozen thin, fleshy tentacles extrude from around the mole-rat's snout, latch around the bird, and suck it into the toothy maw.

A horrible crunch, a gulping swallow, and then silence.

The entire attack took barely longer than a second. The mole-rat settles down in the grass.

The Prince holds me, my back against his chest. I'm not sure when his hand moved from my mouth to my stomach, but I'm glad of the comforting warmth there.

He leans down and speaks, barely above a breath. "Don't move. It can feel vibration. We must wait."

Panic bolts through my gut. What about Clara? She went to get water—what if she comes back to the ledge looking for us? What if that *thing* consumes her, rips her to shreds in its razor maw before we can stop it?

My whole body begins to shake. I can't help it.

The Prince tightens the pressure on my belly and throat, a clear warning for me to be still. But I can't. I've gotten no rest for hours, I've defied my godfather, battled rat-soldiers, almost suffered rape by an Unseelie, shed my blood to lighten the Nutcracker's curse, and now I must wait helplessly while my sister walks right into danger.

No. I cannot simply stand here. My dagger is hanging at my hip. The Prince has his sword, and there are more weapons in the bag that lies not far from where we stand.

I lift my face to the Prince's again, and he bends his ear to listen.

"Let me go," I breathe. "I'll fight it."

"You're trembling," he whispers back. "You can't fight in this state."

"You then."

"I don't have my powers. It would devour me in a moment."

The mole-rat stirs, lifting its head, nosing around. It looks so stupidly innocent, the nasty yellow tusk-teeth the only sign of the monstrosity within.

"You're shaking too hard," breathes the Prince. "It can feel the vibration through the ground."

"I can't stop."

A snarl begins in the mole-rat's throat.

The Prince moves swiftly, lightly, scooping me off the ground. One of his arms curls around my back, the other under my legs, crumpling my skirts.

He stands stock-still, legs braced, while I tremble against his chest. I truly can't stop shaking. My body is beyond its limits, overtaxed and overanxious. My nerves are singing with panic. I need to cry, to scream, to *move*—anything to release this horrible tension. I can't bear it.

The mole-rat's growl subsides, but it remains reared up, its head swiveling this way and that.

The Prince curls me closer to his chest. I'm still shaking, and anger swirls with my raging panic—anger at myself, because I'm the strong one, the adventurous one, the rebel, the risk-taker—yet I can't control myself. I'm collapsing, crumbling internally, sweating through my fine gown.

Anguished, I stare up at the Prince. There's still a stiffness about him, and I can't tell if it's the curse or his personality. Now that he's less Nutcracker and more Fae, he's honestly the most beautiful man I've ever seen. Which only makes it worse that he's seeing me in this shattered state.

A swell of anxiety rolls through me, a paroxysm wrenching my whole body, and I nearly let out a whimper.

But the Prince senses my distress, sees my lips part—

And muffles the sound with his mouth.

He keeps his lips sealed over mine. They're smooth and soft, warm and salty. I exhale into the dark heat of his mouth.

Tentatively I touch my tongue to his, and when he doesn't pull back, I sweep my tongue along his teeth. He tastes like my blood, and also a little woodsy, like cedar or oak.

I've kissed many people, all humans. Some of those kisses were wonderful. But this kiss— it's melting my fear, blurring my anxiety, softening the edges of my panic.

Carefully he ends the kiss, exhaling quietly. I have a mere second to regret the absence of his mouth before it's back again, molding to mine with a quiet urgency that sends a flare of need through my body.

He opens his jaw wide, silently allowing me full access. I lash my tongue through his mouth, and he responds with a languid swirl of his own tongue. The act of being inside each other this way floods my body with heat, dampening the area between my legs.

And that, of course, is not what he intends. He merely wants to calm me, to help me make it through these perilous moments of waiting. He's trying to keep me quiet.

Kissing is meaningless. It's a simple, temporary, mutual pleasure, and this kiss is no different.

So why am I compelled to slide my hand up to his neck? To open wider as if I need him to plunge deeper inside me?

We separate to breathe, and then he ducks his head again, capturing my mouth. His strong arms are locked around my body. For a moment he savors my lips, then probes inside again. Each flick of his tongue sends a wicked tingle right to my clit.

I shouldn't be kissing him like this, feeling like this, when my sister is out there in the Fae forest, helpless to anything that might come along.

But my trembling has stopped.

We keep kissing a while, until my underthings are soaked and I'm like melted wax in the Prince's arms. If he wanted to slip inside me right now, I would let him. It wouldn't be the first time I've let a stranger fuck me.

Suddenly he lifts his head, tilting it as though to catch a sound with his sharp ears.

A few heartbeats later, I hear it too—a thrumming purr like a hummingbird's wings, only louder.

A tall, pink-haired faerie appears beyond the lip of the ledge, blue wings whirring. He's carrying a half-naked Clara in his arms, much the same way the Nutcracker Prince is holding me.

The mole-rat whips toward them, screeching, its maw wide and eager.

The winged faerie darts backward, quick as lightning, but the one of the mole-rat's snout-tentacles curls around his foot. The winged faerie struggles, but he's being drawn closer to the open gullet of the monster.

The Prince drops me and we both race into the open, drawing our weapons. Part of the mole-rat's body is stretched out, extending beyond the edge of the bluff, so we can't reach its head and neck. But the Prince begins slashing at the creature's body, and I join him, thrusting my dagger into the pale flesh over and over. White ooze spurts out and I gag.

"I was right," I shout, breathless with effort. "It's an oversized cock, complete with cum."

"You're disgusting, mortal," says the Prince, sawing at the creature.

"That's not what you thought a few moments ago."

"That?" He scoffs. "It was nothing. I knew you were a licentious woman, and I wanted to distract you so we wouldn't die. Kissing you was a dull task, but an effective strategy."

The mole-rat releases the winged faerie's foot and thrashes around, humping and lurching. The pink-haired faerie deposits my sister in some bushes, flies over the mole-rat's head, and sprinkles some rainbow flakes on it, scooped from a pouch at his waist.

The mole-rat's entire flaccid body shudders, then goes still.

The winged faerie tugs two knives from his boots, lands by the creature's neck and slices its head clean off with a sweeping crisscross stroke of both blades. They're either very sharp knives, or he's incredibly strong. The Nutcracker has cleft a decent valley into the creature's body with his sword, but he wasn't able to sever it completely.

Sweating and furious, I stop stabbing the carcass.

"A dull task?" I snap at the Prince. "How can you say that?"

He shrugs. "I can't help it that mortal women are foolishly susceptible to a little oral stimulation."

"Oral stimulation?" The winged faerie walks toward us, grinning with sharp teeth. "Good gracious, what have you two been doing? Sounds fun."

"We've been *not dying*," says the Prince coolly. "Nothing more."

Clara fights her way out of the bushes she was dumped in and charges toward me. I meet her halfway, and we clasp each other tight.

"I almost died," Clara confides.

"So did we. Who's your friend?"

"He's an asshole."

"I'm beginning to think all Fae males are." I cast a glare over my shoulder toward the Prince, but he doesn't notice. He's talking to the winged faerie.

"We thought you were dead," says the newcomer.

"By the stars' grace, no," replies the Prince. "How did the girl find you?"

"I found *her.* Saved her from a monster. The Rat King is saturating these lands with his foul creatures."

"You two know each other?" Clara disengages herself from our hug and moves toward the two men, frowning.

"This is my cousin, the one we came here to seek," says the Prince.

Clara's eyebrows rise. "You're the great warrior?"

"Can you doubt it?" The new faerie grins, spreading his arms wide.

"You're so colorful and sparkly," I add. "I think Clara and I were expecting someone grimmer and more majestic."

The new faerie claps the Prince on the shoulder. "This one has enough 'grim and majestic' for both of us. Runs in the family. Did he mention his father banished me from court?"

"You were consorting with Unseelie Fae," says the Prince.

"And because I choose to have friends and lovers of all kinds, that makes me untrustworthy?"

"You know I never agreed with the way he punished you."

"Ah, but you said nothing on the topic, except to me, in whispers." The new faerie is still smiling, but his voice has gone hard. "You did not come to my defense then, and now you expect me to come to yours?"

"Not for my sake," says the Prince. "For the sake of the kingdom. For the sake of all the gentle Fae who will suffer torture, rape, and death at the hands of the Rat King and his ilk. You know what they are—fiends thirsty for pain, lustful beasts who like to hear their victims scream before they grant the mercy of death. Is that what you want? For this kingdom to be ravaged and corrupted like the Dread Court?"

The new faerie isn't smiling now. "Of course not."

"You have always ridiculed customs, defied laws, and flirted with wickedness," begins the Prince.

"Not just flirted. I've outright fucked with wickedness," interjects the winged faerie. "Go on."

The Prince shoots him a rebuking look that reminds me of Clara's expression whenever she's displeased with me.

"And yet, I believe you have a good heart," continues the Prince. "You're the only one I know of in this sector who might be willing to help us. We need an escort to the Unending Pool so I can dispel this curse fully."

"Yes, on the way over Clara said something about your cursed form and how blood can temporarily restore you. She said you were *drinking* blood from her sister? How very Unseelie of you."

"Desperate times require desperate acts," mutters the Prince.

I snort loudly, and Clara looks over at me, then at the Prince. She pulls a little frown as if she's trying to figure out the fresh vitriol between me and the Nutcracker.

"Once I reach the pool, dispel the curse, and reclaim my powers, it will be an easy matter to remove the Rat King from these lands," the Prince says. "If you want to continue living as you wish, with the freedom to engage in any darkness or debauchery you like, and without the constant threat of Unseelie beasts, you should help us."

"You'll need more fighters than just me if you're to reach the pool," says the pink-haired faerie. "I may know a few. But first, you'll return home with me. The sun has set, darkness will fall soon, and you don't want to be caught out in this part of the forest at night. Besides the monsters and rat-soldiers, the nights are terribly cold. Seasons change quickly in Faerie," he explains aside to Clara and me. "The turning of the year is nearly upon us. Winter will fall any day now, and frigid nights are the first sign of its coming."

"We'll stay the night with you," says the Prince reluctantly. "But first thing in the morning—"

"Ugh, how I hate those words," says his cousin, with a roll of his golden eyes. "Tomorrow I'll gather a few allies, while little Clara here fulfills her bargain with me."

The Prince turns to my sister, alarmed. "You made a bargain with him?"

"Nothing salacious," says the pink-haired faerie. "She's going to paint something for me."

"Paint what?"

"That's yet to be determined." The faerie bounces into the air, his wings humming to life again. "The sun has set, my loves. Let us depart."

9
CLARA

As we follow the two Fae males through the darkening forest, Louisa leans toward me, nodding in the direction of the pink-haired faerie. "He's a bit extravagant, isn't he? I like it."

"I thought you might. You like everyone far too quickly."

"Not the Nutcracker." She glares at his red-coated back.

"Did something happen between you while I was gone?" I ask. "You disliked and distrusted him before, but you seem to almost hate him now."

"Nothing happened," she says, too quickly.

Before I can press her for the truth, my stomach growls. Loudly. So loudly that both of the Fae glance back at us.

"Hungry, are we?" asks the winged faerie. "It's a long walk—you'll need sustenance to make it there. I'd offer myself as a snack, but I think you'd prefer this." He bounds into the air, plucking two pink fruits from a willow tree like the one I saw by the stream.

He tosses one of the fruits to each of us. The skin is a crystallized pink, as if it's been coated in sugar, but it's not a hard coating. I bite through it easily, into the pulp beneath. Sweet juices burst over my tongue, lighting up my tastebuds.

"God, what is this?" Louisa hums through her own mouthful. "I've never had anything so delicious."

The Fae males exchange a look I can't quite interpret, and the sharp-toothed Faerie licks his pink lips. "There are far more delicious things in this realm, I assure you. These are sugarplums. My favorite fruit."

"He used to eat them so often as a boy that he was nicknamed 'Sugarplum' among the court ladies," the Prince adds, with a sly twist of his mouth.

"And then *someone* persuaded all the youths of the court to call me that as well." The winged faerie flicks his cousin's shoulder. "I decided to embrace the name. And when I became fully grown, it took on a different meaning." He winks at me.

I can't imagine what he means by that, nor do I care to surmise. All I want is to keep eating this incredible fruit forever. But something from an old tale enters my mind—a warning about not consuming any food offered by the Fae.

With my mouth full, I pause on the path. "What will this fruit do to me?"

"Nothing terrible, sweetness," the winged faerie assures me. "It will only ease your hunger a little and make you feel a bit happier, like a glass of good wine."

"Oh. Then may I have another?"

He laughs and jumps into the air again, plucking another fruit from a different tree.

The Prince keeps walking, while Louisa trails reluctantly behind him, but the Sugarplum Faerie lands on the path in front of me, blocking my way with his body like he did earlier. A whiff of his fragrance—peppermint, chocolate, and snowfall—teases my nose. In the dusky depths of the forest behind him, fireflies light up—but they're not the yellow ones from home—these are blue, purple, red, and green.

His eyes shine buttery yellow in the gloom as he hands me the second fruit. "Take a bite."

The flavor that explodes in my mouth is different this time, but just as delicious.

He chuckles at my astonished expression. "A different flavor every time. Can I tell you a secret? It's rather naughty."

I want to say no, but he did save my life—twice if we're counting the mole-rat situation. "Very well."

"Nowadays, people call me Sugarplum because I have the same delightful quality as these fruits. I'm deliciously flavored, and I taste different every time."

"You—you mean your personality?"

"No." His lashes lower, hooding his eyes. "I'm not talking about my personality. I'm talking about my cum."

Warmth spreads through my sex, and it's all I can do not to press my legs together to soothe the tingling there.

"All Faeries taste divine in that way, especially to humans," he says, walking on. "But my particular gift is unique."

Dazed, I manage to walk beside him, trying not to picture him naked and flushed and coming hard—trying not to imagine myself catching the sweetly flavored release on my tongue.

I swallow reflexively, and then, to distract myself, I blurt out the question I've been wanting to ask. "Why does my godfather hate the Fae?"

"Some of us are worth hating. Perhaps he encountered a few of those and thought to paint us all with the same brush. But I don't know his specific reasons, sugar. You would have to ask him."

"I'll probably never get the chance now. He left us behind and closed the portal we used to get here. So my sister and I are stuck in Faerie."

"Not forever," he assures me. "There are other ways to pass between the realms. Fewer than there used to be, but you need not remain here forever, unless you wish it. And you may decide you want to stay. Humans who reside in this realm age far more slowly than they would in their own realm—a distinct advantage, if you can survive the other dangers here. Unfortunately, even in the Seelie kingdom, human life expectancy isn't as long as one might wish. There are so many little ways to die."

The smile he gives me is pure savagery, sharp-toothed and wicked. "Eat your fruit, darling. We'll be home soon."

"This house once belonged to an *abhartach*," says the Sugarplum Faerie, flinging the door wide and holding it open for us to enter. "Instead of craving the blood of humans, he craved the blood of the Fae. He pretended to be a dealer of rare magical ingredients, specifically banned ones. He would disguise himself in various ways and appear at Night Markets in both the Seelie and Unseelie kingdoms. Whenever someone questioned him about dark, illicit substances, he would arrange to meet them in secret, claiming to have the item they needed. And then he would drain their blood, every last drop."

"You're a wonderful storyteller." Louisa pushes past him into the house. "We certainly won't have nightmares after that lovely tale."

Normally she would be dancing through the place already, exclaiming over all its quirks. She's definitely not herself, and I don't think it's only because of the mind-bending changes and life-threatening peril we've encountered today. Perhaps I can find a moment to talk with her about it.

The Prince enters the house next. I take a last, long look at the blue-and-purple forest, at the soft multicolored lights winking through the trees, at the huge white blooms nodding near the door of the rambling house. My mind is no longer overcome by the Faerie landscape, but I don't think I could ever get used to such beauty. I think, if I returned to the mortal plane now, everything I saw would seem dull and drab by comparison.

"You really are an artist," says the Sugarplum Faerie.

I glance at him, quirking an eyebrow.

"The way you're devouring the scene. Not just admiring it, but swallowing it whole. Saving it, so you can mull over it later."

"I suppose." I'm about to pass through the doorway when he bars my way with his arm.

"Someone has taught you to feel shame about your needs, both artistic and primal." His golden eyes pierce mine. "Your guardian, I presume."

"We spent less than two days with our guardian."

"A parent, then."

"My father."

"Interesting. You and your sister had the same upbringing, yet she seems more open than you, swearing, yelling about cocks and cum and such things during our battle with the mole-rat. And I do believe she was doing something naughty with my cousin before we showed up."

"I wouldn't be surprised." Then I bite my lips and look away from him, feeling as if I've betrayed Louisa in some way.

"She's the experienced one." He leans toward me, mischief in his eyes. "But you're the secret freak, aren't you, darling?" Closer he bends, inhaling, his lashes drifting shut. "I can smell it on you—the delicate sweetness of your lust. Like melted sugar, sliding between your legs."

My skin is fire and ice at once, burning and chilling with a fever beyond any illness.

When my sister used to sneak out, at night or during long, dull afternoons when my father was working, I stayed behind. I knew she didn't go far—she couldn't, without someone noticing and telling our father. And she didn't always leave the property—she had ways of bringing the fun into the cellar, the garden shed, or the stable.

I knew what she was doing. And even though I refused to accompany her, I took care of my needs in other ways. I would crawl into our dark closet and touch myself, over and over, sometimes coming three or four times before I was sated. I couldn't do it on the bed, because Papa refused to let us lock our door, and I didn't want him to surprise me in such activities. But just as Louisa had places for her trysts, I had a place of my own.

All the dark fantasies that played through my mind during those stolen moments—I have never spoken of them to anyone, not even my sister. I fear they are too shocking, even for her.

The Sugarplum Faerie's pink lips open, and his breath sifts into my parted mouth. A slight shift forward, and he would be kissing me.

"Clara!" My sister's voice, a sharp tone I've rarely heard from her. "Are you coming in?"

The Sugarplum Faerie drops his arm, smirking, and with a sweeping gesture invites me to enter the house.

It's warmly lit by lamps unlike anything I've seen—floating glass balls filled with dancing flame, fueled by magic. Wooden paneling gives way to plaster halfway up the walls, and the beams overhead are thick, glossy, and well-worn, etched with runes.

After the tiny entry hall, there's a great space upheld by thick posts, also rune-covered. Couches, cushions, and low tables litter the room, all of them draped in lush blankets and covered with pillows. The walls are lined with cubbies, cabinets, and shelves, each packed with glass jars.

And every glass jar is filled with candy.

Small barrels stand here and there, each one packed to the brim with toffees, sugared nuts, caramels, and other candies wrapped in twisted paper or colorful leaves. At one end of the room, tall glass canisters contain chocolates, gumdrops, and pebble-sized crystals in a hundred different hues.

With a little of her usual spark, Louisa darts forward. "Have you ever seen so much candy in your life, Clara? This is more than we saw in the shop Papa took us to that one year!"

"It's a sweetshop of sorts," says the Sugarplum Faerie. "But not the kind you're thinking of."

"In one respect, my cousin isn't so different than the former resident of this house," says the Prince grimly. "He is a peddler of spells—some of them quite illegal."

"This is Faerie. Nothing's illegal, even if your pompous father tried to make it so," snaps Sugarplum. Here in the house, his wings are relaxed, clinging to his back like a filmy extension of the shoulder cape he wears. He throws himself onto a couch, not seeming to mind that he's sitting on the wings. "Go on, girls—have a look. Everything's labeled."

"Mimicry spells." Louisa taps her fingernail on one of the jars. "What does that mean?"

"If you look into someone's eyes while you're chewing a piece of that candy, it will glamour you to look exactly like them for a short time. This particular mimicry spell is immune to glamour detection. When it starts to weaken, the glamoured form flickers."

"Interesting." Louisa reads off more labels. "Beauty spells, sound suppression, tidying spells, lightning storms, deflection, healing, enhanced pleasure—oh, the pleasure ones sound interesting. Can I have a few?" She gives Sugarplum her best smile.

"They were formulated in Faerie, for its inhabitants, and their effects on a mortal could be unpredictable."

Louisa pulls a disappointed face.

"Ah, don't look so sad!" he cries. "I can't bear it when pretty women look sad in my house." He leaps up, collecting her hand and pressing a kiss to her knuckles. She melts into a smile.

I swallow hard, turning my back to them and pretending to inspect the labels on the jars. Why should I care if Louisa has charmed both of the Fae males we've met? I'm used to men liking her better than me.

"We need food, yes?" cries Sugarplum. "I'll take a dive into the pantry and see what we have. Who wants to help me carry it out?"

I half-turn, ready to volunteer, but Louisa is already scampering after him.

The Nutcracker Prince drops into a chair, extending first one stiff leg, then the other. Since he drank Louisa's blood, he moves more easily, but it's obvious he still isn't quite comfortable. There's an element of woodenness in the way he moves and speaks.

Keeping my eyes on his face, I plant myself in a chair across from him and wait until he looks up.

"What do you want, Clara?" he says.

"What happened between you and my sister?"

"We were hiding in the trees from the mole-rat. She was panicking, drawing its attention. I kissed her to quiet her."

"And that's all? One kiss?"

"Why do you care?"

I consider pointing out the change in her demeanor, but I don't owe him an explanation, so I merely shrug and settle back into my chair.

My sister and Sugarplum are gone for a long time. Finally they troop back into the room, carrying trays laden with sausages, smoked meat, cheese, bread, and an enticing array of small cakes and cookies. There's also a big bowl filled with fruits I've never seen before.

They return to the pantry for wine, and then we all dive in—except the Prince, who eats nothing and takes only the tiniest sips of wine. I'm not sure what the curse has done to his internal systems, but I can understand him not wanting to consume much.

With my stomach finally full, I'm so weary I can barely keep my eyes open. Louisa and the Sugarplum Faerie are taking bites of all the decadent desserts he brought out, laughing with their mouths full while the Prince slides morosely lower in his chair, glowering at both of them.

I lean on the armrest of my own chair, warm and drowsy. I feel safe here, though I probably shouldn't.

Sometime later I'm awakened by claw-tipped fingers scraping the hair back from my forehead, sweeping it around my ear.

"You have the loveliest hair, Clara," murmurs a voice. The scent of warm chocolate and fresh snow whisks over me, and I blink awake, staring blankly at the Sugarplum Faerie. He looks even prettier now than he did when I met him. Maybe it's the wine I drank.

"You fell asleep," he says softly. "We let you rest while your sister bathed, but I thought you might want a bath as well. Or rather, I must *insist* you have a bath, so you don't smear dirt and blood all over the sheets."

His eyes dart downward for a second before he pulls them back up to my face. I glance down—and realize that my breasts are practically bulging out of my ruined dress. One nipple is on full display.

But he didn't touch me, and he doesn't mention it as I sit up and adjust what remains of my gown.

"I've conjured a nightdress for you," he says. "And the water is hot. Come, and I'll show you."

10
LOUISA

I pass Clara and Sugarplum in the narrow corridor of the house. I'm wrapped in a fluffy towel, my hair in a knot on top of my head, and I have to squeeze myself against the wall to make space for them to pass.

"The water is magical, Clara," I tell my sister. "See?" I hold out one arm. "My bruises and cuts are all gone! And my ribs don't hurt!"

"You're welcome," says the faerie with a wink. I grin at him and pad down the flat carpet of the hall in my bare feet. He said he laid out some nightclothes for us in one of these rooms— this one, I think—

I push the door open. It's a bedroom, but it can't be mine and Clara's, because His Royal Asshattery is sitting on the bed, staring at his hands.

My good mood dissolves like the sugary orbs our host dropped into my bathwater. I'm instantly furious, because His Moroseness picked me up as if I were lighter than air, and I'm not, yet he held me in those strong arms and kissed me into a glorious sexual haze… and then he pretended he felt *nothing*.

I kick his bedroom door open wider, and he looks up, startled.

"You said it was a dull task," I seethe.

He sighs. "Are you still going on about that? Let it go, mortal."

"No." I march into his room, clutching my towel. His eyes fall to my wet cleavage, bulging a little over the towel's edge, but I don't care. Let him look.

"You said I was a licentious woman," I continue.

"Aren't you?"

"I've had lovers. I enjoy sex. Why would you judge me for that? The Fae are notoriously licentious."

"I'm not."

"But you've slept with women."

"Two," he says. "Just two."

I think I might burst right out of my body. It's all I can do not to scream at him for the wasted opportunities. "You're a prince of Faerie, with liberty and luxury at your disposal, and you've only slept with two women?"

"Someone in my position has to be selective."

"Why the hell? There are kings, princes, and lords all over my world who use their position to enjoy extravagant amounts of pleasure."

"Ah, but you see, I want to be a good ruler, not a careless rake." He rises, his eyes snapping. "And you... what do you want to be? A hole for every man who makes you wet?"

"No," I snarl. "I never said that. But what if I did? What if that's what I want, what I like? Seems as if I'm the more honest one of the two of us. You can't admit what you enjoy."

"Yes, I can."

"Then prove it. Admit to me, right now, that kissing me wasn't a dull task. Because I know it wasn't. I could tell you were enjoying it. You were—savoring me."

The Prince laughs, hard and caustic. "You're imagining things."

"Is that so?" My voice shrills. "I've kissed many people—don't roll your eyes like that—and I know when someone enjoys kissing me."

"But you've never kissed a Fae male," he says coolly. "You don't know what we like. Truly, I felt no sexual inclination toward you whatsoever."

I clutch my towel in both fists. "So you can lie."

"Perhaps. That doesn't mean I'm lying now."

Heaving angry breaths, I brush back the locks of wet blonde hair that have straggled into my face. "You can't have felt nothing. That isn't possible. No one feels nothing when they're with me."

He scoffs lightly. "You have a very inflated opinion of yourself, for a human."

"It's not vanity," I say. "I'm a damn *treat*. Want to see?"

His eyes widen, and his lips part, but he doesn't say no—so I open the towel, showing him my body—every lush, creamy curve, from my heavy breasts and rounded belly to my thick thighs.

The Prince stares. After a moment he presses his lips together and turns away. "You're very beautiful," he says quietly. "I never denied that. You're stunning, in fact."

"Then why are you—" I halt, grappling with a realization. "Wait—can you not feel arousal until the curse breaks? Do you have your—your cock?"

"I do have it, and its current level of functionality is not your concern," he says evenly. "What you seem to be unable to grasp, in your urgent desire to couple with the nearest male, is that I've been a nutcracker doll for weeks."

There's an edge to his voice now, a hint of anger, and part of me rejoices because I'm finally breaking through his apathetic calm.

He continues in a tight, fierce tone. "I have been captured, tortured, cursed, shrunken, handled by strangers, forced to stand stiffly in a human's mansion while my people suffered invasion by dark forces—and now I am grappling with constant changes in my body depending on how long it has been since I've drunk human blood. Not to mention I've had to fight to protect myself and two hapless human girls, while navigating my conquered kingdom and trying to find allies. So forgive me if I don't feel like coddling your human vanity tonight!"

His voice is much louder by the end. The door creaks behind me as the Sugarplum Faerie looks in.

"Everything all right?" he asks, and then his eyes pop wide at the sight of me standing there naked. "Bless the stars, that's a fine view! My best wishes to you both." He exits hastily, closing the door. Shutting me in with the Prince, who has stalked over to the fireplace and is staring glumly at the dancing flames.

"You should go wet his prick again," the Prince says gloomily.

"Who? Your cousin?"

"Isn't that why you two took so long fetching the food?"

"You think we were fucking? For a handful of minutes, in the pantry?"

The Prince shrugs. "He has accomplished conquests in far less time, and in far worse places. Who's to say you weren't… sampling the contents of his sugarplums?"

I stifle a snort-laugh. "Well, I wasn't."

"I don't care if you were," the Prince says hastily. "I don't care if you do it now. Do whatever you like, but do it elsewhere. I'd like to see if I can sleep."

I pick up my towel and wrap it around me again. Without another word to him I slip out of the bedroom and close the door.

The room next to the Prince's has a large bed with two nightgowns laid out on it—flouncy, gauzy things, with embroidered flowers in strategic places. I pull one on and lay the other over a chair. Then I braid my wet hair and flop onto the bed.

Perhaps I was being selfish, thoughtless, and inconsiderate. Clara tells me I am, sometimes. She's always quick to enumerate her own faults after she tells me mine, as if she doesn't want me to think she considers herself flawless. Perhaps her self-critical habits have made it too easy for me to ignore what she was trying to say.

I barely considered what the Nutcracker Prince has gone through, until he vented his thoughts to me just now. Certainly I wanted to help free him, but I've been mostly focused on what that means for *me*—which, at first, included adventure, exploration, and new sights—and then, once we arrived, I switched my focus to survival. I fixated on what *I* was enduring, how *I* could be safe, and how I could protect Clara.

I'm not responsible for what happened to the Prince, or how he feels about it. But if I'm trying to be a friend, or even a temporary tryst, I should try to be more considerate of what he has endured—what he's experiencing every hour, every day, until the curse is broken. The strangeness of living in a body that betrays you unexpectedly, that won't function to its full capacity, that forces you to treat your condition in a way you despise—it must take a toll.

From now on, I must attempt to show human decency to him. Even if he is sometimes an asshole.

11
CLARA

I stand beside the tub, still muzzy with sleep. It's a beautiful pink-marble oval with contoured edges, like nothing I've seen in my world. I remember the Sugarplum Faerie saying something about heating the water with magic. How convenient that must be.

My eyes feel heavy, so I rub them a little. There's a toilet in the corner, smooth marble like the bathtub, so I relieve myself and then strip off the ragged gown. It peels away easily, and so do my shredded petticoat, my panties, my corset. I bend over the tub, trailing my fingers through the water.

"Here we are," says the Sugarplum Faerie, bustling through the door of the bathing room. "I knew I had one of these left. I'll just drop this in and—"

He freezes, his golden eyes blown large at the sight of me.

I gasp, snatching a towel and holding it in front of myself. "Why are you in here?"

"I did say I would be back in a moment," he falters. "I thought you would wait to undress. I had to get this." He holds up a small orb, blue as winter sky. "It's a healing spell that diffuses into the water. I used one on your sister. I don't make many of these, you see—it's a complicated recipe, and most Fae have their own healing powers, but I thought you—with those—" He nods to the scrapes and bruises thatched along my arms. "I thought it might help."

"Oh." I hold the towel against my shoulders. "I—I didn't hear you say that. I think I'm still half asleep."

He paces forward, dropping the orb into the bathwater where it fizzes pleasantly and begins to color the water a lovely azure. But he keeps coming closer, until his black nails touch the corner of my towel, right near my fingertips.

"Perhaps it isn't safe for you to bathe alone in this state," he says softly. His upper lip hitches, showing a few of his pointed teeth.

My bare skin prickles with warmth. How can he still affect me like this, bone-weary as I am? My one foray into the world of sex with men wasn't nearly this exciting, and he hasn't even touched me anywhere salacious.

"Your nails are so sharp," I whisper.

"Do the claws frighten you, sweetling?" He lifts his hand, and a ripple of iridescent magic passes over his fingers. The claws disappear, leaving his nails smoothly rounded. "I can eliminate the danger if I need to, for certain— activities."

I swallow hard, willing the pulsing heat between my legs to dissipate. "I think you should go."

"Very well." He backs away. "I won't enter unannounced again, but I may call to you, and if you don't answer I will come in to make sure you haven't fallen asleep and drowned yourself."

"That seems wise." I give him a small smile, and his eyes light up. His answering toothy grin is terrifying, so alien to my weary mind that I stifle the urge to scream.

He doesn't seem to notice. After pointing out the soap, he saunters out of the bathing room and closes the door behind him, until there's just a thin crack.

He's Fae—an exiled, rogue Fae—and there is no guarantee he won't watch me bathe through that crack. But in truth, I find the idea titillating. I shouldn't, but there it is.

The water eases my discomfort in the most wonderful way. I use the soap, and then I pick up the straight razor by the soap dish and tend to my legs and underarms. I'm in the middle of carefully shaving the stubble beneath my left arm when the door of the bathing room bumps open and three skinny white shapes snake into the room, scuttling across the tiled floor.

I yelp and startle, and the blade of the razor slices into my breast. Gasping with the pain, I let the blade fall into the water and cup my breast, scrambling to my feet and staring wildly around the room. I can hear tiny feet, tiny nails, scrabbling across the tiles.

Then I catch a glimpse of something crouched under the washstand. The second I lay eyes on it, it moves, streaking across the floor to vanish behind a stack of multicolored towels.

The door opens wider and the Sugarplum Fae dashes in, his gauzy wings stirring with alarm. "What is it? I heard you scream."

His eyebrows fly up when he sees me standing in the tub, blood running from my breast through my fingers, down my side.

"There are *things* in here," I pant, staring wildly around. "Creatures, like little white rats, but longer."

"Not rats," he says. "Those are my pets. I have three weasel-cats who deign to visit me from time to time, and they like the bathroom when there's hot water and steam. I'll shoo them out. Lie down in the bath, sugar. The water will heal you."

"Why didn't I think of that?" I mutter, sinking back into the water.

"Because you're exhausted," he says brightly. He crouches, clicking his tongue, and three white furry shadows slink toward him. He scoops one up—it's smaller than a cat, fluffier than a weasel, with a plumed white tail.

"See?" He comes to the edge of the tub and holds the little thing closer to me. It has enormous eyes and the cutest tiny face, complete with long white whiskers. Its two miniscule front paws are cupped over the top of his hand. Though its pink nose is quivering wildly and nervously at my scent, it doesn't struggle to escape. It trusts him.

"This is Ferra," he says. "And the others are Shae and Kriss. Come on now, loves. Out you go." He herds them gently to the bathroom door. They scurry into the hallway, and he closes the door behind them once their tails are clear.

"I didn't know Fae had pets," I say.

"Why shouldn't we? Because we're monstrously wicked?" He strides back to the tub and kneels beside it. "Maybe I only keep them because I'm planning to sacrifice them for some fell ritual."

"Then why did you name them?"

"Ah, you've got me there." He flashes me a smile. "Now let's see what you've done to yourself, darling."

I'm mostly submerged in the water, which is colored deep blue but still transparent. He can see me—all of me.

Slowly I rise a little higher, until my breasts are above the surface. The cut is still bleeding.

"When your pets startled me, I accidentally cut myself with the razor," I explain.

"Why were you using a razor?"

"Back home it was the fashion to remove body hair. Papa didn't like us doing it, but Louisa and I prefer it."

"I never use one," he says. "Most Fae don't have body hair to remove. I only have this razor because my last overnight guest brought it with her and left it behind. She's a fenodyree, a very hairy species of Fae. Not that I minded, but she liked to keep certain areas trimmed. You're lucky it was here. Or unlucky, depending on how you look at it."

He reaches into the water, right between my legs, and plucks the razor from the bottom of the tub. He doesn't touch me, yet my inner thighs and my entire sex come alive with tremulous sensation at the mere proximity of his hand.

His gaze lingers unmistakably on the delicate folds between my thighs. He takes his time admiring every contour of my body, from my legs, to my flat stomach, then up my ribs to my chest.

And I don't say a word in protest.

"I should check the depth of that cut." He cups my arm and lifts it. "May I?"

He doesn't need to touch me. It's an excuse, and we both know it.

I nod anyway.

When his fingers contact the thin skin of my breast, I bite back a little gasp. His fingers shift, grazing the heavy lower curve, then gliding around my areola. My nipples tighten to beads, and I pin my thighs together, conscious of slickness between my folds, under the water.

His thumb slides over the cut, which is a faint scratch now. "All healed," he murmurs, withdrawing his hands from my breast and my arm. "I'll let you dry off now. Your room is down the hall to the right. Third door on the left."

He's getting up. His wings have lifted, fanning gently behind him.

As he moves to the door, I murmur, "Please… stay."

Slowly he turns, biting his lip, heat in his eyes.

"In case I have another accident," I say.

"You do seem rather prone to peril. You realize I've saved your life twice? Three times, if we count feeding you sugarplums before you perished from hunger."

A smile starts deep inside me, spreading like sunshine until it reaches my face. He catches his breath and then exhales, slowly. "Stars, you're exquisite."

I rise unsteadily in the tub, and he moves in, catching my hand, my arm, helping me step out. There's a towel spread on the floor, still damp from when my sister stepped onto it.

I'm not sure what I'm doing. I don't do *this*—the reckless lust, the seduction of strangers. I'm not even sure who's seducing whom. This feels more like a gradual intertwining of desires and actions and movements. Like a dance.

The Sugarplum Faerie turns me so my back is against his chest. We're facing a full-length mirror I didn't notice before, a lovely gilt-edged thing heavy with gold roses and gemstones. I see him in it—indecently beautiful, with his feathery pink hair and soft pink lips. He's framed by those gauzy wings, and his black claws clasp my shoulders delicately.

I'm on full display—my slim, pale, human shape—full breasts, tapered waist, hips slightly tilted, long legs. My auburn hair is darkly wet, plastered to my sides and back, a few curls clinging to one breast and then dangling down to my waist.

"You see yourself," murmurs the faerie in my ear. "You see how beautiful you are."

Magic ripples over one of his hands, smoothing the nails, and he slides that hand down my body, squeezing my breast lightly, smoothing over my stomach, headed for lower parts. Part of me wants to tighten my thighs to prevent access—but that is the Clara from another world, another time.

This new Clara hungers for his touch.

I widen my stance a little, opening my pussy for him, and he hums against my cheek as three of his fingers slip between my folds, parting them. I release a tiny whimper as his central finger strokes deeper, slowly, tenderly.

"Look at this little swollen bud," he murmurs, patting it with a fingertip. "These wet lips, so beautifully soaked. I'll make you come so sweetly for me, darling."

"I thought you wanted Louisa," I say, breathless. "She knows how to make love better than I do."

"You're much more interesting, sugar."

Never in my life has anyone told me that. Louisa is the conversationalist, the fun one, the flamboyant one. I am the quiet one, the dull one, the reader and painter.

"That doesn't make any sense," I whisper.

"Does it have to?" He's still stroking me, gentle slick circles over my sex, each one sending a slow surge of pleasure through my belly. "Hush, sugar, and watch yourself come."

And he thrusts two fingers deep inside.

Another tiny sound escapes me as my body sucks him in, welcomes the invasion with a fresh flood of wetness.

His two fingers thrust slowly, exploring my insides, while his thumb flicks over my clit. His other hand cups one of my breasts, lightly squeezing the flesh, tending to the peaked nipple.

A shift of his hips brings his front against my rear, and I feel a thick hardness pressing my backside through his trousers. But he doesn't ask to be inside me. He holds me steady while I instinctively grip his bicep. My body, overly sensitized from the day's events, is already quivering on the edge.

"Move your thighs apart a bit wider, darling, so I can see that sweet pussy of yours," says the Faerie. "Such a tender little mortal, so sensitive. I have a gift for you before you come on my fingers. Are you ready?"

I suspect the gift is his cock. And yes, I am desperately, helplessly ready.

But when I nod, he says, "I have a rule that if I see someone naked twice, I must give them my true name. It keeps me from forming unwise attachments with anyone I don't trust. And I've seen you naked twice, so I think it only fair that I tell you my name. You won't scream it tonight, but I hope to hear it one day when I taste that melted sugar between your legs. Do you feel how slick you are, Clara? You're so close to coming for me. See how flushed your body is—your breasts, your pussy, your neck, your cheeks—I'll tell you my name if you come for me, you adorable, lickable creature. Come for me, come—"

He pulls his fingers out of me and rubs my clit, swiftly, delicately, the perfect amount of pressure. The pleasure crashes in like the tide, a cleansing wash, a blissful wave expanding through my insides, weakening my thighs and tightening my stomach.

The Sugarplum Faerie sinks his fingers into me again, letting me clench around them while his thumb presses comfortingly against my clit.

"Keep your eyes open," he whispers. "Look at yourself."

My face and body are flushed, my hair curling damp around my shoulders, my sex cupped by his hand, my legs trembling with the force of the bliss. Soft gasps escape my lips, while I shamelessly arch, urging my sex against his palm.

"My name is Finias." He nibbles the curve of my ear with his sharp teeth.

"Finias," I whisper.

When I descend from the crest of the climax, I feel light-headed, melted, glowing and limp. Finias wraps me in a soft pink towel that matches his hair and walks me down the hall.

I cannot believe what I did. It's something Louisa would do, not me. Strange how Faerie seems to be distorting everything, eliciting new qualities from each of us.

Or perhaps they aren't new. Perhaps they were only buried.

Finias pushes open the door of a bedroom. There's a tiny magical orb-light floating near the bedside, and it reveals my sister, splayed across the bed, occupying the entire space. She's flushed, snoring faintly.

"Let's not disturb her," whispers Finias. "You can take my bed." He snatches a gauzy nightdress off a chair nearby and guides me out of that room to another, larger one. The bed is big enough for three or four people.

I look at it, then at him.

He shrugs. "In the past I've enjoyed taking more than one person to bed. These days I prefer one at a time, someone I can trust. Which means I rarely entertain anymore."

That's what I am to him. Entertainment.

It should bother me, I suppose. But I'm actually relieved. I don't want him staking some sort of dramatic Fae claim on me.

"I'll sleep on one of the couches if you like," he says. "But I'd rather share the bed."

"It's enormous. We can share." I take the nightgown from him and pull it over my body. It is by far the most scandalous thing I have worn, except for my shredded gown from earlier.

I hook an eyebrow at Finias, and he gives me a shrug and an unrepentant grin. "Two beautiful women in my house. I might as well enjoy the sights."

He must notice the change in my expression, because he adds hastily, "I won't be finger-fucking your sister, sugar, or taking her any other way. I do believe she's trying to entrap my cousin, without much success. They can't seem to speak to each other long without arguing."

"Hm," I reply, sliding into the sheets. I love my sister, and it bothers me that she's unhappy. But I'll talk to her tomorrow. She needs her sleep, and I cannot function anymore tonight.

The Sugarplum Faerie strips down to a pair of short pants and settles himself on the opposite side of the bed. The glowing orbs in the room dim even further without a word from him; he must be able to control them with his mind.

I'm deliciously comfortable between smooth, warm sheets that smell of vanilla and cinnamon sugar.

"What shall I paint for you tomorrow?" I murmur.

His voice reaches me faintly as I drift into dreams. "Whatever you think I would most like to see."

12
LOUISA

When I wake up, Clara isn't in the bed we were supposed to share.

Small wonder, I suppose, since I tend to flail in my sleep and I'm taking up all the available space.

I rise, shivering a little. The rooms are much chillier than they were last night. Perhaps winter has come suddenly, as the Sugarplum Faerie said.

Snagging one of the blankets from the bed and wrapping myself in it, I make a quick stop in the washroom before going in search of my sister.

It doesn't take long to find her. She's in a large bedroom decorated with a confection of vibrant tapestries and outfitted with stenciled wooden furniture, lying on a bed that's more pillows than blankets. In the center of the pillowy nest lies the pink-haired faerie, shirtless, on his side with his pliant wings draped behind him—and Clara is tucked against his chest.

His arm drapes her waist. With the brown-sugar dusting of freckles across his nose, he looks very young, though as a Faerie there's no telling his true age from appearance.

Clara is a year older than me. Usually she's every inch the protective older sibling—responsible and cautious. But I'm defensive of her too, especially in situations where I've had more experience. I may never have slept with a Faerie, but I've dealt with plenty of lustful men. I know their tricks, and all the ways they can cause a woman pain.

I stalk up to the bedside, lean over the pink-haired Faerie, and flick his cheek sharply with my fingers.

He's on his feet in a blink, poised lightly on the mattress, his eyes sharply alert and a blade in his hand. He moved so deftly, so smoothly, he didn't even wake Clara.

Hiding my shock under a frown, I beckon for him to follow me out of the room. When he does, I pull the door shut.

"What did you do to my sister?" I hiss.

"That is her business and mine." He's no imp of mischief now, no saucy laughing charmer. This is him, woken out of a sound sleep by a perceived threat—sober and unsmiling.

"It's my business because she's my only family," I tell him. "She was exhausted beyond reason last night. This—" I gesture to his bedroom door— "it's not like her. It's not something she would do."

"I didn't force her." He flips the knife in his hand. It vanishes with a twinkle, and I inhale sharply. That teases a smirk out of him. "I didn't even fuck her," he continues. "I gave her what she needed, and then she shared my bed since you were using the whole bed in the guest room."

Narrowing my eyes, I examine his face, searching for signs of deceit. He stares back, brows slightly raised, his gaze open.

"Fair enough," I say at last. "But don't be getting any ideas about using her for your pleasure and hurting her feelings. She's important to me. Harm her in any way, and you'll regret it."

I half-expect him to react with haughty defiance and some comment about his own power compared to puny mortals, but he simply laughs aloud, all his triangular teeth showing.

"You're so delightfully defensive. I love it. Trust me, I won't use your sister unless she wants to be used. In which case I will use her most enthusiastically." He sticks his tongue out at me with a lascivious wink, then saunters down the hall. "We'll have breakfast, and then we can leave Clara to paint while we gather some allies to escort us to the Unending Pool."

I'm uncertain about leaving Clara alone, but when we discuss the plan over breakfast, the Sugarplum Faerie assures me his house has protection spellwork in place. And Clara seems so eager to paint again, so happy with the supplies he gives her—paints in more colors than I knew existed, along with canvases and thick, smooth, heavy parchment. He's something of a painter himself, it seems—he creates the intricate decorative labels for his spells, and he did all the stencil-work on the furniture throughout the house.

He sets Clara up in his spacious, sunny workroom on the second floor, where she can gaze out of the large windows and draw inspiration from the landscape.

Reluctantly I leave her there, barefoot, in a blue dress he conjured for her, biting her lip as she begins to sketch the outline she'll later fill with colors.

I'm wearing a scarlet tunic and leggings, rich and warm. The black fur around my neck and wrists is flecked with white, and gold thread winds over the bodice in intricate designs.

"Do you have no tailors in Faerie, then?" I ask.

"Of course we do. Conjured clothing only lasts a few days," the Sugarplum Faerie tells me. "We prefer to have actual garments made. But in a pinch, I can make a decent outfit with magic." He steps back and nods, satisfied with his work on my clothes.

The Prince comes up behind him, eyeing my ensemble with a dour expression. "A little flashy, isn't it?" he says. "We're gathering allies, not attending a midwinter revel."

The Sugarplum Faerie is unperturbed. "Louisa deserves to look fantastic."

"I like this outfit," I say crisply. "And if your Cursed Maleficence wants another sip of my blood later, I think you'll agree that it's perfect."

The Prince frowns. "Are you trying to bribe me?"

"Why no. I believe it's called *blackmail*."

The Sugarplum Faerie laughs. "Come along, both of you. Surely you can argue and walk at the same time? You've got your weapons, yes? Let's be off."

The forest looks far different than it did yesterday. All the foliage has either turned brilliant yellow or has transformed into transparent skeleton leaves. Frigid air nips at my fingers until the Sugarplum Faerie conjures me a pair of little black gloves.

"Don't you have autumn here in Faerie?" I ask him.

"Not much of one," he replies. "A day or two at most."

"How strange, to switch directly from late summer to winter!"

"We don't think of it that way here," he says. "For us, the seasons are warm and cold, rejoicing and rest. Two sides of a coin—one for growth, the other for quiet reflection. Did you know some Fae hibernate, like certain animals in your realm?"

"I didn't know." I rub my arms swiftly against the chill.

The Sugarplum Faerie touches my shoulder. Warmth suffuses the fabric of the overdress and leggings, until I'm walking in perfect comfort despite the cold.

"That feels wonderful. Is *his* magic as strong as yours?" I nod ahead, indicating the Prince.

"Are you joking?" says the SugarPlum Faerie. "He's the *Crown Prince of Faerie*."

"So… yes?"

The Sugarplum Faerie lowers his voice. "When Lir is at his full strength, with the might of the throne and the crown behind him, nothing can resist him."

"Lir?" I whisper.

"Damn it." The pink-haired faerie closes his eyes. "I have a bad habit of letting names slip. Yes, he's Lirannon, and I'm Finias. His father the king—my uncle—died recently and passed his royal power to Lir. As far as the magic of the land is concerned, Lir is the true king. But the official coronation hadn't taken place yet when he was captured, and Lir, being the stickler that he is, refuses to call himself 'king' until the ceremony is complete."

Before I can respond, the tall faerie ahead of us calls back dryly, "I've heard you say my name at least four times now, Finias."

Finias wrinkles his freckled nose, glancing at me. "It's rude to tell a human another faerie's name without their permission."

"Such private information is best saved for when the faerie in question is ready to divulge it." The Prince turns around and walks backward for a moment, looking sternly at us both. Though he has discarded the hat, he's still wearing his scarlet uniform, and despite the hours that have passed overnight, he looks remarkably un-cursed. His black hair is wavy, his mouth mobile and soft, and his green eyes quick and cool. There's no hint of the wooden doll about him, except a very slight stiffness in his gait and bearing.

"If you were anyone else, I would ask you to punish me for my foolishness," says the Sugarplum Faerie, with a plaintive sigh. "I do love being punished. But since you're my cousin, that would be more irritating than pleasurable."

"I'll let it pass," says the Prince. "Since you're aiding me in this quest of mine."

The look he gives Finias shies nearer to true thankfulness than any expression I've seen from him.

"Look at you, being grateful. It's fucking adorable." With a burst of humming wings, Finias flies ahead and gives his cousin a hearty kiss on the cheek.

"Ugh, get off, Fin." Lir shoves him away, but he's half-smiling.

A companionable silence follows, but it doesn't last long, because Finias likes to talk almost as much as I do. After answering some of my questions about Faerie, he begins to complain about the pace at which we're traveling.

"I forgot how slowly one must go when humans are along," he groans. "You see, Louisa, if you were Fae and Lir wasn't cursed, we could go much faster. All it takes is a bit of magic, and—"

He speeds off, zigzagging among the trees until he's out of sight.

Lir glances at me. "Don't worry, he'll be back in a moment."

"I assumed so." I look away from him. "I want to apologize to you for my thoughtlessness last night."

"Very well." A moment's silence, and then he raises his eyebrows. "Was that it? Was that the apology?"

I glower at him. "Yes."

"Humans," he scoffs. "So lazy when it comes to making amends."

"Forget it," I snap. "I take back the apology."

"You can't take back what never existed."

"My *god*, you're maddening," I gasp. "How much time have you spent in the human realm? You pretend you know everything about humans, but I'm convinced most of what you *think* you know is hearsay and prejudice!"

He flushes faintly. "I—I've read books about humans. And some of them live in this realm. They're usually cursed humans, or slaves to the Unseelie, or temporary guests, or visiting conjurers, but—"

"So you know very little about average humans living normal lives."

"Hypocrite," he says scathingly. "You know even less about my kind. Beyond the pain iron causes us, and the fact that we're long-lived and have magic, what more do you know? You asked me if I could lie, for stars' sake. Of *course* I can lie. The idea of Faeries not being able to lie is a foul deception of the Unseelie, a way to convince humans they're in no danger right before they're dragged into some hideous Unseelie bower for pleasure sport."

"You admit that Faeries kidnap humans and ravage them, then?"

"The Unseelie," he says, slowly and distinctly, as if he's talking to a small child. "The Unseelie have no morals, and they do such things."

"Yet your cousin has Unseelie friends. Apparently not all of them are as horrible as you would have me believe."

"Think of the rats we fought yesterday, and judge for yourself!" he exclaims.

"What if I brought you a rapist and murderer from some dungeon, and told you to judge all humans by his deeds?" I'm nearly shouting at him now. "You can't take the actions of one and infer the wickedness or unworthiness of all!"

Finias whizzes out of the trees and comes to a sudden stop in front of us. He's carrying a basket he certainly didn't have before.

He cocks his head. "You two were traveling pleasantly when I left. What happened?"

Lir and I begin talking loudly, gesturing at each other while Finias recoils.

"All right, all right! Maybe this will settle your spirits." He lifts the checkered cloth over the basket, and a puff of sugar-and-cinnamon air wafts from the interior. "Hot cinnamon buns, glazed in Mother Tollison's best icing."

"We just ate breakfast," says the Prince.

"Your point?" Finias plucks a fat bun from the basket and sinks all his sharp teeth into it. His eyes roll back. "If these don't make you forget your quarrel, you may strip me naked and hang me upside down from the tallest tree in the forest."

"No one is stripping you naked," grumbles Lir, but as he stalks past his cousin, he snatches a roll.

I take one as well. "Thank you. I do hope a few simple words of thanks is *sufficient* in this realm." I shoot a pointed glance at Lir's back. "After all, I do remember someone barely being able to force the words 'thank you' out of his mouth the other day."

"My thanks comes easily when it is deserved," snaps the Prince.

"Who threw the bombs that saved your hide?" I exclaim. "You called me a hapless human girl last night, but who protected you from the iron shrapnel? Who kept a rat soldier off your back? Who gave you blood from her own vein so you could function better? Who—"

"Enough!" he bellows, whirling around. "Thank you, oh most gracious and most demanding of human women. Thank you for defending me, and thank you for allowing me to save *your* life as well. I will be forever indebted to you for that dubious honor. If I hadn't kept you quiet, the mole-rat would have gotten you and I wouldn't have the delight of this stimulating verbal conflict, this insufferable poisoning of an otherwise pleasant morning. So yes, Lady Louisa—thank you." He ends with a flourishing, extravagant bow.

I stare at him, my mouth full of shockingly delicious cinnamon bun.

"So *that's* how a proper thank-you is done," I say through the mouthful. "I always wondered."

The Prince stares at me, breathing hard. And then—something in his expression cracks, and one side of his mouth quirks upward. He tries to force the expression away but he can't— he's grinning, and he's—*goddamn*, he's beautiful. His teeth aren't all sharp like his cousin's, but he has a pair of wicked-looking canines above and below.

The smile only lasts for a second before he manages to get himself under control and continues down the path. Fin elbows me approvingly and then begins to explain Fae speed, how far and fast they can go, how much magical energy is consumed in the process, and how different species of Fae have various speeds and distances of which they're capable.

I'm not sure how much time is passing, or if days in the Fae realm are even the same length as ours; but at last Finias tells me, "We're nearly to the tavern. I sent off messages last night while you were bathing and Clara was napping, so if we're lucky, several potential allies will be there. Lir, I'll conjure you a hooded cloak, since we can't have every patron in the place knowing your identity. Don't tell them the exact nature of the curse, either."

"Why not?" Lir frowns. "These friends of yours—can we not trust them?"

"I never said they were friends. Said they were potential allies—for a price. There's a scarcity of folk loyal to your throne in these parts, cousin. Besides which, few dare to travel through the most heavily occupied territory of the Rat King—which is where we'll need to go to reach the Unending Pool."

My nerves have been strained all morning, my gaze darting into the depths of the wood as we walked, searching for signs of hulking bodies or rat tails. I don't know whether chance or some magic of Fin's has kept foul things from accosting us today, but the thought of venturing through an area more thickly infested with the Rat King's soldiers makes me quake inside. Clara and I might not survive such a journey. We might only serve to slow the others down, or endanger them when they're forced to defend us.

But we have to go along. Lir will need blood every so often to keep the effects of his curse at bay.

"How long a journey is it?" I ask.

"Two weeks if we must walk at a human's pace," replies Finias. "We may be able to use horses, but we certainly can't use airborne forms of transportation or we'll risk drawing too much attention."

That's it, then. Clara and I must go with them.

"Do I have your authority to bargain on your behalf?" Finias asks the Prince. "I assume the royal treasury will bear the burden of whatever price we must pay?"

Lir nods grimly. "Whatever it takes. But do try to keep it reasonable."

Fin splays a hand over his heart. "I'm nothing if not a skilled bargainer."

"You're many things, and a spendthrift is one of them," mutters the Prince. "Do your best not to bankrupt the kingdom."

With Lir draped in a conjured cloak, we round a clump of trees and step onto a new path, one paved with flat rocks that shine golden in the bright air. Leaves of ruby-red or aquamarine flutter in the trees, or drift in jeweled splendor through the haze of sunshine filtering through the branches.

As we walk, I become conscious of a faint pattering and thumping that seems to come from all around us. It sets my nerves on edge, even though the two Fae males don't seem concerned.

"Do you hear that sound?" I ask. "Is it hoofbeats? Footsteps?"

"It is the heartbeat of the trees," replies Lir. He pauses, laying a palm gently against a bluish trunk veined with gold. "This area is an extension of the Living Forest, one of the most precious places in the Seelie realm."

"The trees of the Living Forest hold the spirits of dryads," Fin explains. "Most are sleeping now, but every fifty years they emerge, and then—ah, what delights!" His yellow eyes brighten, and he tosses back his pink hair. "You've never fucked a dryad, have you, Lir? Ah, you've missed out. It's an ethereal experience. Bit of an acquired taste, I suppose, but then, I've never been too particular."

"What are dryads like?" I ask curiously.

"Like willowy saplings, but in female shape," he says. "But they can *stretch*. And some of them have two vaginas, and three or four breasts. When their sweet sap is running they'll let you suckle like a hungry babe—"

"Oh, for stars' sake, stop!" Lir shudders.

"Two vaginas?" I breathe, fascinated. "Can they both orgasm at once?"

"They *can*."

"I'm so jealous. That must feel incredible. And it must be a delight to watch."

"It is," Fin assures me. "I've always loved watching women come."

Lir marches ahead, his back stiffer than ever as he puts distance between himself and us.

"He has never liked open discussion of sex," Fin says aside to me. "A bit of an oddity among the Fae in that respect. Most of us will fuck anyone, anywhere. And most of us enjoy a good orgy. Once you've been to enough of those, though, it all becomes rather hollow. Last one I attended I found myself simply going through the motions, wondering when it would be over." He laughs ruefully, his gaze turning distant.

Much as I like sex, I don't believe I'd want to engage in it in front of others, or in groups. I would rather claim one person as mine and learn all the little ways I could make him come undone.

It's odd how casually I can discuss sex with Finias, just like we talked about Fae speed or the seasons of this realm. I'm a little aroused—not because of him, but because I can't help imagining Lir in the center of an orgy, looking very shocked and displeased. I picture taking him by the hand, leading him somewhere private, stealing the haughty words right out of his mouth, and replacing them with helpless groans.

It would be such delicious fun to dismantle the Prince.

Now I am much wetter. Damn it.

"Lir is walking very fast for a curse victim." Chuckling, Fin tugs a peppermint cane from a pouch at his belt and begins to suck on it. "We should try to catch up with him. The tavern is just ahead—you can see it there, through the trees."

Right before we reach the tavern, Fin turns me to face him and touches the tops of my ears. A prickling sensation dances across my cartilage.

"There," he says. "Pointed ears. I already altered your scent this morning, so you wouldn't draw monsters so readily."

"Thank you?" I arch an eyebrow. "But why would my scent attract monsters? I bathed thoroughly, trust me."

"It's not that," Finias assures me. "Humans have a more carnal scent than the Fae. It incites lust or hunger in darker beings of this realm. Lures them, like a beacon. Seelie Fae can smell it, too, but its effect is less powerful with us."

"So I smell like food?"

"No." Lir eyes me sternly from the shadow of his hood. "You smell like food *and* sex. And… more."

Finias glances at him sharply. He seems about to ask something, but then he pops the peppermint stick back into his mouth, where he holds it between his teeth like a pipe.

"In we go," he says around the striped candy. "Lir, pray don't reveal yourself until I give you the signal."

He leads the way to the tavern's front door, over which swings a creaky sign with a crowned toad on it. The toad's tongue lolls from its wide mouth rather lecherously.

I follow the two Fae into the tavern, staying close behind them. We wend our way through the noisy front room into a bigger back room, not quite as busy. There's a large booth built into the corner, where several figures are already sitting. Finias makes for that spot.

"Good cheer, friends!" he calls merrily. He tosses a handful of rainbow dust into the air, but instead of settling it rises up to the ceiling, swirling and sparkling, illuminating the other guests' faces a bit better. "I know you've all missed me terribly. Achorn, for you." He tosses several wrapped candies to a burly man. "And for you, Theanne my love—" and he draws two crystalline balls from his satchel and passes them carefully to a leather-clad Fae woman with hair the color of fresh blood.

While he's passing out more treats to the others at the table, Lir pulls up a chair for me and for himself. I had thought we would sit in the booth, but I immediately understand his reasoning—in chairs, we can be part of the conversation, but we can also be ready to run or fight if we need to.

My heart is pounding, but I try to appear calm as I take my seat. I let my fingers play across the hilt of my dagger as Finias perches on the corner of the table and props one of his boots on the bench.

"You come bearing gifts as always, Sugarplum," growls the big man, Achorn. With his furred calf ears and slightly bovine features, he seems to be a different sort of Fae than Lir and Finias. "Yet the more gifts you give, the more suspicious I get. Why have you called us here at such a time? The charms on this place may have held against the Rat King's soldiers so far, but the host tells us they press him harder every day. This could be the day they finally break through and swarm in, and I'd rather not be here when it happens."

"And why is that?" asks a grating voice. Its owner has flatter features than most humans or Fae, partly covered with bluish-green scales. "Why shouldn't the folk of the Dread Court enjoy Seelie hospitality? Do you despise them simply because they look different from you?"

"I despise them because they are bastards," growls Achorn.

"Friends, friends." Finias takes the peppermint stick from his mouth. His tongue has sharpened it to a keen point. "You know I have had allies, acquaintances, and lovers from both Courts. I am a neutral party, am I not? Yet even someone like myself, with a heart wide enough for both courts, can see that the invasion of the Seelie kingdom is throwing our realm off balance. Things were comfortable, yes? Plenty of goods and pleasure to be had, and work enough to keep us busy, if we wanted it. The coming of the Rat King has thrown all that into disarray. Personally I've had enough of these mindless rat-beasts rooting around—the mole-rats, rat-bears, and other strange creatures assembled by the dire magic of the Unseelie King. And I don't take kindly to certain lovely parts of this land being soiled."

"So you're taking a side at last, Sugarplum?" asks Theanne, the leather-clad woman.

"Not exactly." Finias winces as if the idea pains him. "I'm merely saying it may be in all our best interests to restore this realm to its former balance."

"And how will we do that?" demands Achorn. "The uppity princeling has fled, or was stolen. His claim and his powers are the only way to push the Rat King back into his own kingdom."

"What if the uppity princeling wasn't quite gone?" says Finias, with a waggle of his brows. "What if he was simply—indisposed? What if he needed an escort to some place of ancient importance—say, the Unending Pool? And what if some of us could provide said escort, so that the uppity princeling could be restored to his full power and return everything to the way it was?"

"That's what you're after." It's a Faerie who hasn't yet spoken, one with long, feathery, gray antennae, like a moth's. At her back is a brown and gray bundle—her wings, folded. "You want us to help you get through the Rat King's conquered territory so you can reach the Pool. The young Seelie prince must be cursed, then. Who did it? The Rat King himself, or someone else?"

Finias looks around at them, all playfulness gone. "Drosselmeyer."

It's as if he has spoken the darkest curse known to Fae-kind. The reptilian Fae hisses, Theanne's fingers tighten to fists, and the moth Fae turns deathly gray. A dark-skinned, white-freckled Fae with antlers murmurs to a chubby pink-skinned male beside him. Even burly Achorn recoils.

"Drosselmeyer took the prince?" says Theanne. "And he escaped?"

"He did." Lir leans forward, pushing his hood back slightly. "And your king needs your help."

The reaction to the Prince's revelation is much different than the response to Drosselmeyer's name. A restless energy travels through the gathered mercenaries, and they exchange wary glances. Finias lets out a huffed breath, as if slightly frustrated that Lir didn't wait for his signal.

"Your Majesty," says Theanne, bowing her head. After a moment, the others follow her example.

"You may call me 'Prince' until I claim the throne and am officially crowned," says Lir. "Until then, I require your assistance."

"Require, but with *money*," intervenes Finias, with an ingratiating smile. "The Prince recognizes that these are difficult times, and he is prepared to offer a substantial reward to those who aid him in breaking his curse and recovering his throne."

"What is this curse?" asks the reptilian Fae.

"That's not important," says Finias quickly. "What's important is that, in these troubled days, we are prepared to offer remuneration in exchange for what you already do best—fighting."

They begin talking about distances, risk involved, the inclusion of meals, and other factors, along with quantities of a currency with which I'm unfamiliar. Instead of listening, I watch their faces, intrigued by the shift of each Fae's unique features.

Until the Prince reaches over and grips my leg, just above the knee.

It's a frenzied grasp, one that transmits his panic as clearly as words.

He has ducked back into his hood, so I can't see his face—but when I look at his hand, I note the change in the quality of his skin. A shift in the color, a faint wood grain beginning to appear.

"Excuse us, would you? We must have a word with the tavern cook about the Prince's meal. He's very particular," I say to the others. "Carry on."

Finias picks up the flow of conversation smoothly, commanding attention by juggling a few of his candy spells while he's talking. Thanks to that distraction, the other Fae don't seem to notice that the Prince has to use my shoulder to pull himself upright, or that his movements are increasingly stiff as he and I move toward the back of the common room.

There are a couple of doorways, so I choose the darkest one, the one that looks least frequented. It turns out to be a short hall leading to a back door—probably the way to the privy or the outhouse. There's another door in the hall, half-open, revealing a clumsy stack of extra chairs, a few buckets, a couple of mops, and some jugs that I'd guess contain strong soap for cleaning.

"The Fae have to clean?" I ask.

"If they're not gifted with that kind of magic and they don't have such spells on hand, yes." The Prince's voice sounds different—throatier, raspier as he transitions back to his Nutcracker form. "Some of Finias's most popular spells are cleaning spells. He can barely keep them in stock. Ah!" His body jerks, and his elbow creaks woodenly as he braces himself against the doorframe.

"Get in here." I pull him into the closet and drag the door shut. Instantly we're engulfed in blackness.

"I don't want to drink human blood again," he rasps.

"You don't have a choice." Fumbling in the dark, I push back the hood of his cloak. "My arm is healed, thanks to Finias's bathwater. I'll have to make a fresh cut."

"It's happening—faster—this time," he gasps.

It's going to take me a few moments to draw my dagger and carefully slice my skin in the dark. Judging by Lir's voice, he doesn't have that long.

To buy time, I bite my own lip, hard, until I feel salty blood welling out.

I reach up, find his lips with my fingers, and stand on tiptoe so I can press my mouth to his.

A hungry groan breaks from him, harsh and sudden, as if he's trying to hold it back and can't. His lips are stiff and hard, but I keep pressing my bleeding mouth against them, and after a moment they soften again. He begins sucking on my lower lip, drawing it into his mouth.

I've been in my share of closets with men. But never have I shared such a dark, close space with a man who needs me so viscerally, yet dislikes me so much.

I'm gripping his shoulders so I can hold myself on tiptoe and keep my mouth against his. He doesn't touch me at first, just keeps sucking my lip as if his existence depends on it. He's breathing hard, and each huff of warm air from his mouth is also mine—I can taste the cedar bitterness and the vanilla warmth of him, mingled with the saltiness of my own blood.

My lip pops free of his mouth, wet and swollen.

"I need more." A shameful whisper in the dark.

"Very well." I hesitate to try and slice my own arm in the dark. But there's another option.

I unbutton the top two buttons of my overdress and pull the furry collar aside, off my shoulder.

"Here." I cup the back of his neck and pull his mouth toward the curve of my shoulder, above my collarbone. His body creaks as he bends. "Just bite me here. I can cover it easily."

"No," he growls.

"I know you have the teeth for it. Do it now. We need you at your best."

"My best." He scoffs lightly, but he lets me pull his head closer, until his lips brush the warm skin between my neck and my shoulder.

"The scent of you," he murmurs raggedly, and the words send a shiver of yearning through my whole body.

Then he bites.

Pain spears through my shoulder, and I gasp. He clamps his jaws firmly into my flesh and sucks, and sucks, while I instinctively clutch his upper arms. I can feel their stiffness receding as he gulps my blood.

His hand slides around me, across my lower back, pulling me closer.

Savoring the swollen bit of my wounded lip, I let my hips sway against his. And just as I suspected, there's another kind of hardness poking against the fabric of his cloak, his uniform jacket, and his pants. He must have very fine equipment for it to make that much of an impression through all those layers.

While he's still occupied with drinking, I slide my hand from his bicep along his side, then squeeze it between us, working it beneath his cloak until my fingers encounter the firm ridge of his cock beneath his clothes.

He freezes, his teeth still buried in my flesh. His hair is tickling my neck and cheek.

"Look at this," I say softly. "Seems you still have wood here."

A tremor runs over his body as I rub my palm along the bulge.

"I think I could make you come in your pants, Your Highness," I whisper.

He unlatches his mouth from my shoulder and straightens, his chest heaving.

My fingertips slide upward, under the hem of his soldier's jacket, to the edge of his pants. I tug them slightly down and away from his body.

When he has my blood in him, the clothes are separate from his skin, no longer painted on. Yet he hasn't changed his outfit, and I'm not sure why.

My fingers dip into his pants, grazing the flat heated skin of his lower abdomen.

And then I touch the head of his cock.

It's a smooth, damp bulge, with a tiny slit that's seeping wetness. I dab my fingertip over that spot, and the Prince shudders again.

I nudge the tip of his cock out, above the edge of his pants, so that it's pinned to his belly by his waistband. I can't see it in the dark, but I trace its shape with my fingertips again, pressing lightly just beneath the head, where it meets the shaft. I stroke that spot, now and then rubbing my palm over the ridge that's still hidden under his trousers.

"Such a nice cock," I murmur. "It's so happy to see me. You should let it out to play more often."

He doesn't answer, only releases a shuddering breath.

"My clit is so tingly right now," I whisper. "And my pussy is so wet. I want to slide this hard cock between my pussy lips, deep into my body. I want to suck it all the way into my tight hole."

"Filthy mortal," he gasps. "Stop it."

I pause, unsure if he means it.

He pushes me back. It's not a violent shove, merely a decisive one. There's a rustle of fabric; he's probably putting his dick away.

"I don't have sex with dirty-mouthed human sluts." His tone is harsh, a blow in the dark. "I only sleep with people I care about. And you will never be one of those people."

He yanks open the door and flings himself out of the closet.

I crumple to the floor, listening to the beat of his boots recede as he returns to the common room.

13
CLARA

The painting is nearly done.

Unfortunately I can hear the others returning—the banging of the front door downstairs, the clomp of boot heels, and the light, merry voice of the Sugarplum Faerie, muffled by the ceiling and walls. A deeper voice responds—the Nutcracker Prince. I don't hear my sister, though.

Footsteps on the stairs. Frantically I lay aside the brush and leap up, racing for the door. I reach it just as it opens, and I hold it firm, just a crack of space no wider than three fingers.

"I'm not finished yet!" I cry. "No one can come in!"

"But it's my house." A laughing male voice with a pleading note. "I want to see my painting."

"Not yet."

Rivulets of rainbow magic engulf the door, and it disappears entirely, leaving me standing far too close to the tall Sugarplum Faerie, who grins down at me.

"Please." I back away, holding out my arms as if to block his progress. As if I could stop him. "Please, it's nearly done. Please wait."

His sly grin fades. "Have you eaten anything while we were gone? Drunk anything? You know I told you where to find food, water—"

"She doesn't eat or drink while she's working." It's Louisa's voice. She's standing right behind him. "And it causes her real distress if anyone looks at the piece before she's ready."

"A true artist." Finias still looks concerned, but he bows to me, taking my hand and kissing my paint-stained fingers. "Very well. I won't look, if you promise to drink some water."

I nod. "And then you must leave me alone. It will take me several minutes to get back into the right frame of mind, now that you've interrupted me."

"I'll fetch the water." The faerie races down the hall.

Louisa steps into the room, which is bathed in the amber light of the sinking sun. "It felt wrong, leaving you here alone today. I was worried."

"I was perfectly safe. I enjoyed having some peace and quiet after yesterday."

I want to sink back into the mesmerizing creative space I've enjoyed all day, but my sister looks dejected. Sorrowful. So I don't ask her to leave, not even when Finias returns with the water.

"Half of it sloshed out while I was running," he says ruefully. "Drink the rest, and I'll get some more."

"This is enough for now," I tell him. "Please make another door on your way out."

He cocks an eyebrow, glancing at Louisa, who has just sunk into a chair nearby. "*She* gets to stay?"

"She's my sister."

"Oh, very well. But you must promise to talk to me later. I'm a very needy host and I require the charming company of my gorgeous guest."

The heated look in his eyes sends a flurry of delighted anticipation through my stomach. "Later, I promise."

With another bow, he leaves the room, and a door solidifies in the doorway again, shutting with a click.

Sipping the water, I walk to Louisa and lay a hand on her shoulder. "Did things not go well?"

"Oh, they went fine." She cups her fingers over mine. "We've secured the services of five mercenaries for the trip. They need some time to make arrangements and gather supplies, so we'll leave the day after tomorrow."

"Were you attacked on the way?"

"Not on the way to the tavern. On the way back we encountered three rat-soldiers, but Fin and Lir made quick work of them."

"Lir?"

"The Nutcracker." A muscle flicks in her temple when she speaks of him. Which gives me a clue about what's bothering her.

"Was he unkind to you today? The Prince?"

"I tried to seduce him again. He rejected me. Why does he keep rejecting me?"

"Perhaps he is simply uninterested in sex? Can he even interact that way, with the curse in effect?"

"Oh, he could. And he wants me—there was ample proof of that. Or rather, his body wants me. Mentally he hates me, I think. He called me a slut."

My fingers tighten on the mug in my hand, my pulse quickening with anger. "He didn't."

"He did."

"I'll have a word with him." I stalk toward the door.

"Don't, Clara. I'll speak to him later. Men have called me that before, when I lost interest in them, but it didn't hurt when they said it. It hurt from him, because I *want* him. I want him badly. And I don't understand why, because we argue constantly, and he's so damn infuriating, and prejudiced, and proud. But the way he craves me sometimes—I can't describe it. It's as if he has bound himself with so many chains, but underneath he is a creature of incredible passion, capable of caring and feeling so much if he would just let himself go, just *once*."

The intensity of her tone surprises me. "I've never heard you talk like this about anyone."

"I've never been rejected over and over like this." She laughs a little. "I don't like it. I wouldn't recommend it. Lucky for you, Fin seems utterly captivated by your charms."

"I don't think so." My cheeks warm, and I quickly drink down the rest of the water.

"Don't let him cajole you into anything you don't want," says Louisa. "Men like him will play awhile, but their interest doesn't last long. Still, he seems kind enough. I like him. We talked about orgies and dryad anatomy."

Jealousy forks through my heart, sudden and sour. "You did?"

"Yes. He has had a lot of sex. Far more than I have, and with a wide range of Fae species, apparently."

"Oh." I chew my lip, feeling unaccountably downcast. Why would such a Faerie be interested in sex with me?

Louisa rises and pulls open the door with a hint of her usual gaiety. "I'll let you finish your work. If I don't see you before bed, good night. I'll try to stay on my side of the mattress in case you'd rather not share Fin's bed of debauchery."

She dances out, and I stand still, gripping my cup.

I love my sister. But I also know her faults as thoroughly as I know my own. When she's feeling despondent or rejected, nothing cheers her up faster than discouraging someone else. I'm not sure if she does it purposefully or unconsciously, but it holds true every time. Once she passes on some mildly upsetting bit of news or a depressing piece of information, her spirits immediately rise, as if she has handed some of her sadness over to them.

Glumly I return to my seat and stare at the canvas propped on the easel. Besides my concentration being broken, a little of the joy has gone out of the process for me. It's not as if I care how many partners Finias may have had—after all, every story I've read mentions the licentiousness of the Fae, their insatiable lust.

I can't truly *care* for someone I just met, beyond a casual liking and a shallow physical attraction. So it shouldn't bother me that he and my sister discussed sexual topics, or that he likely views me as nothing but an exotic human lay, an attractive opportunity for release.

I'm not interested in him beyond a little fun. I'm *not*.

What bothers me is the image I've put onto the canvas for him. It's raw, open, intimate. I'm ashamed that I thought he would want *this*, over everything else I could have painted for him.

But I can't change it now.

Reluctantly I pick up my brush and keep working. At least the piece is nearly complete. Just a few final touches. Slowly I immerse myself in it again, not with the same passionate intensity, but with pride in my work, a determination to finish the art to the best of my ability.

I have no idea how much time passes, only that the light outside is gone and a collection of glowing orbs near the ceiling have automatically illuminated to compensate for the darkness.

Movement startles me—someone's in the doorway. I didn't even hear the door open.

Finias is lounging against the doorframe. He's shirtless, his translucent blue wings shimmering at his back. His long legs are crossed one over the other, dark pants slung low on his hips, angled ridges of muscle disappearing beneath the waistband. His pale skin has a faint sheen to it, like snow gleaming under lamplight. His feet are bare.

On his slim, splayed fingers he's balancing a covered tray, and a lollipop stick protrudes from the corner of his mouth. His pink hair is rumpled, as if someone has been playing with it.

I try to ignore him and continue with the final touch-ups.

He pushes himself away from the doorframe, sets the covered tray on a worktable, and takes the lollipop from his mouth. My gaze can't help traveling to that lollipop, in spite of myself. It's orange, shiny and wet.

"It's been hours," he complains. "I got tired of waiting. And I've brought you food, sugar. You must eat—I command it."

"Hmm," I murmur.

"Tell me it's done. I want to see it."

"No work of art is ever really done."

"But at some point, one must call it finished and leave it alone," he says, prowling nearer.

"I suppose you're right." Sighing, I set the brush aside.

Now that it has come down to the moment of revelation, my stomach is twisting in anxious knots. "You told me to paint something you'd want to see."

"I believe I said, 'paint what you think I would most want to see,'" he corrects me.

"Yes, well... I don't know you. So it's quite possible I've got it wrong." A hot flush is creeping up my neck, and blood pounds in my head, in my ears. I've never been this worked up about someone seeing my art.

I rise from the chair and step back. I feel as if I must go and hide while he looks at what I've painted for him.

"Human talent is a precious gift, a worthy bargain, especially if the talent is plied with both heart and mind behind it," he says, approaching the easel, circling around it. "And when it's—"

He stops speaking. Draws in a quick breath.

Stares at what I've created for him.

It's me—my face and shoulders, crafted with creamy hues of rose and peach and milky white—all the colors of my skin. In the painting I'm flushed and dewy, my brown eyes glossy and dilated, my hair in damp auburn curls around my cheeks and temples. My shoulders are lifted, my collarbones sharply delineated, my neck arched. It's me as I looked in the mirror last night, when I came on his fingers.

The Sugarplum Faerie is still staring, the lollipop hanging forgotten between his fingers. His lips are compressed, his eyes wide and bright.

"It's not what you wanted," I breathe, my heart sinking. "I can make you something else, something better—"

"No." His sharp tone makes me jump a little.

"I'm sorry," I whisper.

Very deliberately he places the lollipop on the table where the paints are set up. Then he stalks toward me, his wings lifting and stirring like gauzy petals caught in a storm.

He cups the back of my neck, hauls me against him, and sinks his mouth to mine.

His lips are faintly sticky, and sweet as candy. A breath of orange-and-peppermint air flows through his lips into mine. I let my tongue slip out and travel over his mouth, tasting him, but I don't venture near his sharp teeth. They still scare me a little.

"You blessed genius," he whispers. "The technique is exquisite, the artistry superb, but the *subject*—damn me, it's perfect. How did you know?"

"I didn't know," I breathe. "I suspected, but—I'm so glad you like it."

"Like it?" He cups my face in his hands, impulsively kissing first my forehead, then my nose, then both my cheeks, until I can't help giggling. "I adore it. I worship it. The way you put yourself into this for me—in Faerie that has meaning, and I want you to know I value it."

"Well, you did save my life."

"And you tried to run from me afterward." A mischievous, serrated smile widens on his face. "That was fun, wasn't it? I do wish you would run from me again. Not here, of course—it's no fun indoors. Maybe while we're traveling…"

My pulse skitters again, arousal blended with fear and excitement at the thought of me running blindly through the forest, dodging branches, while he stalked me, hunted me, chased me down, and—

He bites his lip, grinning. "You're imagining it, aren't you? Picturing what I'd do to you when I caught you. You want that peril, that passion—I can smell your sweet wetness."

"You can?" I swallow hard, pressing my legs together.

"Oh yes." His fingers curl around my shoulders, and he leans in, his breath feathering against my ear. "I want to bathe you with my tongue, lick you all over, but especially there, between your legs. I want to savor all that sweetness flowing out of you. What I did to you last night was barely a taste of what we could enjoy together."

I can hardly breathe. My head is swimming, my world tilting into a glorious whirl of color and sensation where he is the only thing in focus—his pretty face, golden eyes, cinnamon freckles, and soft pink hair.

"Why me?" I falter. "Louisa said you've had many Faerie women—"

"And men. Faeries of every gender and species. Humans too."

"—and she said you've been to—to orgies—you've had multiple partners at once—"

The glow on his face dims. "It's true. I understand if you don't want me, if you think I'm too—well-used." The smile flickering across his mouth doesn't reach his eyes. His hands fall from my shoulders, and he turns away. "No harm done. You should eat something, and then rest. You've been working all day." His tone is light, almost brittle.

I could leave it alone. The shy Clara, the one who stands by and observes, but doesn't join in—she would let the matter drop, before it became too intense, too intimate.

But I shed one layer of that Clara with him last night, and I'm determined to push through the old veil of resistance again.

"That isn't what I meant at all," I say firmly.

He keeps looking at the painting, but tension thrums in the tight lines of his shoulders and arms. "No?"

"I only meant—how could someone like me be appealing to you? When you've had so many more intriguing people?"

He traces the top of the canvas idly with a pointed black nail. "Doing a thing over and over can be pleasurable, but without real emotion, it drains the soul. I've always been popular at orgies because, as I told you, my cum is a different flavor every time I orgasm. At parties and revels, everyone wants to sample me. They work on me ceaselessly, wringing out my pleasure, but I'm merely a novelty, a party trick. A joke, sometimes. They want my delicious release, but not me."

There's a soft pathos in his voice. He reaches into his pocket and pulls out a grape-sized orb, which he crushes into powdery rainbow dust between his fingers. Instantly the paint disappears off the used brushes, and all the little stray daubs of color on the worktable evanesce. The brushes return to their holder, and the paint pots tidy themselves into neat rows in their case.

"Eventually I became so jaded I couldn't come at all, despite the wildest and most depraved stimulation," says Finias. "So I changed my ways."

"And that helped you?"

"Yes. But the difference is not the sexual acts themselves." He turns to face me. "I've done every possible act a hundred times or more. The difference is the person with whom I choose to be intimate. I've become much more selective in the past few years. I don't regret my decades of debauchery—I had fun, but I need something else now. I need to connect to someone first, before I fuck them. Much as I tease my cousin for his near celibacy, I do respect his choice. There is a wisdom in it—taking care to save your keenest moments of pleasure to share with a being who sparks more than a passing lust. And you, darling, have charmed and intrigued me since the moment I first saw you. It's your scent, your skill, your spirit—all of that, and something *else*—damned if I know exactly what it is."

He chuckles, with a look of merry confusion.

I can't restrain my own smile. I let it flood my face while I take a step toward him.

"Did that answer your question?" he says, low, his gaze warming.

"Definitely." I press my hands to his pale chest, and his breath hitches. His wings give a quick, rippling flutter.

"You have depths no one has explored yet," he whispers. "And I intend to be the first to explore them, if you'll allow it—as much as we can, anyway. The timing is shit, of course."

"The worst possible timing." I tilt my face up to his.

His kiss blooms across my mouth, trickles along my throat like honey, races warm through my veins. I'm flushed, flooded with molten desire, forgetting everything except the feel of his hard, smooth body beneath my palms, the graze of his nails against my back, through the gown. I want to tear off my clothes and bare myself to him again.

But as I sway my body into his, with a little moan of eagerness, he breaks away, panting, and holds me at arm's length.

"No," he says firmly. "First you will eat, and drink. You haven't taken care of yourself today. Have you even paused to piss?"

I wince. "Once, I think?"

"Come with me." He takes my hand and hurries me along the hall to a small washroom. "Relieve yourself. Now."

"It's strange to me that the Fae have these bodily needs too," I muse, stepping inside, surveying the washstand and toilet.

"Do your business." He gives me a stern look. Somehow he looks even more handsome with that sober expression than he does with his usual laughing demeanor. I'm intrigued, so I decide to push him a little.

"I'm not a pet," I tell him. "You can't command me to piss."

"Yes, I can, because you're a naughty human who forgets to care for yourself. Which means I must see to it that you do. If you don't get busy, I'll vanish this door and watch you until you're done."

I give a little panicked screech and shut the door.

He chuckles from the other side. "I could remove the obstacle, you know."

"Don't," I beg. "And don't listen, or I won't be able to go."

"I'll go wait at the end of the hall." Soft footsteps retreat, and after a moment I'm able to relax.

When I come out of the washroom, he's halfway down the hall, smirking. "How were you holding so much liquid in that little body?"

"You liar!" I push his shoulder. "You said you wouldn't listen."

"I said I'd wait down the hall. But yes, we can lie. Comforting, isn't it? That's one more way we're like you mortals."

"Not comforting at all," I mutter, re-entering the work room. The tray he brought is still on the table, so I lift the lid. There's a steaming portion of tender-looking meat, some boiled potatoes with butter, and a handful of green vegetables I can't identify. Some sort of leaves, sauteed and crispy at the edges.

"This looks delicious. But what about the Prince and Louisa?"

"Oh, we ate hours ago," he says. "It's actually quite late. Nearly midnight."

"I didn't realize."

He lifts his hand, and the chair I was painting in vanishes from its spot, reappearing again on this side of the long table, near the food. I start to lower myself into the seat, but he slides in first, pulling my bottom down onto his lap.

I suck in a breath at the feel of him. His cock is huge, a thick rod pinned between his thighs and my ass.

"Eat your dinner." His voice is a velvety purr.

Obediently I lean forward and take a bite. When I rock back onto him, he hums in bliss at the contact.

I manage a few more bites, but the grinding thickness of him against my sex is too tempting, even with the layers of fabric between us. I lift myself off his lap, just enough to gather my skirts all the way up, around my waist, revealing my soaked underwear.

"Sit, sugar," he murmurs.

This time when I sit down, I voice a shrill gasp that's half-moan. I can feel him so much better now. I shift, rolling against the hard ridge of his cock. If I can just move like this a few more times—

But his hands clasp my hips, stilling the motion.

"No, naughty girl," he says. "You may not come until you've eaten some more of your dinner. Stand up for a moment and take another bite."

I lift off him briefly, placing a forkful of greens in my mouth.

When I lower myself toward his lap again, I encounter the hot, silky head of his bare cock, jutting upward, pressing against my pussy lips.

The bastard vanished his pants, and my underwear.

I start to sink onto him, but he pinches my ass cheek. "Not yet, sweetness. Another bite."

Poised over his cock, my thighs quivering with the ache of hovering in place above his lap, I manage another bite.

"Good girl," he says. "You may sit down. But don't come yet."

His fingers brush against my bottom as he angles himself for entry. I sink lower, feeling his cock head nudge into my slit, squeezing deeper and deeper, then sliding in all the way to the hilt.

He throbs a little, a warm, silky thickness inside me.

"Fu-u-uck," he groans. "By the fucking stars, you feel divine."

I can only whine in response, fully seated on him, my legs between his.

"Another bite," he says hoarsely.

I lift up a little, leaning forward to take the bite, then impaling myself fully on him again. The surge of his hot shaft through my folds is a stimulation more exquisite than I've ever imagined. Much different from the quick, awkward encounter in the garden shed with the postman's cousin.

I think I'm going to come without him even touching my clit.

"Why can't I come yet?" I breathe.

"Because it's more fun this way." He leans forward, aligning his chest to my back. And then, with a shiver of magic, my dress is gone, and I'm sitting nude on his lap with his cock inside me. "Take another bite."

When I rise this time, my pussy makes a squelching sound around him. I gasp, embarrassed, and he laughs. "Don't be shy, darling. I love it. Give me every crude, naughty, sloppy, wicked sound from your beautiful body."

He pulls me back down, thrusting upward into me, and a small burst of pleasure arcs through my belly. Not there yet, but almost, so very near that I want to cry from the exquisite suspense.

"Have you pleasured yourself before?" Fin whispers. "I think you have."

"Many times," I admit, breathless.

"And what did you think of while you teased your pretty pussy?"

"I... I..."

"Words, darling."

"I can't tell you. Not yet. But if I'd known this was possible—this would have been one of my fantasies."

His cock flexes inside me, and a little thrill runs through my clit. "Oh, god, Finias, I can't take any more—please, I need to come. Please."

Another twitch, deep inside, and he moans. "Since you said my name so sweetly... go ahead, sugar. Fuck yourself on my cock."

With a soft cry, I grip the table with both hands and I obey him. I fuck myself on him, shamelessly, noisily, shrill gasping moans bursting from my lips with every thrust. He never lets go of my hips; he follows my rhythm, surging upward when I descend. He's groaning—he sounds more young and vulnerable and broken than I expected—he's losing himself in me, and I love it, I need it, I—

Oh—it's—

God—

I can't I can't *I can't—*

It's too much, it's too beautiful—it's an explosion inside me, glittering shrapnel raining along every nerve.

I'm caught in the violence of the orgasm—I convulse soundlessly, rigid, my hands spastically clutching his thighs. He tucks three fingers against my clit, and a second wave of excruciating bliss hits me, carrying me out of my body—almost. Almost, because when his hips buck compulsively upward and he comes, gasping and groaning, I feel it. I feel him pressing my clit with those careful fingers, his thighs shaking under my hands. I feel him wrap his other arm around me, across my breasts. His chest heaves against my back.

He lifts me then, tilting me forward until my front is pressed to the table and he's standing erect, still inside me. There's a soft whirr, and in my peripheral vision I see his wings snap out wide. He was sitting on them, but he's flaring them now, stretching them.

"Your wings show your moods," I said faintly.

"Sometimes," he admits. "I try to control it. Sometimes when I'm aroused, or coming, they want to rise too." He clasps one cheek of my bottom, easing himself out of me. "Fuck, sugar. I can see my cum inside you."

My pussy spasms a little at the comment, at my name on his lips.

"It's oozing out of you, Clara," he says quietly. "Would you like to taste it?"

I inhale, ready to say no; but I want to.

I want everything.

"Yes," I breathe.

He dips a finger at my entrance, and I put out my tongue.

He's creamy, vanilla-sweet with a hint of cinnamon and—maybe a twist of brandy?

"Oh my god," I whisper. "Sugarplum Faerie indeed."

"I can be rather addictive." Finias chuckles, swipes another dollop, and places it on my tongue. "Would you like more?"

But before I can answer him, a violent crash resounds through the house.

14
LOUISA

Throughout the evening, Finias keeps pacing and fretting about Clara not eating or drinking enough.

"She is fine," I tell him. "She does this sometimes. When she gets into her creative zone, it's best to leave her alone."

I wander around his living space, touching every one of the candy jars until Lir, draped on the sofa, growls, "Is possible for you to be still?"

"Of course I can be still." I plop onto the sofa, and he scoots farther away from me.

I try not to move. I really do. But despite the day's travel, my body is buzzing with nervous energy. I jiggle first one knee, then the other. When I manage to force both knees to stop moving, I start rocking a little, back and forth, while picking at the hem of my overdress.

"I should take Clara some food," says Finias.

"Louisa said to leave her alone for now," Lir responds. "By the old gods, both of you are maddening." He rises from the sofa, snapping his fingers. "Fin, music."

"Of course, music!" cries Finias. He yanks open a drawer, shuffles through the tissue-wrapped toffees inside, and selects one. "Here, we'll share so we can all hear the same song." He opens the paper and tears off stretchy pieces of the candy. "Chew these, and then we'll dance."

Curious, I chew the sticky treat. It's delicious, and the minute my teeth sink into it, I begin to hear music—a distant, jaunty beat, growing slowly louder, joined by a flow of strings and a delicate flute. The music fills my mind, lighting up my body.

Lir's green eyes meet mine. "Go on, little mortal. Dance."

He doesn't have to ask me twice. Moving to this exquisite music is the most natural thing in the world. My whole body yields to the melody, swaying, sinuous, flowing just like the notes, then sashaying to the beat. It's a blessed relief to channel my jittery energy into the movements.

Finias is dancing, too, along the tops of the chairs and sofas, buoyed by occasional flutters of his gauzy wings. "Dance, cousin," he commands, and Lir let himself go too, his dark lashes hooding his eyes. His motions are stiff, a little jerky, but somehow the moves fit the rapid, off-kilter beat of the song.

My skin is heating, flushing, so I strip off the overdress and leggings and toss them onto a chair, dancing in just my bustier and lacy undershorts. We're in the center of the room now, all three of us, dancing in a circle, hands raised above our heads. Sometimes I catch Fin's hand in mine, and sometimes my fingers lace with Lir's. It's dizzying, decadent, a haze of glorious motion, bodies sliding and slithering with the endless chain of notes.

I swallowed my bit of toffee a few minutes after Fin handed it to me, but the music continues for a long time—maybe hours. At last it fades, and I collapse on the couch, utterly happy and thoroughly exhausted. With a sidelong glance at me, Lir slinks off to his room, while Finias declares loudly, "*Now* I really am going to take some food and drink up to Clara." He disappears in the direction of the kitchen.

With the departure of the two Fae, the lighted orbs in the living area dim slowly, until they're barely glowing. In the soft, quiet darkness, in the faint amber glow, I trace my fingertips along my body, over my generous curves and soft swells. I love every part of me, and right now I feel more luscious, desirable, and aroused than I have in days. Must be the magic toffee.

The living area is silent and empty, so I tuck my fingers beneath the band of my lacy undershorts, and I begin to toy with my clit—two fingertips massaging lightly.

I hear Finias heading upstairs. Since Lir is in his room, that means I am truly alone. I let my fingers travel deeper, between my labia, nestling into the warm heat there, teasing out the slickness.

Tilting my head back, I let a soft moan of satisfaction escape me. This feels wonderful, and also naughty because I'm in a stranger's house, right in the open, not behind any closed doors. I doubt Fin would mind, though, even if he knew.

I shimmy down my underwear and toss it aside. Then I tilt my pelvis up for better access, bending my knees and spreading my thighs apart. My eyes close as I slide my fingers through my folds, over and over, feeling the slow build of pleasure in my belly. Pushing two fingers into my slit, I open my eyes to watch them emerge, glossy and wet.

And when I open my eyes, Lir is standing at the end of the sofa, a tall dark figure in the gloom.

I'm splayed wide open, my fingers sliding out of my pussy, my breasts spilling over the top of my bustier, and my long golden hair scattered all over the sofa cushions.

I can see the Prince's features dimly in the faint glow of the orbs overhead. He's looking right at me—at my face, not the rest of me.

My breath catches, and I freeze, while my pussy flutters with delight at having an audience.

Lir doesn't move. Doesn't speak.

Tentatively I place the two wet fingers on my clit and begin to slide them in careful circles.

His eyes travel from my face to my swelling breasts, to my stomach, to my pussy. And there his gaze remains, while I tighten the circles I'm making—tighter, faster—I'm jiggling my clit desperately now, tiny soft sounds on my lips as my belly and my inner walls tighten.

The orgasm spears my clit—sharp and keen, tracing a lightning path up through my abdomen, shearing through my chest and my limbs. I buck on the sofa, gasping, my fingers still pinned to my clit while my sex quivers.

As the pleasure fades, I shift my fingers lower and spread my lips open so the Prince can see my insides pulsating through the final throes of bliss.

He already thinks I'm a slut. And I've just confirmed his opinion of me.

But he watched. Which means he is just as slutty as I am.

When his stormy eyes lift to my face again, I give him my sweetest, most cheerful smile.

"I hate you," he whispers.

Maybe the words should upset me, but there's an agonized rasp in his voice, a violent desire he's barely restraining. So I consider those three words a victory. Vengeance for the way he has treated me today.

He might hate me. But he couldn't resist watching me just now. And that gives me all the power I crave, and the peace I need to sleep soundly tonight.

I pull my undershorts back into place, pressing them over my wet pussy lips until a damp spot soaks through them. Then I rise from the sofa, pick up my dagger from a chair nearby, and walk past the Prince, letting my arm brush his. I half hope he'll reach for me, but he doesn't.

However irritating he may be, I have to admit that his force of will is incredible. I'm not sure any other unattached, femme-attracted male would be able to resist the juicy pussy I just showed off to him.

Feeling triumphant, I return to my room. A different set of nightgowns are laid out—I'm not sure if they were conjured by Finias or pulled from a storage trunk somewhere. I pull on the pink one decorated with embroidered white snowbloom, and I crawl into bed.

It's odd how very safe I feel in this house, with these two Fae males, especially considering my suspicions when we first agreed to help the Nutcracker. I can still hear the echo of Drosselmeyer's warning:

Don't go with him. He's not what he seems. You don't know who they are, what they do—stop, you idiot girls! You'll ruin everything!

A faint unrest stirs in my heart.

But I ignore it, and go to sleep.

I'm awakened by a loud *bang* from somewhere in the house.

At first my bleary mind thinks it's Clara and Fin, having loud sex somewhere upstairs.

But the *bang* is followed by a horrendous crunching sound, ear-splittingly loud, and a violent quaking of the house as if it's being slowly, inexorably ripped apart by a giant.

Screaming, I scramble out of bed, snatch my dagger and belt, and flee into the hallway.

Half the hallway doesn't exist anymore. It has been chomped and ripped away by the jaws of an immense rat the size of a building, with chitinous armor-plating on its sides and back. Strapped around its neck is a kind of saddle, on which are perched two rat-soldiers. More rat-soldiers are skirting around its paws, climbing into the wreckage of the house. A pair of them shout at the sight of me.

I scream again, not because of them, but because the bedroom where Fin and Clara slept last night is gone—crushed, demolished, eaten. Pieces of it are sticking out between the titanic rat's yellow teeth.

"No!" I shriek. "No, you fucking bastards!" Stricken, I draw my dagger and charge toward the oncoming rat-soldiers.

A strong arm wraps around my waist and carries me off, in the opposite direction from the soldiers, toward the second-floor stairs. It's the Prince, uniformed as usual, his rapier in his other hand.

"Stop!" I yell at him. "Put me down! They killed Fin and my sister—they have to pay!"

I beat at his neck and face with my free hand, but he doesn't put me down, only jogs toward the staircase.

Finias comes running down the steps, stark naked, with my sister behind him—also naked. The next second they're both engulfed in a rainbow whirl of Finias's magic, which solidifies into conjured clothes and shoes. I barely have time to process my relief, because a pair of sturdy boots forms around my own bare feet, and a cloak swirls around my shoulders, pinning itself in place.

"Back door!" shouts Finias. "Take the girls, Lir. I'll hold them off and meet you later."

"No!" screams Clara, but the Prince seizes her wrist in a vise-grip and drags her along with us.

I look back and see Finias striding toward the oncoming invaders, his wings flared, his tall figure uplit by the glow of his broken house and the torch-bearing soldiers. He looks easy, careless, perfectly relaxed.

A volley of tiny rainbow orbs flies from his hands, zipping and diving through the air, slicing straight through the chests of a dozen rat-soldiers. He follows it up with a rain of striped darts—I could swear they're sharpened peppermint sticks—and more rats fall, speared through the eyes or throats. Over it all, Fin's laughter rings out, maniacal and delighted as he takes to the sky, wings whirring, dodging crossbow bolts, balls of fiery magic, and thrown spears.

I don't get the chance to see how he'll attack them next, because Lir is dragging Clara and me out the back door of the house. It looks like a seamless wall until we're charging through it, and when I glance back afterward, I can't see a door at all, or any windows on the back side of the building. Since the rear exit is invisible, no rat-soldiers are posted back here to keep us from fleeing. They're all at the front of the house.

"They'll kill Finias," gasps Clara.

"They won't," says Lir firmly. "He's incredibly powerful. He doesn't let many people see it, but he's a superb warrior. He can hold them off. Why do you think we came to him for help? Why do you think we only hired five others to accompany us to the pool? He's a small army, all by himself."

"Oh." My sister's panic eases, admiration bleeding through the anxiety on her face.

"We have to run now," says Lir. "As fast as we can."

"Are you all right to run?" I ask him.

"I'll do my best. This way."

We jog through the forest. It's freezing cold, but fortunately it isn't pitch-black. Tiny red and green lights wink on and off among the trees, providing just enough visibility for Clara and I to keep track of Lir's tall form as he forges ahead, guiding us.

"Someone betrayed you," I say.

He glances back, a reluctant surprise in his eyes. He has given me the same look a couple of times—when I threw the bombs that saved us in the forest, and when I suggested fighting back-to-back afterward.

"Your instincts are correct, I believe," he says. "One of the people we met with today decided to sell us out. Whom would you guess to be the traitor?"

I think back, pulling the mercenaries' faces from my mind, churning through their words and expressions.

"Theanne," I say. "She showed you subservience first and asked the most questions, which shouldn't make me suspect her—but there was something in her eyes, in her manner when she left the tavern—she was too excited about the prospect of the journey, while the others seemed sober and reluctant. I've faked enough enthusiasm myself to know when the emotion is false, when it's present to hide a different feeling."

"Interesting theory." Lir's back is to me now, but I sense the dejection in his tone, in the slump of his shoulders. "If it is Theanne, that would be unfortunate indeed. She's an old friend of Fin's."

"I could be wrong," I offer.

"Not likely," Clara puts in. "Louisa knows people. And she generally sees good things in everyone, so when she does pass judgment, it's typically true."

"I wasn't right about Drosselmeyer," I say. "I liked him at first."

"We both did." Clara is breathless as she jogs beside me, but she manages to reach over and squeeze my arm.

"I was also wrong about you, Lir," I say, before I can stop myself. "I disliked you from the first night—still do, sometimes. But I don't believe you mean us harm."

"Very astute of you," he says dryly. "But perhaps that's simply because I need your blood, and if you're killed I can use your sister's."

I catch my breath, casting a side glance at Clara. She shakes her head and gives me a little smile.

"We don't believe that," I tell him. "We're so charming, both of us. Admit it—you like having us around."

"I'd like it better if you were *quiet* while we run from our enemies," he retorts.

"Fair enough." But Clara and I exchange a smirk and a silent laugh.

"You're mocking me," the Prince throws back over his shoulder. "I can feel it."

Clara pulls a haughty, prim face that's such a perfect imitation of Lir I can't help giggling.

The Prince whirls around, stopping us both in our tracks. "Enough." His tone is low, but his eyes flash with frustration. "We are *fleeing*. And my cousin is buying us time to get far away from here. You can make jokes later. For now, shut up and run."

We run until our lungs ache and our legs burn. We run deep into the night, until I think I can't keep going, I *can't*—and yet somehow I do. Lir lets us slow down occasionally, because Clara and I are children of a quiet, sedentary household, unused to running for any sustained period of time. But after every period of walking, he makes us jog again.

After hours of traveling as fast as we can manage, Clara looks up, her face brightening. A second later I hear it, too—the hum of whirring wings.

The Sugarplum Faerie lands lightly beside Clara. He's smudged with smoke. Bloody wounds glisten raw on his bare chest and arms.

"I killed them all," he gasps, and smoke issues from his cracked lips. "Even the big one." He coughs up more smoke.

Clara makes a pitiful sound at the state of him, but Lir says crisply, "Don't fuss. He will heal quickly."

"You're welcome." Finias glares in his cousin's direction. "I questioned the leader of the group before I ended him—he told me Theanne betrayed us."

My instincts were right.

Lir shoots me a look of startled admiration. "Really?"

"Unfortunately, yes," says Finias. "Lucky for us she only told the local commander of the Rat King's forces, and he attacked us without sending word to the Rat King himself. So I believe we're safe to continue our quest."

"How do you know he wasn't lying?" I ask.

"Truth candy." Finias gives me a half-grin. There's blood on his pointed teeth. "Very rare, very difficult to make, but we needed to know if the Rat King has heard of the Prince's return. For now, he's still in the dark. We must take full advantage of the time we have." He adjusts the large satchel he's wearing so its strap sits between two of his wounds. "I brought what I could pack in a hurry. I'm afraid most of my spells were ruined, and I couldn't find the bag of weapons Louisa brought with her, either. We'll have to do without some of the things I'd planned to bring. As for supplies, horses, and food, I'll send messages for our allies to meet us as Dellwyn Ford."

"Messages? How?" I ask.

"Magic."

He seems too tired to provide further explanation. Just as well, because I'm probably too tired to listen. My brain is content to accept "magic" and move on.

Clara lays a hand on Fin's arm as we begin walking again. "Are your little pets all right?"

"Yes, they're fine! A nose for danger, those three. They would have run off long before the rest of us knew there was anything wrong. They have their own tunnels in and out of the house, as well as their own burrows in the forest. They'll be all right."

"Oh good." Clara sighs with relief. "I'm sorry about Theanne betraying you."

"She and I had a falling-out some time ago," Fin says. "I thought I had softened her up with my gift today, but perhaps she still holds a grudge. She always hated your father, Lir, but she despises the Rat King, too, so I thought she would be a safe choice. She's a wonderful fighter."

"We'll have to do without her," says Lir. "Send your messages to the others, and we'll make for the ford as fast as we can. The humans will need to rest eventually, but we can go on until dawn, then find a place to hide and sleep."

15
CLARA

Louisa and I have never had to travel any significant distance on our feet. And the only journeys we've made on horseback have been afternoon rides with Papa. The two days' journey to the ford is beautiful, because we're walking through Faerie—but it's painful, too. Despite the comfortable nature of the boots Finias conjured for me, my muscles still scream, and I still get blisters.

I try not to complain, but somehow Fin can tell. "I'm sorry," he whispers to me once. "I would use a healing sweet on you, but we need to save them in case of greater wounds later in our journey."

Of course I understand. But his sympathy doesn't make the walk any less painful or wearying. Besides the gorgeous scenery, the only other pleasant thing about trudging through Faerie is the conversation. Both Fin and Lir tell us more about their realm, and about themselves. How they grew up together at court, how Fin's parents died saving a village in the South from a rogue leshy, how Lir's mother contracted a rare disease and passed when he was small, and how Lir's father the king, being ancient even for a

Fae, eventually let himself fade and released his spirit, leaving his son to rule in his stead.

They're sad stories, but the pair of them seem to have plenty of good memories as well—pranks played at court, merry dances and drinking parties, hunting Unseelie monsters with friends, training with their favorite weapons and spells.

By contrast, what Louisa and I share of our quiet lives seems very tame and dull. But the two males seem fascinated by our confined, routine life, and by the way Louisa and I each managed to find an outlet—her by sleeping with anyone she could get alone, and me by immersing myself in art.

When we finally reach the ford, we meet four others—a big fellow named Achorn, a moth girl, a reptilian person, and a dark-skinned Fae with white freckles. They've brought horses along, and weapons, and supplies.

They seemed surprised that Louisa and I are part of the group, and that Louisa is human, not Fae. Apparently Fin disguised Louisa with a glamour during their meeting at the tavern. But Fin skillfully fends off their questions about who Louisa and I are and how we're connected to the quest, basically by hinting that we are a pair of mortal pets or slaves who belong to the Prince. He doesn't say it outright, so I don't protest, but the implication is clear. After some displeased looks, the mercenaries seem to accept us as part of the group, and we continue our journey on horseback.

I'm glad my feet get a rest, but riding for hours every day causes a different kind of discomfort. So much chafing. And it's more difficult to chat with Finias and Lir. Besides which, the spell Finias has been using to deter any monsters that might be nearby doesn't work for such a large group, and we have to fight a number of stray creatures—or rather, our escorts do. Most of the monsters are easily scared off once they've been stung by multiple spells or blades, but a few persist until they are killed.

"They can smell the humans," growls Achorn after one such encounter, wiping blood off his great heavy blade. His fingers are still soot-stained from his use of fire spells.

"I'm doing my best to cloak their scents," says Finias. "But my charms keep wearing off faster than I expect, especially with Clara. She smells so fucking good."

A blush burns on my cheeks. "I'm sorry."

"Don't apologize, sweetness." The Sugarplum Faerie licks his lips and winks at me.

My stomach flips as I remember being on his lap in the workroom. I haven't gotten more than a few hasty, stolen kisses from him in a week. We're always with other people, either traveling or hastily cramming food into our mouths before collapsing into our bedrolls. I usually sleep sandwiched between my sister and the moth-girl for warmth during the freezing nights.

"We should stop and make camp soon," Finias says, his eyes still on me.

"Yes," says Lir fervently. His voice sounds raspier than usual—it's usually the first sign that he's reverting to Nutcracker form. Whenever that begins to happen, he and Louisa slink off into the trees together. The others in our party probably assume they're having sex, when in reality he's drinking her blood. She keeps her arms covered, not only because of the cold but because of the bandages around them, concealing the places where he has bitten her. I only know of the bites because I saw her washing one morning in a cold stream before anyone else was up.

I'm not sure why she's letting Lir bite her, instead of using a knife for a cleaner cut. The two of them have the strangest dynamic—they're either bickering endlessly or not speaking to each other after a hearty fight. Yet when he needs her blood, she goes with him quickly, almost eagerly, and they both return flushed.

We continue walking until we enter a part of the forest where the trees bear huge white blossoms the size of my head. Each bloom consists of a myriad of enormous, delicate petals, layered together, coated with frost. Icicles glitter along the black branches of the trees, and pink afternoon light bathes the ground, which is a motley of rich black soil and clusters of white crystals.

My mind, which has become more accustomed to the startling beauty of the Fae realm, quakes a little with the wonder of this grove. Again, like on that first day, I feel compelled to be still, rooted to the spot while I try to take it all in. I pull my horse to a halt.

"This might be my favorite part of Faerie so far," I breathe.

"Then here we shall camp," Finias declares. "That clearing looks promising. And I do believe I smell fresh water nearby."

We turn our horses aside into the space he indicated. The mercenaries immediately dismount and begin setting up for the night, while Louisa and Lir sidle away into a clump of trees whose low-hanging boughs and blossoms will offer them concealment.

"Do they think they're being subtle about it?" I ask Finias with a smirk.

"If they do, they're wrong." He reaches up, and I hop off the horse into his arms.

He holds me against his lean chest for a moment, and I savor the heat radiating from his skin. I've noticed he doesn't wear heavy cloaks or clothing like the rest of us, yet he doesn't seem to be cold.

"You're always so hot." I press my palm to the center of his chest.

"Of course I am." He winks again.

"Is it part of your magic?"

"It's a trait of mine, yes. Different Fae have different aspects, attributes, and gifts, as I'm sure you've realized by now. Some of them are inherited, but mostly our gifts and magical abilities are determined by the alignment of the stars when we were conceived, by the location and timing of our birth, and by the intensity of magical influence around us at the time. Many Fae scholars have studied the topic, but none have been able to successfully predict a Fae child's aspect, powers, and traits."

"That's so interesting." I touch his face, rubbing my thumb along his jaw. "You know, I'd love to paint you sometime."

"I hope you'll get the chance. Most of my home was broken and burnt, but the workroom remains intact, and the painting you made for me is safe. I placed a sealing spell on the undamaged part of the house, to protect it from the elements until I can return and make repairs."

"So handy to have magic. I wish I did."

"You have a magic of your own, darling. Your talent, your kindness—and that maddening scent." He inhales deeply from my hair, then lowers his voice. "I'd like to eat you whole. I *need* to have you again, sugar."

He presses his lean body tighter to mine, while his wings flare outward, stiffening and thrumming. The hard outline of his cock nudges my belly, even through the warm layers I wear.

I quiver in his arms, my breath shredded with arousal and with the cold. There is a waking dream I've been amusing myself with lately, when traveling becomes too dull to bear—a dream not unlike the naughty fantasies I used to have back home, when I made myself come in the dark closet.

Rising on my toes, I tip my face up and murmur in his ear. "What if you wanted me, and I said no? What if I ran from you into the forest, but you couldn't hold yourself back, so you chased me, and then you threw me down and rutted into me by force?"

I can't believe the words that just left my mouth.

Now he will think I'm wretched, sick, wicked and twisted. He'll despise me.

Ashamed, I start to pull away, but Finias grips the back of my neck, his chest heaving. "What if, indeed? What if that happened tonight, while the others sleep?"

A degenerate hope blooms in my chest.

"What if," I breathe.

His hands tighten on my neck and waist briefly before he lets me go and stalks away to help with the preparation of the campsite. His role is to lay spells of protection and warning around the area, including something he calls a "watchman spell," so we can all rest during the night and no one has to sit up and keep watch.

My job is to see that the horses are watered and fed. Louisa is supposed to assist me with those chores, though she usually finds a way out of it. Today I can't insist that she help me, since she is getting her blood sucked by a cursed Fae prince. So I find the nearby stream and tote water for the animals, cheering myself by imagining the keen pleasure that awaits me tonight, when Finias and I play our perverted game.

16
LOUISA

"That's enough," I gasp. "Enough, Lir."

He hums against my flesh, still drinking greedily.

"Lir." I smack his cheek.

He pulls his mouth off my arm, his lips and teeth drenched with glistening scarlet. His eyes shine with a maddened, dazed look I've become all too familiar with.

During the past week, I've fed him every other day so he can maintain his form—and each time he takes a little more than he did during the last session. Each time it's a little harder to get his attention and make him stop.

I fear the Prince of Faerie is becoming addicted to my blood.

Finias has been giving me pebble-sized candies to chew—a restorative to help my body renew its blood supply faster. But although the candies help prevent dizziness and weakness, they can't keep Lir from one day deciding that he's going to drink me dry.

I haven't told anyone my fears, not even Clara—because there's a seductive madness in Lir's compulsive need for me. I love it, and I don't want it to stop.

He's looking at me now, his lips glazed with my blood. His tongue runs out, juicy red, and swipes some of the blood from his mouth.

"I went too far again," he says hoarsely.

"It's all right."

"No. It isn't." His jaw clenches. "I'm slipping, I can feel it. Drinking human blood is an Unseelie practice for a reason, Louisa. It does terrible things to a faerie. I'm—changing. Becoming someone I don't recognize. I hate it."

"You're going to make it. We have one more week of travel," I tell him. "Then you can bathe in the pool and be restored to yourself."

There's another reason I love these feeding sessions with him. When we're with the others, he and I can't seem to stop fighting over one thing or another. But when we're alone like this, we don't fight. He lets me stroke his glossy black hair while he drinks from me, and when he's done we talk a little, quietly. He has never mentioned the night when he watched me touch myself, and neither have I. If that night didn't make him want me, I don't know what else to do.

The Prince steps over to a large white bloom, detaches one of the enormous petals, and wipes the crimson blood from his mouth onto it. He lets the scarlet-stained petal flutter to the ground.

I suck in a quick breath as he approaches me again. But he only takes my bandages from where they're hanging on a branch, and he begins to bind up my forearm. His touch is slow, gentle. Almost caressing.

"Are you afraid of me, Louisa?" he says.

A glib "no" springs to my lips. But I swallow it back, and I let something else slip out—a visceral truth. "I'm afraid of how you make me feel."

His lashes flick up, his gaze meeting mine. Words drag out of him, so low they're barely audible. "The fear is mutual."

My stomach does a slow dive before soaring upward, straight out of my body.

What does that mean?

Did he just admit that I make him feel something?

I could press him for more. But I'm learning that this man is unlike anyone else I've met. I can't dance gaily and carelessly into his heart, or fling myself onto his cock. I have to move slowly, patiently. I have to consider before I speak, calculate before I move.

I've never met anyone for whom I was willing to be so slow and patient.

Instead of pushing him to speak of his feelings, I shift the topic. "Sometimes I wonder what Drosselmeyer meant when he warned us to be careful of you. That you aren't what you seem."

His green eyes lock with mine, serious and open. "I am what I've told you. A Prince of Faerie, soon to take my place as the true King of the Seelie. I have no magic now, but once my curse is broken, I will have unfathomable power. Perhaps that inherited magic is what your godfather meant."

I wince. "Don't call him my godfather. I don't want that connection with him."

"And yet, when all this is done, you'll return to him."

My mouth opens, but I can't make a sound.
Go back to Drosselmeyer?
Beg his forgiveness and hope he'll let us remain under his roof? Submit to his approval regarding my choice of a husband? Remain at his mercy until I can claim my inheritance?

"He left us to die." My voice is hoarse and brittle.

"Do you have any other kin? Any other protector in your world?"

"You know we don't." I shoot him an accusing glare. "We've told you everything during these days of travel. You know Clara and I are alone."

"Yes, well…" The Prince clears his throat. "You're both resourceful, brave, and intelligent. You can leave your guardian and make a life of your own."

"Ingenuity, bravery, and intelligence should be enough, yes. But in our world, it isn't. Connections, luck, and a smart marriage are the best things women of our class can hope for—at least in our district. If we do go back, I'll have to grovel before Drosselmeyer and then marry whomever he approves as quickly as possible.

Only then will I have some level of financial independence—unless my husband refuses to let me control my own money. If I'm able to, I'll give Clara what she needs to begin her own life as a painter, in a city where people will appreciate her talent."

"And what will you do?"

"Me? I suppose I'll cheat on my husband. Probably once a day." I laugh, but it's hollow. The joke isn't a joke; it's my future reality. "Sex has always been an escape for me—especially when it's forbidden. That naughty thrill, and the excitement of the seduction game, is all I will have left once I marry. I'll enjoy it until I'm too old to attract any fine gentlemen or pretty ladies anymore—or until I perish from some venereal disease."

"Venereal disease?" The Prince frowns.

"When you fuck a lot of different people, there can be consequences," I tell him. "I take certain tonics to prevent pregnancy and stave off some diseases, but others cannot be prevented."

"We have no such diseases in Faerie," says Lir. "Which is fortunate for my cousin, or he would be riddled with them."

He attempts a smile, but I can tell something I said has troubled him deeply.

Impulsively I say, "What if we stayed in Faerie?"

"No." He finishes with my bandage and tugs my sleeve down to cover it. "You can't. I won't allow it."

"Why not? You told me once that some humans do live in Faerie. We could stay here."

"It's too dangerous for humans here. They're always delighted with the prospect of not aging, but they don't realize how many other dangers exist in this realm. Most perish before they can enjoy the lengthy lifespan they hoped for. And what would you do in Faerie? How would you earn your keep? Your sister can paint, at least—the Fae do love a human with talent— but what can *you* do? Besides fuck?"

I stare at him, my lungs and throat tightening, tears stinging my eyes. "You keep doing this. Reducing me to a slut, a whore."

"Because that's how you've presented yourself to me. By word and deed, you've told me who you are. Own it, or change it. There is no in-between."

"You keep making me hate you," I whisper.

"Good." A muscle flexes in his temple. "That will make everything easier."

He stalks out of the clump of trees, leaving me alone in the beautiful grove, with the blood-stained petal at my feet.

17
CLARA

I'm too excited to fall asleep.

I lie in my bedroll, with the moth-girl Cahren on one side of me and Louisa on the other. Above me arch black boughs and snowy blooms, with the night-blue dome of the sky behind them. The stars are familiar, but their arrangement seems reversed, and I remember what the Nutcracker said, about our world and this one being two sides of the same coin.

After what seems like forever, a tall, lithe figure moves soundlessly past my sleeping spot. His scent of peppermint, snow, and chocolate wafts over me. Quietly I ease out of my blankets, slip on my boots, and follow him.

Once we reach the edge of the clearing, the Sugarplum Faerie turns, and I nearly gasp at the hectic excitement in his eyes.

He sweeps me into his arms and rises with a quiet hum of wings, expertly navigating tree limbs until we break out into the open sky, hovering in place. It's colder up here—a star-riddled, frozen darkness that bites into my bones.

His hot breath gusts against my ear. "You want this, darling? You want me to chase you, claim you, fuck you by force?"

I'm wet just from hearing the words. "Yes."

"I'll do it. I'll use you however I want—break you down to quivering bones, flay your sweet pussy with my tongue. Tell me a word you'll say if you want it all to stop."

"Drosselmeyer," I whisper, and he flinches.

"Let's hope you won't have occasion to speak that name. And now, sugar, I'm taking you far away, so the others can't hear you screaming."

I don't have time to answer before he streaks away, across the tops of the trees. He keeps flying, skimming this way and that until I have no idea which direction the camp is. And then we drop—a stomach-flipping plunge, right into the center of a snowy clearing.

Finias releases me, but I stay near him, almost touching his chest, looking nervously at the black shadows under the trees.

The Sugarplum Faerie's claws curve under my chin, tilting my face up. He's a different creature out here, in the dark—taller than ever, it seems, with eyes of molten death and teeth like a chain of knives that glitter as he smiles, cruel and mocking.

When he speaks, his usually light, merry voice is far deeper and more dreadful. "You act as if you feel safe with me."

"I do."

"You shouldn't." He exhales, peppermint coolness across my lips. "You realize I demolished the Rat King's soldiers with relative ease. All by myself."

"Y-yes," I murmur.

"Do you know how easily I could kill you?" The words are a lethal hiss, and a tremor of true apprehension thrills through me. "One hand around this little neck, cutting off your breath—or a flex of my fingers—a quick *snap*." He spits the word, and I startle in his grip.

He laughs, low and menacing. "Maybe I've been waiting for just such an opportunity. A little feral play, and then—I take you, torment you, maybe even end you. We only need your sister, after all. Her blood can sustain my cousin. You are the spare. The mouse between the paws of the cat."

His fingers flutter lower, over my heart. He hums with predatory satisfaction when he feels how fast it's beating.

"Maybe I won't listen to your special word after all." He lowers his face to the curve of my neck. "No, I don't think I will. I think I'll do whatever I like with you. Skin you with my kisses, lacerate you with my tongue, cleave you with my teeth."

I feel the ripple of urgency that undulates through his body, as if he's barely holding himself back. That primal shudder, more than anything else, terrifies me. A flood of goosebumps rises on my skin.

"By the gods of old, I can smell every bit of you," he groans, his tongue lashing between his sharp teeth. "You would taste so good. Do you know why the Unseelie consume flesh and blood, little one? Because it gives them more power, yes. But not only that. They do it because it tastes delicious. It yields such exquisite sensations. Practically... orgasmic." He tilts back his head, gazing at me out of the corner of one yellow eye. "Want to know how I know that?"

Horror vibrates in my bones, and I shake my head.

"You'll find out soon enough, sweetness." His voice is nearly a snarl now. "I think you should start running. Because when I catch you, I'm going to claw away everything that hides you from me, and I'm going to fuck every hole you have until you scream for mercy. And I won't grant the relief you crave. I will sink my teeth into your sweet pussy and drink you, devour you. I will savage those pretty breasts and thrust my cock down your throat until you choke. So run, little sweetmeat. Run."

He reaches for me, claws out, a snarl on his lips, and I jump back, my heart pounding from the sight of him, his yellow eyes and lolling tongue. I remember him throwing a sharpened peppermint stick through the jelly of the rat-bear's eye.

He could do anything to me. Anything. And I wouldn't be able to stop him. My safe word might be useless—I'm not sure if he was serious about that part or not.

"I'll count to a hundred," he says through his fangs. "If you can elude me for an hour, I'll spare you. Otherwise—you're mine to do with as I please. Mine to tear, to fuck—or to kill."

My pulse is pounding through my skull, my heart thudding heavily in my chest. My mouth is dry, my limbs galvanized with an exhilarated panic.

He won't kill me. He's been sweet to me, he appreciates my talent—

But the other things he threatened—I'm not sure how far he'll go.

His wings shudder behind him as he lowers his head, then tilts it sharply, an unnaturally quick movement. "One."

I inhale.

"Two."

With a soft squeal I leap away, racing into the undergrowth.

"Three." The word leaves his throat as an exultant groan of anticipation.

Like a rabbit with the hounds on her tail, I run, leaping over logs and roots and rocks, dodging branches, ducking around patches of thorns.

He can smell me. And with my scent uncloaked, there are other things in this realm that can smell me, too, that will want to rape me and devour me. He's taking a risk, letting me run like this. What if something *else* finds me first?

A thorny vine rakes my arm, tearing the skin. Warm blood drips as I keep running. The blood will make it easier for him to track me, so I clamp my hand over the spot, scrunching the sleeve of my tunic together and pressing it to the cut.

I skid down a pebbled embankment and struggle up the other side, cut through a quiet glade powdered with snow, fight my way through a tangle of interwoven black branches.

When I break out of that thicket, I hear him. A quiet, derisive laugh slithering through the dark silence of the forest.

Abandoning all thought, I flee. I thought I was running fast before—this is a speed I didn't know I was capable of.

But he is Fae. A warrior, a tracker, a wielder of powerful magic. There is no escaping him.

"Clara." A disembodied whisper at my ear. Then again, "Clara," this time to my right.

I jump ahead, spurred by terror.

I can't see him anywhere.

The cold air pierces my weary lungs, and each rapid breath shears through my lungs like a blade. Tears of cold and suspense ooze from the corners of my eyes, tracking hot lines down my chilled cheeks.

He appears ahead of me, dark and lean and dominant, with those bright yellow eyes. I scream and swerve, angling to the right. He veers to follow, running beside me now, his wings pinned back, his claws extended. I scream again and dart away. He hisses, leaps after me, and rakes my arm with his black nails.

Then he's gone again.

Blood and pain well up together on my forearm. With agonized clarity I realize how foolish I was to propose playing this game with a faerie I've known for scarcely more than a week—one who was banished from court. One who dallies with the Unseelie.

"Cla-ra…" My name is a delicate singsong through the trees, coming from everywhere, and I pause, my body wracked with exhausted gasps.

I brace my back against a tree and hunt for him with my eyes, raking the shadowy depths of the forest, the gray spaces between the black trees. My breath puffs in ragged clouds of steam, but despite the cold, I'm sweating.

I'm wearing a pair of soft tights beneath my tunic—no undershorts. The crotch of the tights is soaked with my arousal.

In the closet of my bedroom, I used to imagine being chased by hideous or handsome monsters—being thrown down and stripped and taken roughly. Finias is the only being I've shared those fantasies with—and he didn't make me feel ashamed for having them. He agreed to play them out with me.

We're just playing. It's only a game.

Just a game.

Finias explodes out of the night, a beautiful, hideous storm of malevolent eyes and claws and teeth. With a shriek I run again, but he zips in front of me, bars my way with one arm against a tree trunk, like he did on the first day I met him.

I try another direction, but he's there again, quicker than thought.

With a screech of frustration I turn my back on him and race for another gap in the trees.

His claws rake my back, snagging the fabric, the tips scratching my skin.

He clutches a handful of my tunic and jerks me toward him.

"No!" I scream, flailing and kicking. Then I put both arms up and I slither down, right out of the tunic. I'm in a light chemise and tights now, my skin burning despite the cold.

Pelting away from him, I begin to triumph a little over my escape—but his weight hits me from behind, knocking me flat.

He's on top of me, crushing me face-down into the leaves and dirt of the forest floor.

"Scream," he hisses. "Scream all you want. Beg someone to come and save you."

His hardness is grinding into the soft flesh of my ass. I scream, writhing under him, and his cock thickens still more.

His claws snarl in my hair, gathering a fistful, and he yanks my head up, ducking his face down to my exposed neck.

"Such sweet fucking blood," he murmurs against the pulse of my throat. "What if I rip your vein open right now, little one?"

I whimper, and his teeth press lightly to that vulnerable pulse point. He kisses, then sucks my skin—a pinch of pain mixed with a rush of heady pleasure.

I've been still for a moment, but the second he breaks the sucking kiss, I buck hard and wriggle forward.

He snarls, raking me back toward him. I manage to flip over and I kick him hard, first in the stomach and then in the jaw.

With a growl of frustration he drags his claws down my front, shredding my chemise. "I'm going to fuck you harder for that," he seethes.

"You can try." I twist and duck, crawling rapidly away and then rolling quickly, clambering to my feet.

His body slams into mine. Instead of knocking me down he's gripping my arms, wrestling me over to a tree, crushing my bare breasts against the bark. He's naked now—he must have vanished his clothes. But he doesn't vanish mine—he tears my tights down to my thighs, until my bottom is exposed.

He pauses, taking a moment to grasp my flesh, to feel me. He's shaking, breathing hard.

"Fuck, I need you so badly," he says hoarsely. "I couldn't stop if I wanted to."

He grasps himself and wedges his cock into my drenched pussy. I vent a choked scream. His hand curls around my throat, and he thrusts, hard and brutal, still grinding my front against the tree. A broken cry cracks from his lips as he pushes deeper into my heat.

Five rough thrusts, and then he pulls out, throws me onto the ground. I start to scramble away on hands and knees, but he seizes my hips and shoves himself inside me again. This time it's a vicious pounding, frantic and noisy, while his claws grip my waist for leverage.

I'm soaring inside, the pleasure I crave skating closer and closer—but he pulls out again, flips me over, and bares all his glittering teeth in a savage howl of exultation before burying his face between my legs.

I shriek my terror to the sky—but Fin doesn't chew into my sensitive area like he threatened. He sucks my pussy lips recklessly, fiercely, lapping up every bit of my juices, and the tips of his teeth sting me a few times, but they don't hurt.

He lifts his eyes to mine while he's eating me out. One of his hands hovers over my belly, claws pricking my soft flesh—a warning to be still.

A shivering, tremulous climax is building inside me, stronger with every lush lick. He pulls my clit into his mouth, dangerously close to those wicked teeth, and I nearly explode—but he raises his dripping mouth and snarls at me like a true predator.

"You're not allowed to come yet," he says.

Then he crawls up my body, inhumanly fast, turns around, and kneels astride my face. He pinches my nose between two of his claws until my mouth pops open, and then he pokes his enormous, burning cock between my lips, pushing it as far down my throat as he can.

I'm choking, squirming, clawing at him, but he only laughs, pumping deep and slow. "You can't say your special word now, can you?"

I almost bite him, just out of spite. But he withdraws before I can make up my mind to do it. And that mercy of his floods my heart with warmth.

He didn't really bite my pussy, or choke me for more than a second or two. Even though we're playing, he can't bear to do more than scratch me up a little. This monstrous side of him isn't entirely an act, but there's such compassion in him, even threaded through this savage game.

But I'm not ready to end the pretense. I need more from him.

He's still hovering over my face, but he has taken a moment to paint my cheek and lips with the arousal seeping from his cock head, all while humming a soft, wild tune.

I see my chance, and I roll away from him, leaping up and racing naked into the forest.

I don't make it more than two dozen steps before he catches me by the throat and bears me down to the ground again, on my back. I'm kicking, screaming, twisting away every time the tip of his cock gets near my hole. But he's impossibly, beautifully strong, and within moments he pins my wrists together in one of his hands, knocks my legs out of the way, and surges inside.

We're both smudged with dirt, wet with melted snow, and smeared with traces of my blood. He has a bruise on his jaw where I kicked him, and he has never looked more glorious. The tiny lollipop earrings swing in the lobes of his pointed ears as he fucks me, never taking his eyes from mine.

"I can't hold back anymore," he says, terse and strained. "I'm coming—I'm coming inside you—aahh—Clara—fuck—"

He shudders violently, heat flowing through my insides as his cock throbs. The sensation is overwhelming, and the sight of him—blue wings rigid and vibrating, his pale body flexed hard in orgasm—I can't bear it, and I come, too, my legs curling, sharp shrieks bursting from my lips.

The climax is the best I've ever had. Also the longest.

My mind swirls into rainbow darkness, and I'm shaking, venting my ecstasy in a shrill, broken voice.

Fin claws me closer to him, pulling me into a sitting position. We're locked together, chest to chest, still joined. The heat of his body melts into mine, warming me as the cold starts to seep beneath my skin.

"We'll rest a moment." As he speaks, a conjured cape of soft white wool appears, encircling my shoulders. "But I'm not done with you yet."

Finias has caught me for the second time.

This time he has me bound with ropes that smell like black licorice. I'm suspended between two trees, with my limbs extended. Since I'm completely nude, I should be freezing, but by some magic of his, I'm not.

Maybe it has to do with the warm glow of the lights he has conjured, which float around the clearing where he has strung me up. He says the lights are similar to the spells around our campsite—protective and defensive.

Fin is enjoying the sight of me while savoring another one of his peppermint sticks. He's licking it to a point like he usually does.

"Where do you get those peppermint sticks?" I ask. "The night we were attacked, you were naked, yet you had weapons ready."

"I keep them in my pocket." He grins, taking the peppermint stick out of his mouth. "It's a sliver of interdimensional space accessible only by magic. I can store a limited amount of items there and access them at will."

"But how do—"

"No, no, little prey. Hush now." He produces a round pink candy from midair, pops it into his mouth, then approaches me. I turn my face away, but he grips my chin, forcing it back around, and crushes his lips to mine. I open instinctively, lured out of the game by the irresistible sweetness of his mouth, and he pushes the pink candy onto my tongue. A blast of delicious flavor startles me, and I hum with delight.

"That should keep you quiet." He gives me a saucy grin. Then he takes the tapered end of the peppermint stick and touches it to my nipple. I jerk at the cloying, sticky contact. An answering tingle of arousal flickers through my clit.

With the tip of the candy, he draws widening circles on the same breast, until my belly is quivering, my limbs trembling. Tiny bursts of pleasure dance through my clit.

Fin places his warm hand on my stomach, sweeping it over my skin, slowly moving upward until he cups the underside of my breast.

"I have never seen anything as beautiful as you, tonight," he says softly. He sucks on the peppermint stick again, swirling his tongue around its shaft. Then he shows me the keen point of the candy and presses it to his finger. A dot of scarlet blood emerges.

"I'm going to use this peppermint stick to make you come," he whispers. "I'm going to put it on your pretty clit."

"No, no, please no," I whine, pressing my thighs together.

"Don't you trust me, darling?" His lashes lower, hooding his eyes. "Spread your thighs and hold very, very still."

I shake my head, keeping my legs pinned together.

With a sigh he conjures more of the licorice ropes, which snake between my legs and loop around my thighs, pulling them apart, spreading me open to him.

A breathless whimper escapes me as he kneels, his face level with my pussy, and touches that sticky, pointed end to my clit.

It's a pinprick of sensation. A dot of scintillating awareness.

I hold my breath.

Again he touches, this time on a different part of that tiny nub of tender flesh.

And then he jiggles my clit lightly, with the tip of the peppermint stick.

A sharp thrill races through my stomach, and I gasp. "Oh…"

Another delicate touch, a prick that's nearly pain but not quite.

I sob, my body rigid with the effort of holding still.

"I can hardly bear to do this," Fin says thickly. "It's all I can do not to toss this aside and taste you again. You smell divine, sugar."

He looks up, into my eyes—not the predator this time, but a torturer, mischievous and mad, and entirely obsessed with me.

"I like you kneeling there," I whisper.

Fin chuckles. "Don't make me laugh, dearest. I need a steady hand for this."

Dearest…

He hasn't called me that before.

It doesn't mean anything.

We're just playing, he and I. Amusing ourselves, taking advantage of the strange fate that has brought us together. At the end of it all, we'll separate, and I'll return to my own world. I will never see him again.

He's stroking my clit delicately with the tip of the candy, its stickiness tugging at the tender skin. I can barely think beyond the wriggling lines of pleasure expanding from that spot—my stomach and thighs are tensing, my insides tightening.

"It's coming," I breathe. "Don't stop, don't stop, keep doing that, please, please, I'm begging you—Fin, Fin—ah—"

His warm breath fans across my sex as he traces the same path, over and over, keeping the rhythm and pressure precise—until a lightning crack of ecstasy snakes through my clit, quaking through me in a storm of soaking release.

The Sugarplum Faerie drops the peppermint and grasps my thighs, leaning in to savor my wetness, licking me through the ebbing pleasure. When he's done, he vanishes my ropes, and I collapse onto the soft white-wool cape he spread beneath me.

I lie there, boneless and blissful.

Finias crawls over to me, pressing a palm to my cheek. "Open for me, little prey," he says, and I let my lips part for him.

"You exquisite creature," he breathes, stroking his rigid shaft. He's panting, his eyes raking over my whole body until they finally meet mine, and when they do, I smile at him, openmouthed, putting out my tongue. His eyes widen with startled joy, and he groans faintly, lines of his cum painting my tongue and lips.

This time he tastes like strawberries and the frothiest sweet cream. I take every drop he gives me and suck the tip of his cock to extract the last delicious bit of his release.

He collapses beside me, swearing softly, over and over. I don't recognize some of the words he includes—a Fae dialect, maybe.

"I never thought I would be able to do things like this, with anyone," I murmur. "I thought I would marry a staid businessman and keep house for him, warm his bed, have his children. If I was lucky I'd get to paint a little. Either that, or I'd remain single, focused on my art, pleasing myself when I had the urge. This is—like a dream."

I roll onto my side, gazing at him while he lies there on his back, his pink hair tousled and his face flushed.

"You're very good at all of it. I know you've had decades of practice but—" I sigh contentedly. "You're wonderfully talented. What you did just now—you knew exactly where to touch me."

"That's because I can feel it, with you," he says slowly. "I'm connected to you somehow—

not magically, nothing so concrete or precise—
but I have a sense of your body, your mind, your
pleasure. I can't explain it. And I've never
experienced it this strongly with anyone else."

He pushes himself onto one elbow and
leans in, sliding his hand across the back of my
neck, under my hair. "You, my dearest darling,
are someone I've only dreamed of meeting. I'm
very afraid I won't be able to let you go back to
your world. I think I shall have to keep you here,
with me."

A delicious chill runs up my spine. "Keep
me? For how long?"

"Maybe forever," he whispers, pressing his
lovely lips to mine.

We don't speak of the future again, but we
kiss for a long time before he conjures me a fresh
set of clothes, picks me up, and flies me back to
camp, just before dawn. When we land, he slips
me a gumdrop and murmurs, "This will help
with the scratches, blisters, and bruises. And it
will keep you from being too tired."

No one noticed our absence—or at least,
that's what I think until the next evening, when
Louisa goes with me to fetch water at our
campsite.

"I wish faeries could conjure water," I
complain, swinging the waterskins.

"It's a 'vital element' or something," she
answers. "Only certain Fae can produce it, just
like only certain Fae can produce fire.
Apparently conjuring water is a rarer gift—it's

harder to make it in any decent quantity. Fire, on the other hand, grows by itself when given enough fuel."

I raise an eyebrow at her, and she blushes. "Lir told me all about it.

"How is he? With the blood and such?" I ask. "You two sneak off almost every day. The others think you're fucking."

"No, still not fucking." She plops onto a rock. "You and Finias are, though."

"Hm?" I keep my eyes on the stream as I scoop water into one of the bottles.

"Last night? You two sneaked out of camp and didn't come back for hours."

"Oh. That."

"What were you doing? It doesn't take hours to have sex."

"Sometimes it does," I say primly. "If you're playing games."

"Oh my god," she breathes, grinning. "Games? What games? You must tell me everything."

"No, I mustn't." I can feel my blush deepening, my smile spreading.

Louisa watches me in silence for a moment. "Clara," she says soberly. "Do you love him?"

"Of course not," I say with a breathless laugh. "What a silly idea."

"You can't, you know. When this is done, we're going home. They don't want us here."

I try to bite back the words, but I fail. "You mean Lir doesn't want *you* here. Fin wants me to stay."

"Did he *ask* you to stay?" she says doubtfully

"He said, 'I think I shall have to keep you here, with me. Maybe forever.'" I shoot her a defiant look.

"That's very noncommittal. Did he say it right after an orgasm?"

"That—that's beside the point."

"Ah, he did." Louisa laughs. "You're very inexperienced with men, sister mine. Anything they say right after an orgasm can't be taken seriously. Their brain-blood is still in their cocks at that point, and they may *think* they want you forever, simply because your pussy or mouth did the job well. But they really don't want *you*. Just your holes."

I jam the cork savagely back into the neck of the waterskin. "You know, Louisa—sometimes I really hate you."

"I don't mean to upset you," she says. "I'm only telling you the truth."

"Maybe that's what you tell yourself." I swallow hard against the lump rising in my throat. "But I think you can't bear for anyone else to have something you don't. That's why you always feel the need to ruin everything!"

I pick up the waterskins and march back to camp. And I don't speak to my sister, beyond what's necessary, for the next two days.

On the third day after our fight, she offers to go with me to fetch the water again. "The stream is farther away this time. You shouldn't go alone."

"I'd rather do it alone," I say crisply.

"If you don't want me along, at least take Fin."

"Fin is helping Achorn with the horses." Waterskins in hand, I start to walk away.

"Without me, you'll have to make multiple trips," she calls. "Clara—I just want to talk."

For a moment I nearly relent. This is one of the longest periods of silence and anger we've ever had between us, and I hate it.

But I also hate her for possibly being right. Fin has chatted with me since our night of passion, and he has kissed me a few times as well—but we've been traveling hard, taking detours to avoid monster dens, or to steer clear of the rat-soldier patrols he or the moth-girl spot from the air. There's been no more time for wild forest fucking. The one time I asked him about doing it again, he said the area wasn't safe.

Logically, I know why we haven't been able to connect like that again. But Louisa's words poisoned my joy, like they always do. She introduced doubt where I was feeling so confident, so cherished.

I can't forgive her for that. Not yet.

I trudge onward, ignoring her call.

When we picked the spot for camp this evening, the moth-girl told me where the nearest stream was. It's out of sight of the clearing, but still close enough to be safe.

I step out of the trees onto the bank of the stream. It's a cold, sluggish, gleaming sheet of water with high banks. I walk along it, searching for a jutting rock, a strip of beach—any place where I can climb down for better access.

Something whizzes past me, snatching me up before I can think or scream.

I've been stolen. Taken. I'm being carried along at a frenzied speed, icy wind shearing past my face, whipping tears from my eyes, stealing the air before I can breathe it.

For a fleeting moment I think it's Fin. But he showed me his Fae speed a couple of times during our travels, and he's not this fast.

Which means whoever or whatever has a hold of me is something *else.*

I try to suck in enough air. But I can't—it's flowing by too fast. My lungs and my head feel as if they're swelling, growing, tightening unbearably. I try to thrash, but the force of my captor's speed keeps me pinned.

I can't fight.
Can't breathe.
I'm blacking out.

My head aches. The back of my throat feels sore and cracked, and my mouth is horribly dry.

A swollen heaviness weighs my eyelids.

"Water," I rasp.

"Apologies, human." A reed-thin, high-pitched voice. "I did not realize your kind could die from speed."

Something drips against my mouth. I open wide, desperate for liquid, and more of it pours into my throat. It's water, I think. Nearly tasteless, faintly sweet, and very cold.

I drink until the flow stops, and then I rub some of the water that splashed onto my cheeks over my eyelids. After a moment, I'm able to open my eyes, though they still feel puffy.

The creature before me is the strangest I've ever seen—human-shaped, but with limbs as delicate as flower stems, pale green and tapered. The body is impossibly slim as well, naked and green-skinned, with no genitals, just pale-green smoothness. The Fae's long neck rises to a gracefully tapered skull and a face with large eyes and flat features. They remind me of a blend between a greyhound, a praying mantis, and a delicate flower. Wingless, obviously streamlined for running, yet with an unmistakable plantlike quality.

Maybe it's the ethereal delicacy of the creature that prompts me to speak gently, despite my fear.

"Why did you take me with you?" I ask. "My friends will be worried."

The creature cocks their head. "Friends? You were alone."

"My friends were encamped nearby."

Translucent lids slide over the creature's large eyes for a moment, then retract. "You will not need your friends. You are mine now."

"No, I'm not. You cannot claim a living thing, a being with speech and thought. I must go back to my people. I travel in the company of several Fae, and if you do not return me, they will be angry. But if we go back now, they might forgive you."

"That is not possible," says the creature. "I need a favor from the Rat King. I was hunting for an appropriate gift for him. Imagine my surprise when I smelled you—so luscious, so human. The perfect offering. The stars have sent me a blessing. I shall gift you to the Rat King, and he will grant my request."

"No!" I lunge to my feet, but a wave of dizziness hits me, along with a burst of pain in my head. At the same moment, threadlike vines whip out from the creature's delicate fingertips, wrapping me round and round, over and over, spinning me until I'm completely bound in a cocoon of them. The vines knot themselves tight and detach from their owner's fingertips.

I feel like a fly, encompassed by a spider's webbing, and the sensation only worsens when the Fae scoops me up and sets off through the forest again, traveling at a perilous speed. They must have keen eyesight and quick reflexes, because we streak through the forest without hitting so much as a twig.

This time I don't pass out, since my captor is traveling more slowly. But I almost wish I could sink into oblivion. That would be better than hours of blindingly fast travel, during which I'm utterly helpless, increasingly nauseated, and tormented by dread.

I can't bear to think how far away we are from camp now. It's possible no one has yet realized I'm gone. And once they do realize it, they won't know where to look for me. They won't know I'm being taken to the last place I want to go.

The court of the Rat King.

18
LOUISA

The moth-girl descends from the sky into the center of camp, the gust of her wings putting out the fire over which Finias was cooking dinner.

"Watch it, Cahren!" he protests.

"I was flying over the forest," says Cahren in her cottony voice. "Stretching my wings, looking for prey—and I saw the girl. She was taken."

"Taken?" Finias rises, still holding the pan in which sausage and potatoes are sizzling. "Clara? Was Clara taken?"

"Yes. She was by the stream, and a Racer took her."

Fin drops the pan and bolts through the trees toward the stream.

"A Racer?" My voice shrills as I chase after him. "What's a Racer?"

"A species of Fae gifted with incredible speed," Lir says from behind me. He's running too, but since he doesn't have all his Fae abilities, his speed is a match for mine. Finias has outdistanced both of us. Panic spurs me on, my heart thudding with a sick, growing terror.

When we jog up to the bank of the stream, Fin is crouched by two discarded waterskins.

"She's gone." He looks up at me, his yellow eyes wide and fractured with panic. "It took her. They must be hours away from here by now."

"We can't chase a Racer," Lir says. "Not with me in this state, and her—" He gestures to me. "There's no possible way to catch up."

"What? What are you saying?" I'm shaking, my voice threaded with rage. "We have to go after them. We have to get Clara back!"

Lir turns to me, sorrow in his eyes. "None of us are a match for a Racer, Louisa. She could be anywhere by now. Once I have my powers back, I can find her. I can—"

"She might be dead by then!" I scream. "You said yourself that Faerie is dangerous for mortals. Who knows what that thing might do to her! You have to get her back for me. You *will* get her back."

"I'll have the power to find her once my curse is broken."

"We're still days from the Pool! I can't— you *won't*—" I fly at him, punching his chest as hard as I can. I don't care that the others from camp have arrived, that they're watching. "You fucking bastard! You unfeeling piece of shit, you asshole—"

Lir seizes my wrists, pins them together in one hand, and clamps his other hand over my mouth. "I can't let you speak to me that way in front of our companions," he hisses. "Calm yourself. We'll do everything we—"

"I'll go after her."

It's Finias, white-faced and grim-jawed.

"Not even you can catch up to a Racer, Fin," the Prince says.

"If it's running at top speed, Clara will pass out," Finias says. "Hopefully the Racer will notice and pause to bring her back to consciousness. Then it will have to go more slowly so she doesn't die. It wants her for something. Racers don't copulate, so it's not for sex—and they don't consume flesh. They live off soil, air, and sunshine. It's probably taking her somewhere to sell her, or to sell her bodily fluids." He turns to the moth-girl, Cahren. "Which way did it go?"

She points in a direction.

"They always run straight toward their destination," says Finias. "All I need to do is run in that direction as well, until I find them. And when I find them, Louisa, I will bring Clara back to you. I promise."

I nod, releasing a sob against Lir's palm. Tears overflow, running down my cheeks onto his fingers. He lets me go, his hand cupping my chin in a brief caress, almost an apology.

"I know you need me for the next part of the journey, Lir," Finias says, his golden eyes desperate. "The Ravine will be full of the Rat King's forces. But Clara—"

"Go," says the Prince. "Save her. We'll make it through without you, somehow."

Finias gives him a grateful nod. "I'll meet up with you again as soon as I can. Louisa, take my satchel of spells. There's a guide in the front pocket. Study it, and use them."

"Me?" I gasp. "Shouldn't it be Lir who uses them, or—"

"No, he's right," says the Prince. "You have a warrior's instinct, the mind of a strategist. You will use the spells."

Finias grips my hand briefly, a fierce promise. "I'll save her," he says.

And then he's off, speeding down the bank of the stream like an arrow.

"He'll fly when he needs to," says Lir. "But he's faster on foot as long as the way is clear enough."

The other mercenaries are turning away, muttering amongst themselves as they shuffle back to camp. I face the Prince, gratitude and anger churning in my chest. "Next time, don't cover my mouth."

"I couldn't let a mortal girl speak to me that way in front of *them*." He speaks low, with a jerk of his head toward the mercenaries' receding figures. "They already lack respect for me."

I clench my teeth, hating that he makes sense. "Fine. But I didn't like it."

"Fair enough."

"Thank you, though. For letting Fin go after her."

"I doubt I could have stopped him. There's something between them. I'm sure you've noticed."

"Oh, I've noticed. She told me they've fucked, at least twice. And he watches her all the time, hovers near her, smiles whenever she speaks. It's rather adorable."

"I haven't seen him like this with anyone." Lir says the words gravely, as if they carry a deeper meaning.

"You think he's—in love with her? I thought maybe he just wanted to fuck a human, for fun…" My voice trails off at the stormy look on Lir's face.

"My cousin is the only one who could have ensured our safe passage through what lies ahead—a Ravine overrun by the Rat King's troops and monsters. Fin has abandoned this quest, knowing full well that leaving me now likely means I will fail, and we will all die. Yet he departed without question, without pause. His affection for your sister outweighed his love and loyalty to me, his kin. And his duty to the entire kingdom of Seelie."

The heaviness of dread weighs my stomach. "And you let him go," I whisper. "You gave him permission, knowing his absence might mean capture and death for the rest of us."

"Clara's safety is important to you," the Prince says stiffly, avoiding my eyes. "And I happen to like your sister. She's far less argumentative than you are. Besides, as I said, Fin would have gone after her anyway."

He starts to move away, but I catch his hand. "Lir. Thank you."

A moment's hesitation, and then his fingers curl around mine. Just for an instant, and then he lets go. "Come, we should return to camp. I believe our mercenary friends are unhappy with my decision to let Fin depart."

When we reach camp, the four mercenaries are deep in a heated discussion, which cuts off abruptly at our approach. Achorn steps to the forefront of the group, his burly arms crossed and his bovine features heavy with displeasure.

"We didn't agree to this," he says. "We signed up for this job because Sugarplum was part of it. Now he's gone. He had the magic to get us through. Not just those candy spells but the real goods, his natural skills. And you sent him off."

"I did not 'send him off,'" replies Lir coolly. "He wanted to leave. I allowed it. He will return."

"Who knows when?" snorts Achorn.

"There's no way through the Ravine without him," adds Cahren, curving her moth wings around herself protectively. "I have my acid, my wind spells, my bow, and my camouflage, but it won't be enough."

"I can take on a dozen enemies at once," puts in the dark-skinned Fae with the antlers. "But not five dozen. We told you when we laid our plans at the tavern—we told you the kind of force that's massed in the Ravine. Without Sugarplum, the odds are too great."

"He went to save my sister." I spit the words out, trembling with anger. "Sounds to me as if the rest of you are cowards."

Lir winces at my words, and a venomous rumble travels through the other Fae.

"Cowards, are we? What's your little mortal ass good for except fucking the Prince?" sneers the reptilian Fae. "I won't be called a coward by a leaking fleshbag of a human whore!"

Before the reptile's words can register with me, Lir has him by the throat. He smashes the other Fae into the ground and slams a boot down on his neck.

It all happens so quickly I barely have time to react, to think. But as the mercenaries reach for their weapons, I dive for Fin's bag of spells and snatch an orb out of it. I leap to the Prince's side, holding up the orb, my teeth bared.

"Back off," I hiss at the other Fae. "Or I'll use this. Fin told me what it does, and believe me, you don't want to find out."

They recoil, glaring. The reptilian mercenary squirms under Lir's boot.

"Take it back," snarls the Prince, grinding down harder.

"I take it back," rasps the mercenary. "Your pardon, my lady. Mercy, mercy! I beg your forgiveness!"

"You're forgiven," I say. "But if you want to keep your tongue, I suggest you train it to be more polite."

Lir slants an approving look at me and eases the pressure on the mercenary's throat.

"This is how we will proceed," says the Prince evenly. "I know Fin gave you money to purchase the supplies and horses, which means the provisions and mounts in this camp are not yours. And since you are leaving our company before the job is done, you won't be paid. However, in recompense for your time and effort, you may keep all the horses but two, and you may take with you the supplies we won't need."

"Or we could kill you and keep it all," growls Achorn.

"Wait, now." The antlered Fae shakes his head. "That's too far. I won't be party to killing the future King."

"Agreed," says Cahren. "We take all but two horses, a few weapons, and two shares of supplies. We forfeit the reward, but keep our lives. It is fair."

She looks at Lir, and in her eyes I see a cautious request for his approval. She and the antlered Fae want to depart, same as the other two, but they recognize that if their Prince does happen to survive and make it to the Pool, he might decide to punish them for leaving him in the lurch.

"It is fair." Lir says, with a nod. "Collect your share and begone."

He moves his boot from the neck of the reptilian Fae, and he and I withdraw to one side of the clearing with some of the supplies. I'm already wearing the blue dagger I took from Drosselmeyer's weapon room, and I keep Fin's satchel slung around my body.

Lir and I stand our ground, looking as aggressive and authoritative as we can while the others pack up. I toss the orb I'm holding lightly, a subtle threat. There's no verbal agreement between me and the Prince on our stance or strategy; there is simply an understanding—a seamless, unspoken partnership. Portray strength, and the others won't change their minds and challenge us.

"Do you really know what that thing does?" mutters Lir out of the side of his mouth.

"No idea," I whisper back. "It could be a fizzy bathwater ball or a lethal spell."

He gives me one of his rare grins. "Clever woman."

"I have moments of brilliance."

We maintain our dominant stance until the others have ridden out of the clearing. And then the enormity of what has happened rushes into my heart, and I sink to the ground, tucking the spell back into Fin's satchel.

"We should wait here, shouldn't we?" I say faintly. "Wait until Fin comes back with my sister, and then go on. We can't do this by ourselves."

"The longer we stay in one place, the more vulnerable we are to the Rat King's patrols, or to monsters," Lir counters. "We don't have Fin to cast a shielding spell on your scent anymore. Creatures will be drawn to you."

"Like the mole-rat."

"No, the mole-rat simply decided to sun itself when we happened to be there. While their perception of sound and vibrations is highly developed, their sense of smell is practically nonexistent. But there are many other creatures who will catch a whiff of your decadent aroma from far away, and will try to hunt you down. Our best chance is to keep moving."

He walks over to the two remaining horses, absently stroking the nose of the gray gelding. "I suppose we'll camp here, as planned. Tomorrow we'll ride until we reach the Ravine, and then we can try to sneak through it on foot. Perhaps it's best that the others left. It would be more difficult to slip through enemy lines quietly with so many travelers."

I'm not sure if he truly believes what he's saying, or if he's attempting to reassure me. I think he's trying to feign hopefulness for my sake. In exchange, the least I can do is not collapse entirely and weep for my sister. I'll be strong, and I will see this through. For myself, for Clara—and for him.

19
CLARA

When the Fae who captured me said I was being taken to the Rat King, I pictured two different scenarios.

One, I'd be taken to the royal city or wherever Lir's palace and ancestral throne might be located. The Rat King would be sitting on a throne of pillows, or possibly a very fancy chair, since he's magically prevented from taking the actual throne unless the true King dies.

Two, I pictured being dragged into an enemy camp with lots of tents and horrific-looking soldiers milling around. I thought the Rat King might be in the biggest tent, chomping on a leg of mutton or a giant wedge of cheese.

I have no idea which he'd prefer, or what he looks like. Maybe he drinks tea, with eyeballs in it.

But when my captor dives into a large, ragged-looking hole in the earth, my heart nearly stops.

Why didn't I anticipate that? A rat would of course live in a hole.

For once I'm glad of my captor's speed, because I only catch hasty glimpses of the tunnels we're traveling through. Some of them glow with a sickly green light, others flash with spurts of purple fire or orange flame, and others are lined with luminescent bluish worms. By those dim sources of light I glimpse hulking figures with bristling fur, the gleam of armor plating, the toothy grins of soldiers wearing rat's heads. As we move deeper, the whine of weapons being sharpened and the growls of soldiers give way to screams of agony or shrieks of pleasure. There are twisting naked bodies in the underground rooms, most of them part human and part bestial.

The clang of goblets, the sharp scent of hard liquor, the acrid tang of vomit, and the roars and hisses of undefinable creatures flood my senses in rapid succession. Wings flutter against the ceiling of the tunnel—the shiny black wings of beetles, the leathery wings of bats, and the dark feathered wings of ravens or vultures—but the owners of the wings aren't any of those familiar animals.

"What is this place?" I venture, as my captor slows down to a walk. I'm not sure how they can carry me when their limbs are thin as flower stems, but they seem to be managing easily.

"This is the Rat King's headquarters," they say. "Home to his second army. Most of his forces are gathered in the Ravine, far from here."

"Why so far away?"

"Why should you care, mortal?" Those strange pale-green eyes blink at me.

"I'm merely curious. I can do nothing with the knowledge, either way." Remembering the faeries' affinity for bargains, I add, "You stole me, so it's only fair you should give me the small satisfaction of answering my questions before you hand me over to the Rat King."

My captor runs onward silently for a moment, then says, "The Unseelie forces plan to take possession of the Unending Pool, the source of true magic. But the remnants of the Seelie Prince's army are stationed between them and the Pool. So they are gathering in the Ravine, and when the Rat King gives the word, the Seelie army will be crushed."

"And the royal city? The palace? Are there any Seelie left to defend it?" I ask.

"Some, yes. But precious few. Most of those guards were killed, eaten, or reside in the dungeons far below us. The kitchen cooks up a few of the prisoners occasionally and serves them to the Rat King's favorite advisors and concubines."

I swallow hard, trying to keep from gagging. "And the Rat King plans to use the army gathered here in the caves to overwhelm the royal city?"

"Yes. And now I will no longer speak to you, human. You would be wise to remain silent while I gift you to the Rat King." My captor hurries forward to a gate woven of thorns, jawbones, and antlers. I have a sick desire to sketch it.

"I bring a valuable gift for His Unutterable Majesty, the Rat King of Seelie and Unseelie," says my captor to the guards. "See this human female? She will make a wonderful concubine."

Oh no. Concubine to the Rat King? No, this cannot happen. I try to struggle, but my bonds are so tight I can barely writhe. The most I achieve is a frantic bobbing of my head.

"See how eager she is to serve," says my captor. "Allow me to pass so I may offer this gift to the King and receive his favor in return."

One of the guards, a huge one with a bloodstained leather coat, steps forward. The rat-head he's wearing is white like the others I've seen, and has the same perpetual grin full of serrated black teeth—but the eyes are scarlet instead of ebony, the round ears are studded with silver hoops, and blood flecks the white fur.

He pries open my jaw and thrusts his enormous thumb into my mouth, shoving it so far back I almost gag. But I manage to resist the urge.

With a nod, he steps back and jerks his head, indicating that we can proceed.

My captor carries me along a tunnel so impossibly high that I can't see its roof. It's lined with pillars of an equally dizzying height, coated with glowing cobwebs of orange and green. Bioluminescent spiders dangle from gleaming threads overhead and I shudder, praying to every deity I've ever heard of that the spiders will stay up there and not decide to drop onto my face while I'm bound and helpless.

The corridor opens suddenly into an enormous chamber, so big I almost feel as if we're outside again. The entire arch of the ceiling is a crystalline mass of heated, glowing rocks. Hordes of Unseelie fill the room. Some don't look much different from the Fae I know—colder, maybe, more cruel—but many of them have the limbs or heads of crabs, spiders, or insects. Whether those are actually their heads or merely masks like the rat-soldiers wear, I can't tell. Some of the Unseelie have dramatic body modifications—thick silver chains, huge golden spikes, razor-sharp blades, long rows of brass rings, or actual thorns embedded through parts of their bodies. One Unseelie, who looks otherwise normal, has replaced her spinal column with one of silver.

There's a dais of black rock in the center of the chamber, with a twisted mass of thorny carapaces, titanic bone shards, and cracked skulls forming a wretched-looking throne. And in the center of that throne sits the Rat King.

I expected something horrible. But at the sight of him, bile creeps up the back of my throat.

He has one large head—the head of an immense rat, and it's no mask—the rolling of his red eyes and the champ of his long sharp teeth are unmistakably real. There's a spiked crown of white bone protruding from the top of his head, as if his skull grew into that shape at his will.

He's naked, except for a stained red loincloth that conceals an immense and terrifying bulge between his thighs. His thick torso is human-looking, but gray-skinned, coated with coarse pale hair across the chest. His legs are half-human, ending in paws rimmed with sharp nails. His arms are furred like a rat's, but structured like a human's. He holds a scepter of white bone in one paw.

The most terrifying part of him is the bodies of smaller rats that have been magically fused with his own. They're clearly not part of his consciousness; they twitch and writhe and squeal faintly as if they're trying to get away. But they are definitely built into him, extruding from the muscle and skin of his stomach, his pectorals, his thighs, his arms, even his calves.

Six of the smaller rats' heads form a sickening, ever-shifting collar around his neck. Their heads protrude beneath his chin, their bodies disappear into his sinewy throat, and their tails emerge again just below his collarbone, wriggling constantly.

If I could capture this scene, it wouldn't be a painting. It would be a coarse sketch in dark pencil and charcoal, all tortured lines and black spikes and hollows and coils. It would be the most horrific drawing I've ever done. If I survive this, I think I will have to draw the Rat King, if only to purge him from my mind, or I have the strangest feeling he will linger there, lurking and gnawing, with his blood-colored eyes.

While I've been staring, my captor has been waiting in line behind the other supplicants. But all too soon we're at the front of the line, and my captor sets me down before the steps leading up to the dais.

"A gift for you, O Unyielding and Unfathomable Majesty," my captor says. "A fresh human concubine, yours for the taking. I only ask the release of two of my kind, Racers who foolishly took up arms against your Lordship. I would like to take those two Racers with me, confine them at home, and teach them the error of their ways, convincing them that you are the sole liege of this land, to be honored and worshipped."

The Rat King snuffles and grunts, idly stroking the polished ruby head of his scepter. "Let's see this gift of yours," he rumbles.

Tendrils of darkness unspool from his body, coiling like foul-smelling snakes around my cocoon of vine-ropes. The shadows eat through the vines like acid, and they sear through my clothes as well. Everything melts off my skin, leaving me naked on the floor. I curl into myself, covering my breasts, but the shadows wrap my wrists and ankles and tug sharply, splaying out my limbs so the entire Unseelie Court can see all of me.

"Two Racer prisoners, in exchange for this tasty morsel?" says the Rat King.

The Racer who captured me bows low. "By your grace, my lord King."

"You would offer me a gift, and then propose I pay you for it?" The Rat King's voice rises, and some of his shadows snake out, writhing around the slender body of the Racer. "That is no gift, but a bribe. A foolish bribe, that would see my enemies running free."

He's drawing my captor closer, dragging them up the steps until they're directly in front of him, right between his huge knees. There's a small rat sticking halfway out of his kneecap, scrabbling frantically with its tiny paws, trying to pull itself free.

"I cannot grant your boon," says the Rat King to the trembling Fae in his shadows' grip. "Because I have already eaten your friends. They were crispy and delicious. As I'm sure you will be."

And with that, his jaw drops, his maw expanding to four times its size, glistening throat-flesh lined with razor teeth. He shoves the whole head of the Racer into his mouth and rips it from the body. Clear fluid spurts from the Racer's neck stump, and a loud crunching fills the air as the Rat King chews.

I lie still, transfixed on the floor, still pinioned by shadows.

When the Rat King has finished chewing, he says, "Take my new concubine to be clothed, and then put her in one of the cages. Tonight, we will all partake of my collection of fuckflesh!"

He gestures to one end of the immense chamber, where brass cages are hung from the ceiling at different heights. There are a couple dozen of them, filled with various species of Fae, all genders.

At the Rat King's promise, a great roar rises from the crowd of Unseelie, a roar punctuated by hissing, chattering, and howling. Two servants come forward and begin dragging me away, past jeering, lustful faces and snatching claws.

This is the end of me, then. I will be fucked to death by monsters. Because no one knows I'm here, and no one could possibly have followed me fast enough to reach this place by tonight, and even if they did, they would die trying to get inside. No one can save me.

I dread the horror and pain that will precede my death, but worse is the knowledge that I won't see Finias again. The sweet savagery of him, the laughter blended with compassion, the intense creative skill with magic, the virile beauty—I won't ever experience or enjoy it again.

And my sister—my Louisa—things have been so strained between us, yet I wouldn't let her talk to me. I wouldn't let her try to fix it, or listen to her apology. The chasm between my sister and me is like a ravine through my heart, one I will never get the chance to bridge.

I refuse to cry openly in the Court of the Rat King. But inside, my heart weeps tears of blood.

20
LOUISA

The first night alone with Lir is terrifying. The forest is darkening around us, and he has no magic.

"So we're out here alone, you and I," I say, shivering, "and you have no magic, while I smell like a savory buffet, or like sex incarnate."

Lir's green eyes glow faintly at me. He's crouched beside our scanty supplies, opening our bedrolls. "Yes."

"So we're going to sleep here until they come to devour and rape me?"

"Does Fin have anything in his bag that could protect us?" he counters.

"Shit, why didn't I think of that?" I plop down and open the satchel. There's a guide within, just where Fin said it would be. I'm not sure if he had it all along, or if he conjured it on the spot when he left us.

I pore over the list of spells, comparing them to the colorful sweets and tiny spheres tucked into the various pockets of the satchel. "Here's something to disguise a person's scent."

"How many of those?"

"Just one, I think."

"Save it. We'll need it when we're passing through the Ravine."

Shrugging, I trace my finger down the parchment. "This one is for protection. It creates a dome that lasts for several hours. That should work, yes?"

"Show it to me."

"You don't believe me?"

He gives me a stern look. "Louisa."

My stomach thrills when he says my name. "Fine. Here."

He examines the chart, then inspects the piece of candy. "There's only one."

"Maybe if one of us eats it and we're standing close together, the dome will appear around both of us."

"Unlikely."

"Then we split it."

"We may get two domes and half the protection time."

"Well, we can't ask Fin about it, so we have to try something." I unwrap the sweet. Unfortunately it's not easily divisible; it's a hard, round ball.

"It's meant to be sucked on, I think," I muse, turning it over. "Maybe I can suck it for a while, and then you—"

He's looking at me with the most supremely disdainful expression.

"Or we could suck on it at the same time," I say, just to annoy him.

"That idea has merit," he replies. "It would ensure the dome forms around us both."

My jaw drops. "You—I—then we—all right."

We're already sitting on the ground, so he scoots nearer to me. "Hold it between your lips, and come here."

I place the round candy between my lips, in front of my teeth, and he kisses me. We both open our teeth slightly at the same moment, our tongues sliding out, caressing the sweet surface of the candy. My eyes are closed, my brow furrowed as I concentrate on exerting the same amount of pressure as him so the candy stays balanced between us.

Never have I kissed anyone like this, tongues pressing and gliding, sweetness slipping into both our mouths. The candy is dissolving faster than I expected, growing smaller and smaller until it's a syrupy flow down my throat, but his tongue is still in my mouth and he's not pulling away.

I open my eyes, and his are closed, black lashes traced on pale cheeks. Behind him the protective dome shimmers. It's just the right size for the two of us—a rainbow bubble that looks all too fragile. But I'm sure it isn't as flimsy as it seems. Fin's packaged magic seems dependable, from what I've witnessed.

Unfortunately the horses ended up outside the small dome, but they're native Fae creatures, with shaggy coats to protect them against the elements. Hopefully the dome will muffle my scent so no monsters will come prowling around and put our mounts at risk.

Gently I separate my lips from Lir's. "It's done," I murmur.

He blinks and pulls back. "So it is."

"Do you think the horses will be all right?"

"They have their natural coats and their blankets. They will be fine. Good night."

He drops down to his bedroll, shucks off his boots, pulls the blankets over himself, and ignores me.

I walk over and touch the dome. It seems fairly solid, which probably means not much can escape it, including my scent.

"Will we run out of air in here?" I ask.

"No."

"But the dome will block my scent?"

"Even if your scent does leak out, the Fae magic of the dome should color the fragrance enough that it won't be a problem. Like clear water strained through a freshly dyed cloth takes on the same hue."

"What?"

He sighs gustily. "Go to sleep."

I would, but I'm worried about the deepening cold. I didn't think to gather any firewood before we used the spell.

Uneasily I take off my boots and curl into my bedroll.

My sleep is fitful when it comes, and sometime in the dead of night I wake to the sound of my own teeth chattering. The dome doesn't seem to hold much heat, and the temperature is bitterly cold. I can't feel my toes anymore.

"L-Lir," I whimper into the dark.

"What is it?" He sounds as if his teeth are gritted.

"I'm so cold. I think we should—share heat."

A long silence. Then, "If we must."

"Can you—can you take off the uniform?"

"What?"

"When two people are freezing and need heat, skin to skin is best." I'm shaking so hard I can barely manage the words. "That's what humans do in low temperatures without a fire. I'm not trying to seduce you, I promise. We can sleep—back to back—if you want. Just—please."

There's a rustle of fabric, which I suspect is him undressing. Then he says, "Come."

Trembling, I strip off my traveling tunic and leggings. "Fin conjured these for me yesterday. Will they last until the journey's end, or will I end up naked?"

"There are extra clothes—among the supplies," he says, his voice jerking like mine. So he's shivering too. "They may not—fit you well—but they'll have to do."

Entirely naked, I crawl into his bedroll, arranging my blankets and both our sets of clothes on top of us for extra warmth.

He's naked too, every bit of him. My chilled blood stirs as my skin brushes so much of his body, and warmth spreads through my sex. Wordlessly I turn my back to him, but he says, "It makes more sense to lie face to face. More warmth for the vital organs."

I turn over, my tight, cold nipples brushing his chest. I cringe inwardly—but the shared warmth does feel good. Cautiously I tuck my frozen toes against his.

"So you're Fae-ish right now, but you're lacking certain traits," I whisper. "Can you heal yourself like Fin does?"

"The wounds on my arm would say otherwise."

"Wounds?"

"Feel."

My stomach pitted with dread, I move my hand up his arm—the arm that splintered when I dropped him, the same one that was damaged again when he saved me from the rat-soldier. My fingertips meet a patch of deeply scraped skin along his forearm, then a deep, sticky groove on his upper arm. I jerk back.

"Oh my god," I whisper. "I'm so sorry."

"Finias could not help me. I tried one of his healing sweets, but nothing happened. The structure of my body is different under the curse, and I could not be healed." He clears his throat lightly. "I feared removing the uniform would make the damage permanent."

"Permanent?" I gasp. "Why didn't you say so? I wouldn't have asked you to take your clothes off!"

"Without my heat, you could die."

I can't respond. Can't fathom the kind of person who would treat me like a lower species and then sacrifice his body for mine.

"You don't make sense," I breathe against his collarbone.

"I do, though," he whispers. "To me, this is fair payment, since I've wounded you, too. The bites." His fingers graze the bandages on my forearms.

"I'm sorry I dropped you that first day." I cuddle closer to him.

A hot, hard, satin-smooth length presses against the soft flesh of my lower belly.

"You'll have to ignore that," he says through his teeth. "It's a foolish physical reaction."

"I will ignore it if you like," I say softly. "But if that part of you needs more warmth, I'm happy to help."

Every muscle of his body tightens. I can practically feel his panicked embarrassment, the roaring blush of his skin. Smiling to myself, I snuggle into his heat and breathe deeply until I can relax.

Sometime in the night, I rouse to find him shifting, tilting his hips forward, his cock rubbing up my stomach. Just once he does it, and then he's still. But he's clearly awake, still painfully aroused. The taut need is practically radiating off him.

Sighing as if I'm asleep, I change my position slightly, grazing the underside of his cock again. A soft moan issues from him—the quietest, most beautiful male sound—and my pussy comes to roaring life.

In the darkness I squirm against him, and he chokes out something unintelligible—maybe a protest, or possibly an encouragement. I press my soft stomach to his hard abdomen, rubbing his cock shamelessly between us.

Lir's whole body quakes and cum spurts from him, painting my belly and the underside of my breasts. I can feel his shaft throbbing, his chest heaving.

He's trying so desperately to stifle his gasps, as if he still wants to pretend he's in control, that he's not vulnerable to me. A foolish pretense.

"I'm going to taste your cum now," I whisper to him, and he sucks in a sharp breath.

I sweep a fingertip through the glaze of cum on my breast and put that wet finger in my mouth. It's sweet and salty, and I hum with delight.

My pussy is slick with arousal, but I'm exhausted too. Lir doesn't attempt to pleasure me, and I'm too tired to take care of myself, so I retreat into the glowing warmth of my dreams again, happily conscious that the Seelie Prince's cum is drying on my skin.

Like the night when he watched me play with myself, Lir says nothing of what happened between us in the dark. When our protective dome fizzles with a pop, we dress quickly in the pre-dawn gloom, find some bread and dried fruit in the bags, and mount the horses.

On the way, Lir tells me about the Ravine, a deep canyon cleaved through the northern part of the Seelie kingdom. It bars the way to the Unending Pool, the original source of Fae life and magic.

"When we reach the brink of the Ravine this afternooon, we'll let the horses go," Lir says. "We'll climb down under cover of darkness and hopefully slip through the enemy encampment."

"Why would an army gather in a ravine?" I frown at him. "Seems like a trap not easily escaped. I'd rather have my troops on level ground or high ground, with a way to retreat if necessary."

"Unless your strategy is to hide your numbers, or to hold a certain position," he counters. "The Rat King desires control over the Undending Pool—or at the very least doesn't want anyone else to gain access to it."

As we ride, he informs me about past Fae wars. He explains the battle scenarios, complete with topography and available ground cover, and he waits to hear my thoughts before telling me what actually happened. For me, each scenario he presents is like a puzzle. Condensing and analyzing all the disparate information is an intriguing game, a pleasing exercise for my brain.

"I could do this for hours," I tell him eagerly, and he laughs—a genuine, mirthful laugh. He seems pleased by how good I am at predicting strategies and outcomes.

But by afternoon, neither of us are laughing. We let the horses go early because we have to keep pulling them aside into thickets while rat-soldiers troop past. The first patrol nearly sniffs us out, but I find a deflection bomb in Fin's kit and toss it. The orb bursts in midair, diffusing into a white powder. The moment the rat-soldiers inhale it, they head off in the opposition direction.

"He's a genius, your cousin," I whisper as we extricate ourselves from the bushes after that first encounter.

"He's extremely powerful. And he has the gift of condensing magic into compact, portable, reliable form."

"And a delicious form."

"Yes, it is delicious." Lir's mouth tips up. "I suppose he is a genius in his own way. Other Fae can package spells, too, but the way Finias does it—the flavor and the flair—those are all his own."

I spend the next hour attempting to memorize most of the contents of Fin's satchel. I've never been good at rote memorization, so I allow myself to leap around on the chart, creating an odd little song out of the names of the spells. I'm not sure how much of it sticks in my brain.

After we narrowly escape two more patrols, we shoulder our packs and release the horses. It's much too hard to try to hide their bulk as well as concealing ourselves.

"So we go on foot from here," Lir says grimly.

As the sun sets, we creep through the bushes, careful to stay undercover as we crawl right to the edge of the Ravine. Several winged Unseelie are wheeling in the red-streaked sky, and Lir presses down on my head when I lift it too high.

"Careful," he hisses.

"I'm very careful." Writhing on my belly, I squirm closer to the lip of the Ravine.

Nothing could have prepared me for the enormity of the scar delved into the flesh of Faerie. At the bottom, far far down, where it's already dark, armored figures churn between black tents, uplit by red fires.

"We can't get down there, cross it, and climb back up the other side in one night," I whisper to Lir.

"No, I don't suppose we can," he says glumly. "This is the narrowest part of the

Ravine, from what I can remember. At Fae speed it would be possible to do it in a night, but you and I aren't that quick. And we'll have to go slowly, creeping along."

"We'll get caught, Lir. When dawn comes, we'll be down *there*, and we'll be trapped. There's nowhere to hide, except in one of their tents."

With a grunt of abject frustration, he punches the ground we're lying on, then sets his forehead on top of his fist.

"I should go down there," he says, breathing heavily, "and give myself up."

"Don't say that." I jab him with my elbow. "Don't ever."

"Why not? I've already lost the fight. I was stupid enough to get captured by Drosselmeyer, which allowed my kingdom to be overrun. Now my people are in hiding or dead. Your sister is gone because I let you two come with me. And my cousin, the only person who could have helped us through this part, has run off to save her. Since my father died, it's all gone from bad to worse. And I am the common link in the mess. I ruin everything around me, without even meaning to." His breath hitches, almost a sob. "All I wanted was to be a good, wise ruler. If my father could see this—if he knew how badly I've wrecked his legacy—"

He buries his face in his hands, his shoulders heaving.

Slowly I reach out and run my fingers through his dark hair. I stroke the silky waves, trace the pointed tips of his ears gently. Then my hand travels to his back, rubbing in circles. He's wearing the Nutcracker's uniform again.

I have no words that will comfort him. As I rub his back, I conjure and discard several phrases that might end up being more of a discouragement than otherwise. My brain gives up on the task and begins skipping to new topics, like how difficult it must be to get supplies down into that Ravine for the army, and how crossing the Ravine or moving troops out of it must be a massive amount of work.

And that's when I have a realization.

"They've made ramps," I mutter. "Or lifts, or bridges. They'd have to. It's the only way, unless he plans on moving them with magic."

"What?" Lir mumbles.

"You can see in the dark better than I can," I tell him. "Look as far as you can in both directions. Do you see any towers that might have a lift mechanism? Or bridges?"

"There have never been any bridges here. The chasm is too wide."

"But there might be a bridge now."

"It would take an immense amount of magic, or a multitude of workers," he protests.

"Lir." I snake my fingers through his hair again, gathering a handful and tightening my grip. I pull his face up from the ground. "Just look."

With a doleful sigh, he crawls a little farther forward and cranes his neck, peering in first one direction, then the other.

A frown puckers his brow. "By the stars," he mutters, and squints harder. "I think you might be right. I can't tell if it's a lift or a bridge—maybe both, or neither, but there's a tower on each side of the Ravine in that direction."

"That's our way across. How far?"

"I think we could walk it in an hour."

"Before we go, I think you should drink some of my blood," I tell him. "It's been a while, and we can't have you reverting to Nutcracker form while we're crossing."

He keeps staring in the direction of the towers until I wonder if he heard me. But then he says, "We'll need to find a quiet, safe place. And you should keep your knife ready. Once I start drinking from you, I don't know if I'll be able to stop."

21
CLARA

The "clothing" provided for the Rat King's concubines is scanty at best—black ribbons wound around my arms, chest, belly, and thighs. The broad ribbons cover my nipples, and there's a bit of black lace between my legs, but otherwise I'm bared to anyone's view. My hair is pinned up partway, the rest of it tumbling in long curls down my back.

The Unseelie woman who dresses me adds makeup as well—scarlet lip color, face powder with glints of gold, a little rouge, some kohl around my eyes. If I'm honest, I rather like the look, though I despise the reason for it.

Since my ears aren't pierced, she pierces them three times each, swiftly and expertly. She inserts long glittering earrings into my lobes and two small gold rings in my upper cartilage on each side.

"I'm sorry for the pain," she whispers. "I don't have a choice."

Her ebony skin is pierced along the brows and cheekbones, and ram's horns curl from her abundant hair. She might be from the Court of Delight, if not for the fact that most of the flesh of her chest is gone, peeled back to reveal a live bird fluttering inside the cavity, beating its tiny wings wildly against her exposed ribs and sternum. I can't see any heart or lungs, only a crystallized red interior behind the bird. Was she born this way, or cursed?

"Poor little human." She pats my shoulder, eyeing me from top to toe. "Unlucky."

"Can you help me?" I whisper. "Please?"

She shakes her head. "I wish I could."

I consider telling her about my connection to Lir and Finias, but revealing my link to the true king of Seelie might get me tortured, not freed.

"Here." The woman hands me a tiny green pill. "Keep that with you, and swallow it before they begin to have their fun. It will numb you to what's happening."

"Thank you." I pinch the pill between my fingers.

A pale, oozy-looking Unseelie male with eyes like a frog comes to lead me back into the throne room. He pushes me into an empty brass cage and seals it seamlessly behind me—no door or lock to be seen.

"Don't think of trying to escape, human." Each word is a wet gulp from his throat. "These are Inescapable Cages. They can't be unsealed but by the Rat King's will. And if by some chance he dies, the cage will shrink and crush you."

He must like the expression of horror on my face, because he gives a slow, gurgling chuckle. He lifts a slimy, three-fingered hand,

and the cage rises until I'm swinging above the heads of the Court.

When the froglike Fae walks away, three winged Unseelie take to the air and hover around my cage, sliding various appendages through the bars to poke me.

But the teasing only lasts a few minutes before all three of them are yanked backward by tendrils of the Rat King's shadow magic. He leans forward, palming the head of his scepter.

"My new human concubine is not to be touched until I wish it," he bellows.

Small mercies. I watch, wincing, as he throttles all three of the creatures until they go limp. When he drops them, the bodies are dragged away.

I squint at the Rat King, watching as he removes his paw from the ruby orb at the top of the scepter. Strange how he fondles it whenever he's using his magic. Perhaps he needs it to perform magic at all. Intrigued by the idea, I watch him closely for the next two hours, but he doesn't use the shadows again, although he kills two more supplicants and beats a third nearly to death with the end of the scepter. The others who come to him receive their boons, or a place at Court for the night's festivities, which apparently involve feasting and an orgy.

I curl one hand around the bars of the cage, still holding the pill in my other hand. It's my lifeline, the sole indication that I might survive this night—or at least die in less pain than I'd feared.

"Next!" roars the Rat King.

The tunnel leading to the throne room remains empty. No supplicants appear.

"Next!" he shouts again, spit flying from his lips.

A burst of red light erupts into the chamber. Streamers of it snake up to the ceiling before shattering into a dazzling shower of ruby sparkles. The path to the Rat King's throne sinks, forming a shallow stream bed through which lava flows, molten and steaming. A drumbeat begins, low and powerful enough to shake the entire room.

The Court explodes into a cacophony of voices, some panicked and some excited. The Rat King grips the head of his scepter.

Along the lava path strides a tall, slim figure, clad in black from head to toe, with epaulets of interlaced bone jutting from his shoulders and a dark cloak billowing at his back. The lava hisses around the soles of his thigh-high boots.

My fingers tighten painfully around the bars of my cage.

His hair is pink as ever, but streaked with black and woven with twists of licorice and shards of bone. He's grinning, his cruel teeth on full display, his yellow eyes heavily lined with kohl.

The Sugarplum Faerie.

He spreads his arms wide, and a tempest of wrapped candies flies from his palms, arcing upward and then raining down on the Court in a hail of licorice twists, scarlet gumdrops, and red-flecked mints. Instinctively the crowd reaches up to catch them.

Finias reaches the end of his lava stream and drops to one knee on the wide first step of the dais.

"My lord and king," he says, bowing his head.

"What is the meaning of this?" growls the Rat King.

"A little fun, Your Majesty." Finias looks up, head tilted aside, giving the king an ingratiating smile. "I heard there was a party tonight, and I hoped for an invitation. In exchange I'm prepared to offer entertainment the like of which Your Glorious Eminence has rarely seen."

"Wait." The Rat King leans forward. "I know you. You're that rogue faerie who goes from Seelie to Unseelie and back again, fucking everything in sight and throwing treats at any Fae with a sweet tooth. I remember you from— from—"

"From the Carnage Revel of Imbolc, three years ago." Finias bows again. "I produced a river of honey-milk, spiced with hot cinnamon, in which everyone could swim, and a mountain of chocolate-covered eyeballs so tall no one could manage to climb it. Some of my best work."

"Yes, yes." The Rat King narrows his red eyes. "The Sugarplum Faerie. Stupid title, but apt, I suppose. And you have no quarrel with my conquest of this kingdom?"

"None at all. It's about time someone shook up the sleepy Seelie, don't you think?" He looks around, brows lifted, and the Court rumbles with approval. "No, Your Majesty, I have no stake in kingdoms or conquests, only in parties and the darkest of carnal delights."

The Rat King hesitates, his muzzle twitching. "You, Magda!" He beckons sharply, and a tall Unseelie with the torso of a woman and the legs of a spider scuttles forward. "You introduced this fellow to me three years ago. What say you? Can he be trusted? And bear in mind if you lie to me, it will be his head *and* yours that I swallow."

For a handful of heartbeats, Magda looks at Finias.

I don't know how they know each other, or what passed between them. But I beg her silently, with all my heart, to speak in his favor. I can't watch him be torn apart, or swallowed.

"He can be trusted," Magda says. "His magic is weak, good for little except showmanship and amusement. He's a delightful fuck, though. His cum tastes different every time he ejaculates. It's good fun."

A murmur of hungry interest ripples through the Court. Finias is still smiling, hard and bright. My heart breaks for him, because I know how he feels about being used for his unique sexual attributes.

Somehow he followed me, tracked me, found me. He hasn't cast me so much as a glance, but I know he's aware of my presence. I can feel it.

Where are the others? Are they safe? He couldn't have brought them anywhere near here, not with the Prince so powerless. And I doubt the mercenaries would have agreed to come. It must be Finias alone, then.

What must it have cost him to walk in here by himself? Yet he did it for me.

"You'll stay then," says the Rat King to Finias. "You'll make two pools, right here in this room—one of honey-milk, and one of richest blood, well-peppered. Some more of those fireworks, too, and the kind of sweets my people like, and any other tricks you can manage. If you do well, you may have your pick of my concubines tonight."

He waves a paw toward the cages, and Finias looks.

He looks at me. Right at me.

And in that moment, when our eyes lock, I know beyond all doubt.

I love him.

The briefest glance, not the slightest flicker of recognition, and then he's turning back to the Rat King.

"My liege, your generosity is overwhelming." Finias bows, touching his forehead to the steps. "This will be a revel you will never forget."

22
LOUISA

Lir and I cover about half the distance to the bridge before we find an enormous tree, nearly the size of a small, one-room cottage. Veins of glittering blue slither along its purple bark. There are several of its kind in the vicinity, but this tree split long ago, near the roots, and then seamed itself back together and kept growing. As a result, there's a large hollow in its trunk.

Leaving our packs outside, the Prince and I climb into the space after he has checked it for crawling poisonous things. His movements are noticeably stiffer, wood grain beginning to show on his skin.

"Aren't you glad I suggested a little blood session now?" I slide deeper into the hollow.

"I'd have thought of it before the crossing," he says.

"Of course, Your Illustriousness. You always think of everything." But teasing him isn't as satisfying now that he has stripped his heart bare before me, revealed his doubts and his insecurity. I'd thought him aloof, supercilious, and stubborn. And I suppose I also thought him calm, confident, and perfectly capable of reclaiming his throne. He played that role well.

Maybe that's why he acts so haughty. To disguise the fact that inside, he is wretchedly uncertain.

The tree hollow is an oval shape, and while there's enough room for both of us to stand, it's a bit awkward and the toes of our boots are jammed against each other.

"You should eat that candy now," he says, low. "The one to disguise your scent. We're already dangerously close to a horde of Unseelie, and once the smell of your blood hits the air, they'll come for us."

I reach outside the tree and fumble in Fin's satchel until I find the precious spelled candy. It's white with a green stripe down the center, thick and chewy. It tastes like peppermint and white chocolate.

"Can you still smell me?" I ask, settling back into the dark hollow.

Lir leans closer, inhaling along the side of my cheek. He presses his face into my hair, and my pulse quickens.

"No," he says. "I can't smell you at all."

"You sound disappointed."

"Hm." His nose is still buried in my hair.

"Lir." I press my hand to the back of his neck, pulling his face down to my shoulder. "Bite me."

He resists, pulling back and looking into my eyes. "You have to stop that," he says hoarsely.

"Inviting you to bite me?"

"Saying my name that way. It's too informal. Too—intimate."

"More intimate than you watching me touch myself?" I whisper. "More intimate than you coming all over me?"

The night is cracked with cold, but in the close air of the hollow, his breath is mine, and my heat is his, and desire swirls, fragrant and heavy, between both of us.

"Stop," he says desperately. "Stop this."

"Why, Lir? Why are you so afraid to admit that you want me? From what I've heard, plenty of Fae sleep with humans. There's nothing forbidden about it."

"But I don't merely *want* to sleep with you!" he bursts out. "Gods, I thought when you hid your scent I would get some relief but—it never ends, this battle I must fight when I'm around you. Remember when I said you smell like food and sex?"

"Yes…"

"To me you smell like more."

My heart is fluttering, my pulse racing as if I'm wobbling on the edge of the Ravine itself, about to plummet into depths I don't understand.

"Your scent," he says. "It's like nothing else I've ever encountered. It's—it's mine. It's *my* scent. That's the only way I can describe it. It's not the way I smell, but it belongs to me, it's—tailored to me, designed to be the one fragrance I can't resist. That's how I heard my father describe it when he found his Chosen. My mother."

I freeze, hardly breathing.

"The royal Fae may encounter multiple potential mates with such a scent in their lifetime, or none at all," he continues, his voice tight. "It is not a fated pairing, no forceful hand of destiny—but the scent draws two beings together. And if they should find love, they may become each other's Chosen. It is a bond no others in Faerie experience, only the reigning ruler and their selected mate. And that bond brings with it a more exquisite pleasure, a more abiding loyalty, and a more fulfilling love than most Fae or humans will ever know."

He rests his forehead against mine. "I thought the scent of you was the only thing compelling me—luring me to obsess over you. But your scent is concealed from me now, and I still have these feelings—this inner dread at the thought of losing you, this ache, even when you're near me, because you're not close enough, because I need you—not your body, not only that, but more. I—I admire you, Louisa. I admire your confidence, your keen mind, your beautiful enthusiasm for everything, your courage in crisis. I long to be like you. I wish I could lose myself entirely in you."

His mouth presses to my forehead, a hot seal of yearning.

"You want more than just my body." I feel as if my mind is stuck, gears locked in place over that concept.

Men don't want more than my body. Sometimes they *think* they do, after sex, and then later they change their minds. And I pretend not to notice, or care.

"Yes, I want so much more." He plants another burning kiss, this time on my cheek. "I know I tried to frighten you about life in Faerie—I wanted you to leave, because then I might get some relief from this agony. I told you if you stayed, your life would be cut short. I can't promise that won't be true, but I can promise to stand between you and every danger if you'll stay, if you'll only let me hold you once in a while, and if you—if you will stroke my hair sometimes, like you did tonight."

"What are you saying?" My voice is faint and ragged.

"My heart chose you the moment your blood touched me, the moment I sprang to life in your hands. I fought against it—stars, I fought so hard. My head kept telling me you were a foolish choice, ill-suited for life at my side, as Queen. But you have proven me wrong, so many times. *I* am the ill-suited one. You—you are incredible. You are my Chosen."

I can't bear his fervency anymore. I turn my face away, biting my lip. "This isn't what I wanted. I just wanted to fuck you."

Not to love you.

At my cruel words, he stills instantly—the stillness of a clockwork toy whose key stops turning, momentum arrested, life gone.

I can't bear to meet his eyes.

I pull my cloak and tunic farther off my shoulder, baring my skin to him. "You need to drink, and quickly. We have a long way to go."

A long pause, while I grit my teeth and try not to cry.

At last his mouth descends, the familiar puncture of the bite distracting me for a moment. Only for a moment, because with every sucking pull of my blood into his mouth, I hear another phrase from the confession he spoke to me.

My heart chose you the moment your blood touched me.

I can promise to stand between you and every danger if you'll stay.

I fought against it—stars, I fought so hard.

This ache, even when you're near me, because you're not close enough.

I wish I could lose myself entirely in you.

I play it out in my head—the future I could have with him. A life in Faerie, in this eerie, beautiful, wild land. I picture myself seated on a throne, hearing endless grievances, or getting distracted and bored during meetings of state. As his Chosen I would be bound to him, only him, forever. No secret dalliances, no forbidden trysts.

Is that what I want?

How long have I been thinking about it? How long has he been drinking from me? I'm beginning to feel faint.

"Lir, stop," I murmur.

He keeps drinking.

"Lir, enough now. Let me go." I push against him, but he only growls and nuzzles deeper into my neck, gulping more blood.

"Lir." Tears mingle with the panic in my voice. "I don't want to hurt you, not in this form. You won't be able to heal if I do. Don't make me hurt you, please—please stop."

I'm sobbing now, beating at his cheek, but he's insensible, captive to the charm of my blood.

With one hand I grip the hilt of the dagger at my waist and draw it from the sheath. I set the tip of the blade against his ribs.

My whole body is shaking, a horrible weakness spreading through my limbs. My heart slows, weary and heavy. Then it stutters.

"Lir," I say. "You have to stop. You're killing me. You're killing me, Lir. You're killing your Chosen."

He snarls through the blood. Lifts his head a little.

"Your Chosen, Lir. I'm your Chosen. You have to stop. You promised to protect me."

He's withdrawing his fangs, blood streaming down his chin, his eyes regaining focus. "Louisa?"

Sobbing, I clamp my palm over the wound, but my fingers feel weak and fragile, barely capable of pressure. I step out of the hollow and collapse beside Fin's bag.

"Louisa." Lir's voice breaks with anguish. "I'm so sorry."

"Something for healing," I manage through a sob. "There should be a few left. Find one."

He rummages frantically, comparing a few sweets to the chart before he locates the right piece. I swallow it whole. Mere moments later, my wound begins to close and my dizziness lessens.

"Louisa." Pleading and penitence in his tone.

"We can't talk about this now," I tell him. "No more distractions, or we die. From now on, one single focus. Get safely across the Ravine, then head for the Pool."

"Agreed." The resigned ache, the self-hatred in his voice—they almost break me.

But I've come too far to be broken now. He is fracturing already. And if I let myself crack, even a little, the Prince who loves me will die.

23
CLARA

Finias has outdone himself. I've never been to a Fae revel, but even I can tell.

He created the bathing pools the Rat King wanted, which are now crowded with Unseelie folk slathered in blood or honey-milk—and he made a third pool of warm melted cheese, in which the Rat King himself is rolling and dunking, his fur stuck together in cheesy clumps. It's all very disgusting. But Finias also produced a bowl of candies that, when chewed, clean every bit of the eater's body. Some of the Unseelie are going in and out of the pools and chewing the candies just to watch the magic work.

There's a seemingly endless hiss and crackle of tiny orange, gold, and ruby-red fireworks exploding against the ceiling, and there are great mounds of sugary treats, most of them blended with disgusting things, like peanut brittle with cricket legs, or cotton candy twined with spider silk. He made the chocolate covered eyeballs again, too—several of them are bobbing around in the pools, unspooling melted chocolate and releasing the eyeballs inside.

A number of the Unseelie have sampled Finias's musical toffees, which apparently play a different song inside each person's mind. They're dancing, but to the music in their own heads, so most of them are completely out of sync with the music that's actually playing—a thumping, shaking, virulent roar that nearly deafens me and seems to have no discernible tune.

Finias isn't partaking much himself. During the feast he barely ate, and he didn't touch the roasted meat, for which I was glad since I knew where it came from. Now he's sauntering among the guests, his black cloak hiding his wings, sipping blood-colored wine and looking altogether Unseelie. But I can feel his restlessness—I can see it in the angle of his shoulders and the sharp turns of his head. I can hear it in the edges of his laughter.

He has only glanced at me one other time. Likely because he doesn't want to draw attention to me, or indicate any prior connection between us.

Powerful as he is, he could probably destroy everyone in this room. But what about the rest of the army in the underground lair? I doubt he'd be able to fight them all off before he ran out of energy, or whatever fuels his power.

Fortunately for me, he must have recognized these cages for what they are—inescapable. He has probably seen similar ones before, during his prior visit to the Unseelie Court. He knows he can't kill the Rat King, or every concubine will be crushed to death in their cages.

Which leaves both of us with one option—wait until the orgy begins, and the cages are opened.

This phase of the night's festivities feels interminable. I sit cross-legged on the bottom of the cage, my elbow propped on my knee, and my chin resting on my palm.

Of all the places I thought I would end up after Papa's death, I never imagined I'd be a caged concubine in the throne room of the Rat King of Unseelie, while my faerie lover attempts to charm the Court of Dread long enough to claim me and smuggle me out of an underground lair.

I'm not sure how Fin plans to do the smuggling part. I doubt the Rat King will let the two of us walk away. Even if he was distracted, the guards in the corridor would surely stop us.

The Rat King is climbing out of the cheese-pool. He chews one of the cleaning candies, then picks up his scepter from where he placed it right next to the bath.

He's utterly naked, and the size of his thick, bulbous, gray cock terrifies me. One of the concubines in another cage whimpers at the sight, but she's too far away for me to offer any comfort.

A servant offers the Rat King another goblet, and he drinks the liquor down. Several of the rats protruding from his body, which appeared rather drowned after his cheese-bath, seem to revive.

"Sugarplum," he roars. "Come here!"

Finias skips to his side, bowing low. "My liege. Is there anything else I can do to make this evening more memorable?"

"Not exactly," says the Rat King. "You've done very well, boy. But it's all been a bit Seelie for my tastes. You can't help your roots, even if your heart is with us and your intentions are good." He claps a paw on Fin's shoulder. "I'm in the mood for some hearty fucking. It's time to bring forth the concubines. As I promised, you get to choose one for yourself. Which one will you have? There's a new one there, see?" He points to me. "Human, unbroken. I would take her myself, but I fancy a Seelie rump tonight."

As he speaks, one of the cages lowers all the way down and then melts away, leaving a naked Seelie girl bared to view. She has huge breasts, doe eyes, and tiny antlers. Feathery white wings, soft-looking as clouds, ruffle at her back.

She stands tall, a seductive smile on her face, and paces toward the Rat King, her hips swaying. Either she truly doesn't mind fucking him, or she has learned that going along with it is easier.

The Seelie girl glides around the Rat King, her fingers playing with the rat-tails near his collarbone.

"The collar strips away her magic." The Rat King reaches up to touch the band around the girl's neck. "Go on, Sugarplum, choose one. Any of them. There's a fine Unseelie lad there, or a strapping Seelie male, if that's your preference. Got a few non-gendered folk as well. Or we can pull up some monsters from the pits below, if your tastes run that direction."

"I'll take the human girl, as Your Majesty suggests," says Finias lightly. "A rare treat for me. Thank you, my liege."

"So be it," says the Rat King. "Perhaps I'll find you a permanent place at court, if you promise to darken your festive offerings. Less delight, more dread."

"Of course, Majesty." Fin bows.

My cage begins to sink toward the floor. All around the room, cages are lowering, evanescing, releasing their occupants into the claws of Unseelie courtiers. Some of the Unseelie forgo the concubines altogether, stripping off any remaining clothing and winding their bodies around each other, finding ways to couple even if their species and parts are wildly different.

I try not to watch. I try to let everything else become a blur of squelching, sighing, screaming, sucking, and squealing. I try to keep my eyes, my mind, my everything fixed on Fin as he moves toward me through the churning crowd.

He reaches me. Slides his hand up my arm, whispers, "Are you all right?"

I nod.

He wraps a hand around my throat and leans in, his lips against my ear.

"I've used a lot of magic," he breathes, so softly I can barely hear him. "We can't leave yet. I don't have the strength."

My gaze travels to the dais, where I see the Rat King seated on his throne, with the Seelie girl already bouncing on his cock. The King's red eyes are fixed on Finias and me.

"He's watching us, Fin," I whisper.

"Fuck." He sighs. "You're going to have to trust me, dearest. Can you do that?"

"Yes."

"I'm going to take you now," he breathes. "To refuse would be a terrible insult to the King, and we'd both be killed at once."

"You're going to fuck me while he watches? While they—"

Roughly, Fin clamps a hand over my lips. He looks into my eyes, his own burning with a bright warning. *Trust me*, he mouths.

I relax in his grip. Only then do I realize I dropped the tiny pill I was given. The loss of it burns, because I don't yet know what this night may bring, for Fin or for me.

All around us bodies are twisting, laughter shrilling, voices crying out. A quivering pair of dragonfly wings catches my eye, flexing and sparkling as their owner takes one male down her throat and another under her tail. Two females have their legs interlaced, humping urgently and kissing, not seeming to care that one has a regular mouth and the other has a lizardlike face, complete with scaly lips. Everything blends into a whirl of tilting antlers, parted mouths, slithering tails, and wild shadows dancing on the walls. But beyond it all I'm conscious of the Rat King still watching as Finias runs his hands along my body, toying with my ribbons.

If it were just the sights and sounds, I could shut them out—I'm used to shutting everything out when I paint. But the room reeks of hot cheese and oily blood, of pepper and curdling milk and sulfur and damp fur and sweat.

I whimper against Fin's palm, and he lifts it slightly, bending his head to listen.

"The smells in here are terrible," I whisper.

"Here." He kisses my nose, exhaling gently as he does. The scent of his breath is exquisite, as always.

"Thank you." I nuzzle upward, my lips brushing his.

"We're being too affectionate," he murmurs. "That isn't what this orgy is about. Relax, dearest, and let me fuck you the way he wants me to."

My stomach quivers with nervous anticipation. "All right."

Fin's demeanor changes instantly. He catches me by the back of the neck, tears aside the ribbons across one of my breasts, and grasps it fully in his hand, kneading the flesh savagely. He leans down to my shoulder and bites me, piercing the skin just enough to raise little drops of blood.

Raking his teeth lightly up the curve of my neck, he licks my cheek, marking my skin with my own blood.

I'm panting, inflamed, caught in the storm of feral passion he has unleashed.

"Be as loud as you want," he mutters, grinning right before he kisses me.

The kiss roars through me, whirling my mind away into a glittering field of midnight stars, in which Fin and I dance alone. His tongue tantalizes mine, darting into my mouth before slipping away. He's surging against me, and I don't think he's pretending anymore. The convulsive grinding of his hips against mine sends a flare of heat through my center.

He's moving me, pushing me backward. My spine hits the cold surface of a stone column and I cry out, breathless. He braces one hand against the pillar, beside my head, so the drapery of his cloak partly conceals us both. It also cuts off part of my view of the Dread Court, for which I'm grateful.

"Legs up, darling," he whispers. "Around my waist. Good girl. My brave, beautiful girl—fuck, Clara, I'm about to come in my pants. Shit."

I gasp a laugh, ecstatic because he craves me that much, even here, among the madness and peril.

Quickly I help Fin unbutton his pants, and I free his pretty cock. My center is already aligned with him—I shift a ribbon aside, lift the bit of gauzy lace, and then he's nestling into my folds, sliding deep into my warmth. He feels just as wonderful here, in the Court of the Rat King, as he did in the workroom, or in the forest. I suspect he would feel like this—like coming home, like safety, like comfort and beauty and bliss—no matter where we are.

"Scream," he commands. "Scream for me."

I'm not my sister. I'm the retiring one, the quiet one in the corner, the one observing, not being observed. I don't like drawing attention to myself. But this is bigger than me and the privacy I usually crave. This isn't only about my life, but Fin's. So I scream for him. I scream while he fucks me against the pillar, brutally, mercilessly. He comes after only a few thrusts, and he roars with the force of his release, his hips driving me harder against the stone column, pinning me there.

I scream when he keeps thrusting, when he forces an orgasm out of me and it shatters through my body. I scream into his mouth while he holds me, impaled on his cock, his hands tangled in my hair, near my temple.

He breaks the hot torment of the kiss for a moment, and in that moment I say the words against his lips. "I love you."

No more than a frenzied breath, but he hears me. His hand tightens on my hair, and he crushes himself against my body, his words hot and hoarse in my ear.

"Only you," he grits out. "Only you, ever."

An Unseelie with an exposed jawbone and six eyes sidles up to us. "If you're done with her, Sugarplum, I'll have a turn."

"Does it look like I'm done with her?" Fin snaps.

He pulls out of me and slides his hand to the top of my head, grasping my hair afresh. Violently he spins me around, pushes my breasts against the column, and crowds in behind me. My front is partly hidden by the pillar, my back by his body and his cloak.

Incredibly, Fin is getting hard again; I can feel his rigid shaft poking my bottom. Thank goodness for his Fae stamina. As long as he can keep fucking me, I'm safe from anyone else.

The Unseelie male shrugs and saunters away.

Fin takes me again, pushing in slowly from behind, then assuming a punishing pace that jogs helpless moans out of me. I come on him again, shuddering, clutching the pillar as if it's a lifeline.

"Another hour or two, darling, while I recover my magic," he whispers. "And then we'll give them all a real show."

24
LOUISA

The tower Lir saw marks the head of a bridge across the Ravine. It's also the location of a massive lift that can descend into the Ravine or ascend from it. At this time of night, the bridge lies empty, but the tower bristles with armed guards wearing rats' heads.

The bridge will save us several hours. But how to get across without being caught?

If only Finias had packed invisibility spells. No such luck. But there are two more deflection charms, a spell for high wind, another for mist, and—I wince, trying to remember the jingle I taught myself to remember the available spells. It's too dark to pull the guide chart out now, and we certainly can't risk a light.

Deflection, reflection, mist, mire, and mayhem,

High wind, healing, mimicry and might—

"It's so perfectly simple!" I gasp a laugh, nudging Lir. "A spell of might or strength won't help against so many, but mimicry—that's what we need. We just need to separate one of the guards and get him over here so we can look into his eyes. The effect won't last long, but hopefully it will be long enough."

"Separate one of the guards? Easier said than done," mutters the Prince. "They always travel in packs."

"What about when they need to piss or shit?" I point through the foliage of the bushes in which we're hiding. They're broad, shiny evergreen leaves, the perfect concealment. And there are more of the same bushes clustering around a ramshackle outhouse near the tower.

Lir casts me an admiring look, then reigns in his expression with a sorrowful twist of his mouth. My heart twinges at his pain, at the rift between us, but I can't mend it now. I need to stay focused.

"You've done so much already," the Prince says. "Let me do this. Wait here, and I'll bring one of the guards back."

"This might help." I hand him a noise-muffling orb. "Dash it on the ground and it will mute all sound for a few minutes."

With a nod, he takes the orb and slinks away, swathed in his cloak. His shape practically melts into the dark. I can barely see him as he slips into the outhouse.

Chewing my nails and shivering, I wait.

Finally a lone rat-soldier descends from the tower and trudges out of the circle of torchlight, across the hardpacked dirt, all the way to the shack. He disappears inside.

With no one around and this much at stake, I'm very tempted to start whispering to myself, out of sheer nervousness. I clamp my hand over my own mouth.

Finally a pair of dark figures emerges from the outhouse, moving immediately into the cover of the bushes. I squeeze my hands together, waiting with bated breath until Lir shuffles into my hiding place, dragging a rat-soldier with him.

"Alive?" I ask. "He needs to be alive."

"He's alive. Unconscious, though."

"Gag him, quickly. We'll have to do the mimicry spells once he wakes up."

The rat-soldier begins to stir just as Lir finishes with the gag. I shove my dagger against his throat as an extra incentive for him to be quiet.

"You first," I whisper to Lir. "It's the pink and yellow one. Look into his eyes while you're chewing it." I jam the dagger tip harder against the soldier's neck. "Eyes wide, bastard. And stay silent."

Lir chews the candy, staring at the guard—and then he morphs seamlessly into a perfect replica of the rat-soldier.

"We don't have long until it wears off," I warn Lir, holding out my hand. He places another mimicry candy on my palm.

To the rat-soldier I hiss, "Keep your eyes open, stay quiet, and you'll live." Staring into his beady black eyes, I chew quickly.

The magic prickles all over me, and when Lir gives me a salute, I know it worked.

Swiftly I slice across the rat-soldier's throat, careful to step aside, out of the path of the spewing blood.

"You promised he could live," says Lir under his breath.

"I changed my mind."

We leave our packs in our hiding spot. The mimicry spell doesn't disguise them, and they'll look strange on a pair of rat-soldiers patrolling the bridge. But I keep Fin's satchel with me. Hopefully no one will think anything of it.

It feels idiotically bold and naked to stride out of the cover of the bushes and walk across open ground. My heart pounds as we approach the tower, as we mount step after step, as I try to move confidently, not too quickly but quickly enough.

We pass a couple of guards descending the steps. Now we're walking past more guards—they're muttering in low tones. They smell terrible, like sulfur and copper and bile.

We're on the bridge. On the bridge—oh god—it's terribly, shockingly high. Don't look down, don't look down—one foot, then the next. Firmly, like a soldier. Purposefully, as if I have orders to fulfill, duties to perform.

Lir is ahead of me, but he doesn't look like Lir—he's a greasy-coated, rat-headed soldier with a spiky club.

And I'm his exact image. What if someone notices that the pair of us look a little too similar?

Another step. Another.

The bridge sways, creaking in the cold wind. A suspension bridge, perfectly safe, it has to be perfectly safe—it was built by the Unseelie, and they can't risk having their soldiers topple into the canyon every day. They must have built it well. It's safe. I'm safe.

More steps, more steps, and we're still on the bridge—when will it end? What if I'm not following Lir anymore? What if I somehow got confused and followed a different rat-soldier? They all look so similar—a good thing for us— oh fuck, the wind is coming again—

I grip the rope railing and keep going despite the stomach-dropping sway of the bridge. My teeth clench and grind against my terror.

Frantically I try to focus on good things.

At least I only *look* as if I'm wearing a rat's head. I'm not actually stuffed inside one—I'm breathing the fresh air. I have an unobstructed view of the stars.

Risking a look ahead, I discover that we're almost there. Nearly to the second tower. Just a quick climb down those steps, and then—then we'll be on the other side of the Ravine. We can find cover, plan our next step.

And then, up ahead of me, Lir's disguise shivers.

It's a brief wink—a split-second's glimpse of his true self beneath the glamour. Barely detectable unless someone was looking right at him.

But it's the first sign that we're reaching the end of the spell's potency.

I slip one hand into Fin's satchel and feel for the tiny compartment where I stowed two eyeball-sized orbs and two candies. Palming one of the orbs, I draw my hand back out.

A few minutes later, just as he's approaching the tower guards at the end of the bridge, Lir's disguise flickers again.

I don't think they noticed. But just in case, I flick my wrist, flinging the orb at the side of the watchtower, right below the level of the bridge. It explodes silently into powder on impact.

A moment later, mist begins to rise and to gather around the tower and the end of the bridge, half-concealing me and Lir.

Hurrying forward, I mutter to him, "Time's up."

Lir picks up his pace, and the two of us hurry past the guards at the top of the tower. By the time we're halfway down it, he's blinking in and out of his glamour, and mine is failing too. By some miracle, though, the stairs are empty of soldiers.

As we clatter down the last flight of steps, I drop the second orb to the floor of the tower. In the ensuing cloud of mist we move swiftly out of the tower, across an open space, and into the shadow of a building.

What building it is, I have no idea. But we're facing a larger problem. Because the clifftop on the far side of the Ravine is also a camp, and it's teeming with soldiers.

Rough voices, clanking armor, and leaking fumes of poisonous magic fill the air. Between us and the forest lies a stretch of tents, tables, and campfires.

My palms are clammy, and I can't stop panting.

"Lir," I whisper. "I can't do this. I can't."

"You can."

"You're Fae. You're born with grace and stealth. I'm clumsy. I'll get us both killed. You should leave me, and go."

His strong fingers wrap around my wrist. "Never. We get through together, or we perish together. Now follow me, and do exactly as I do. But—use your instincts too. They've served you well in Faerie so far."

The next hour is a blur of quick, quiet movements, darting from shadow to shadow, holding our breath, crawling beneath carts, slinking along the sides of tents. Most of the time I follow Lir's movements exactly, but twice I get a tingle of apprehension and awareness, so I wait. Sure enough, in both cases, a soldier passes by unexpectedly. If I'd moved right away, I would have gotten caught.

The soul-shrinking, bone-riveting tension of performing stealth in the middle of such peril—it's exhausting. By the time Lir and I reach the treeline, all I want is a good, solid night's sleep.

But there is no rest for either of us. We can't linger so near to the enemy camp. We have to keep going.

"I think they're planning to move out soon," Lir says to me under his breath, once we're deeper into the trees. "They'll head for the Unending Pool and secure it for the Rat King. It's usually under guard, but only by a handful of soldiers. My father thought it was important to keep the place open to all of Faerie, since it's such an important part of our history."

I can't muster the energy to reply. The anxiety of the bridge crossing and the nerve-searing tension of threading through the enemy camp has left me dull and empty. It's all I can do to stumble after Lir for the next two hours.

The darkness in the forest is so thick that I lose him twice, and he has to circle back and find me. After the second time, he unhitches the waterskin from its place at his hip and hands it over to me.

"I'm sorry for this," he says quietly. "For what I'm putting you through. Are you all right, after the—I know I took too much of your blood."

"The healing candy helped," I tell him. "But I'm tired. I want a hot bath, and a hot meal, and a warm bed, Lir. A *bed*."

He stares down at me for a moment. "I wish I could give you those things."

Then he's scooping me up, gathering my curves into his arms as if it's the easiest thing in the world. He strides onward silently, carrying me.

I doze against his shoulder for a while, but my mouth keeps dropping open and my neck keeps lolling at an uncomfortable angle. Just as I've found the perfect position and I'm slipping into sleep again, his grip on my body tightens. "Louisa. Look."

Curses perch on the tip of my tongue, but I hold them back and open my eyes.

The dark world has transformed. As far as I can see the ground is flat, translucent, and luminous, like a sheet of ice or crystal uplit from beneath, glowing blue. White trees, some thin as my finger, grow from the blue stone, and where each emerges, its base is encrusted with orange crystals, also glowing. I have never seen a place so luminously beautiful.

"What is it?" I breathe.

"The Soul Grove," Lir murmurs. "It is said that the souls of the ancients rest here, waiting to be put into new bodies. Sometimes, if you look through the crystal, you can see images of their past deeds as they dream."

"Put me down," I say eagerly.

With a chuckle he obeys, and I kneel on the sheet of crystal, running my palm over the smooth surface. The longer I look into it, the deeper I can see—far, far down into the ethereal blue. Wisps of white dance through those depths, briefly forming images—a pair of Fae dancing, two armies racing toward each other, a woman holding a child.

Lir's warm hand cups my shoulder. "Come. I know it's beautiful, but we can't linger where there is no place to hide. Your scent is perceptible again."

Reluctantly I start to rise—but as I do, something vibrates through the crystal into my palms. I frown, bending down to the surface. "I hear something."

Lir drops to one knee and places his hand on the ground. Alarm wakes in his eyes. "Someone is coming. And they're moving too fast for us to hide or run."

I stand up, fingers closing on the hilt of my dagger. "Then we will fight."

"I think there are four of them."

"Two for each of us." But my heart sinks.

I'm no warrior. I held off one rat-soldier for a while, but in the end, Clara took him out. I'm not sure how I'll fare against two enemies.

In the far distance I can see the figures galloping toward us on—not horses—are those deer?

"White reindeer," breathes Lir, rising beside me. And then he begins to run. Not away from the figures, but toward them.

"Fuck," I groan, and I hurry after him.

Lir reaches the newcomers before I do. Instead of drawing his sword, he calls to them, and one of the riders swings down and wraps him in a rough embrace.

"That's promising," I mutter, letting go of my dagger and slowing my pace. No need to hurry if these folk are friends, so I take my time approaching on my weary feet. Lir is speaking to the newcomers hastily, gesturing more than he usually does.

When I finally reach the group, he turns, his face alight. "Louisa, these are members of the royal guard. And there are more of them encamped near here. They're protecting the Pool."

He introduces me to several tall Seelie Fae, all of them beautiful. Three have long, flowing locks, and one has a crown of neat black braids in tight rows. Their armor shines silver, and they wear heavy dark-blue cloaks trimmed with white. Joy, relief, and excitement shines in their eyes whenever they glance at Lir.

"Come," says the one with the black braids—I think Lir called her Orain. She extends her hand to me with a warm smile. "The Unending Pool is still a long way from here, and the Prince says you need rest and food."

"Breaking his curse is more important," I say stoutly. "I can keep going."

"But I need rest as well," says Lir. "And I must speak with my people."

"The word of the Prince," Orain says, with a smile. "We'll take you to our camp."

Two of them double up on one of the huge white reindeer, leaving a mount free for Lir and me. With a boost from Lir, I manage to swing into the saddle without falling, which I count as a supreme victory. He swings up and settles in at my back, his thighs pressing against mine. My rear is nestled right between his legs, and the tingling awareness of our position floods my lower belly with naughty warmth.

I still want to fuck him. So badly. And I don't want to do it only once, but over and over, until I know all his pleasure points, every tender hollow and bold ridge of his body. I want to dismantle his resistance until he cries out with agonized pleasure. I want to know every sound he makes when he comes undone, and I want to soothe him afterward, to gently pet him as he lies panting and helpless and utterly mine.

Almost without thinking, I lean back against him, ensnared in the fantasy. He's holding the reins, but he switches them to one hand and curls the other around my body, tentatively. I can almost taste the hope in that gesture.

We're in the center of the column of riders—two in front of us and two behind. There's enough space that I don't think they can hear if I speak softly. I turn my head so my mouth is nearer to Lir's face.

"I didn't intend to hurt you, earlier," I murmur. "What you said to me was overwhelming. The scope of this, the Chosen bond—I'm not sure it's something I can handle. The thought of me as the Queen of a land that isn't mine, joined to someone I haven't known very long, for the rest of what might be an unnaturally long or a perilously short life—it frightens me. You ask for too much, Lir."

"I ask for no more than I'm willing to give. Which is everything."

I twist so I can look at him better. "You have the gall to ask me for everything, when we've barely been acquainted for two weeks?"

"The Fae are not slow in matters of love. Once we know our hearts, we act on those feelings."

"And your feelings for me—they are—"

"Love. I love you."

Hearing him say it steals my breath. "You hate me. We fight constantly. How is that a wise foundation for a relationship?"

"We communicate. We find our differences and discuss them."

I snort a laugh, facing forward again. "That's certainly a kind way to put it."

A chuckle rolls through him, and he kisses the top of my head.

I don't know why that sweet, chaste kiss makes me warmer inside than any I've ever received. I'm so wet for him I'm afraid I'll leave moisture on the saddle when I dismount—but beyond that, I think my *heart* is wet for him. It's softening, melting, making me believe that if I just give in to this, if I let him choose me, everything will be all right.

"What would it be like?" I ask abruptly. "What would I have to do? If I—if you—"

"If I marry you and make you my Queen?"

A tremulous delight flutters through my chest. "Yes."

"We could travel together, like this. See all of Faerie, visit the far corners of the kingdom. We could taste the most delectable foods, witness all the most fantastic sights. And when you tired of that we could return to the royal city, where we could host parties, see plays and performances, enjoy music and art. I could take you to the training fields and turn that innate talent of yours into true fighting skill. You also have a knack for strategy. The same mind that successfully planned so many seductions could be invaluable to this kingdom's defenses. I would like to see you as a Captain one day, if you wish it. Or at least an advisor in my Court."

The picture he paints is nothing like the dull, restrictive royal life I imagined, the one I let fear design in my head. His vision of a life together is open and free, a life of pleasure and possibilities.

Why am I holding myself back from this? I was going to marry anyone I could find, just so I could get my hands on my inheritance. Yet when I'm offered the passionate love of a beautiful man, a *king*—when I'm staring at the chance for wealth and travel, beauty and variety, training and authority—I balk at it. Maybe because I fear it can't be true. I've never allowed myself to dream so high, never expected much beyond a comfortable life with a foolish husband whom I'd cuckold frequently for fun.

I think if I told Lir the kind of future I've envisioned for myself, he would frown and think it unworthy of me. Because for all his "little mortal" comments and his sneers about humans, I know he respects me. He shows it by asking for my advice and following my plans, by protecting me and by arguing with me like an equal. He sees more in me than I've ever seen in myself—a queen, a captain, a wife he would cherish for decades, maybe longer. His Chosen.

I've left him unanswered, the dream he shared suspended in the frosty air, fragile as a puff of warm breath, and gone just as quickly.

He doesn't press me for a reaction or a reply. We ride on, until we come to a long line of blue-and-white tents, four or five deep. There are corrals for the reindeer and horses, low fires burning, a few voices murmuring. It's still the dead of night, and not many are stirring. But I see a watchman posted in a tree, and a few guards patrolling the line.

It all looks so neat and lovely at first, but as we pass through the camp I notice the dark circles under the eyes of the warriors who are wakeful. I notice the dents and cracks in their armor, and the patches and scorch marks on the tents.

"I must speak with my people," Lir tells me. "Go with Orain, and she'll care for you."

I nod, too weary to argue, though I feel a little abandoned. He's with his folk now, reconnected with guards and servants who can keep him safe and take him where he wants to go. He doesn't need me anymore.

Orain leads me to a large tent with a big wooden tub. It's already filled with water, and she heats the water with a touch.

"I'll find you some fresh clothes and some food," she tells me before leaving.

The water soothes my aching body, but a restless unhappiness curdles my soul. I try to remind myself of Lir's claim that he loves me, that he wants me for his Chosen. But I don't like being passed off to a servant and sent to bathe, while he strategizes with his own kind. What is he telling them about me, about Clara? Will he divulge all aspects of his curse? Will he curl his lip in disgust when he admits he had to drink my blood to stay in his current form?

I don't like being parted from him. It was rude and unkind of him to leave me alone when this isn't even my world, when I don't know any of these people. How long will it take him to finish with them and come back to me? Or perhaps he'll leave me here while he continues with the quest. Maybe I won't even get to see his curse broken.

After Orain drops off the clothing for me, I continue to soak and fume in the bath. Finally I climb out and dry my skin with the provided towels. I inspect the thick, soft, well-made clothes—silky yet sturdy underthings, a tunic and leggings of rich blue wool, a heavy cape, and a leather belt to which I can fasten my dagger.

As I dress, I chastise myself for my attitude.

I rejected Lir, and yet I want to be the center of his thoughts and attention at every moment? How foolish of me. How selfish.

Part of my craving for him is pure fear. We're still much too close to the Ravine and the Rat King's army. They could reach us in less than two hours. What if they were to attack while Lir is elsewhere in the camp? What if I'm taken away, or killed? What if he's captured, and I can't find him, and I never see him again?

That would be a nightmare. I don't want to imagine it.

And what of my sister? What of Clara, my best friend and companion since childhood, the one person who knew about everything I did? She knew, yet she never told our father, not once, no matter how angry she was with me.

What if she's—what if Fin didn't get there in time, and he can't bring her to us? Not that I want her here, sharing this peril—oh fuck. It's all a fucking mess, and I wish I could tell Clara how sorry I am, for everything I've said that hurt her. I wish I could drag Lir in here and throw him down and kiss his precious stupid face until I feel safe again.

As I'm chewing my lip, bouncing anxiously on my heels, Orain enters. "I've laid out food for you in another tent, where you can also sleep. If you'll come with me, Lady Louisa."

"And—the Prince? Is he—where is he?"

"He's speaking with the captain," she says. "He will go to his rest soon."

I don't dare ask if "his rest" is with me, in my tent. Of course it isn't. He's a king, and he'll sleep in some royally appointed tent, not in the same tent as the slutty mortal girl who damaged his arm and fingered herself in front of him.

The tent Orain gives me is small and cozy, with a thick mattress and blankets laid on a rug over the cold ground. The bed is certainly wide enough for two, but not as wide as a king would probably want. Another sign that Lir won't be joining me tonight.

I sit cross-legged on the mattress and devour the soup, biscuits, fruit, and cold sliced meat on my tray. Then I drink deeply of the wine.

Full and weary, I crawl into the bed. There's no candle to blow out—just a few tiny orbs of faerie light floating near the top of the tent.

I've slept in the company of other people for nearly two weeks now. Being alone in a tent near a potential battlefront unsettles me so badly I can't rest. I flip the pillows over, again and again, and I turn from one side to the other like a pancake being fried.

What if Lir is already gone? What if he headed for the Unending Pool without me?

What if he rides for the Pool, and on the way he reverts to his Nutcracker form, and falls from his mount and shatters into splinters against a rock?

Or what if, after being with his Seelie subjects again, he remembers how much lovelier, wiser, and more capable they are than I am? What if he decides to take one of them to bed tonight?

What if one of his own people is a traitor and kills him in his bed?

What if—

A burst of cold air rushes into the tent, and I spring up, lunging for my dagger.

"Louisa." Lir closes the tent flap and frowns, eyeing the blade I'm brandishing. "You seem agitated."

"Do I?" I toss the dagger aside and rise from the bed. "Do I seem agitated? After you left me with a stranger, in the middle of a war camp? After I was put in this tent alone and told to go to bed, with no news of you and your plans? Why should I be agitated after *that*?"

"Who told you to go to bed?" His eyebrows rise.

"It was implied," I say haughtily, "by the presence of the *bed*." I point to it.

His frown deepens. "You were tired. You said you craved a hot bath, a hot meal, and a warm bed, so I provided those things, and *of course* you're not pleased. I thought you could use some time alone, away from me, since you obviously do not wish to be mine. And *of course* that consideration displeases you as well."

"If you thought I needed time away from you, why are you here?"

"Because—" He clears his throat, his gaze darting around the tent. "Because I… I wanted to make sure you had everything you needed."

"Orain already saw to that. So why don't you run off to your own fancy tent and your royal bed?"

"All the tents and the beds are the same," he says. "After our discussion, I didn't think you'd care to share one with me."

"Well, you didn't ask, did you? And speaking of beds—you're the one who has never been keen to share mine, until your effusive confession today. You want to know what I think?"

"Not particularly," he growls, crossing his arms.

"I think you proposed marriage to me because you are exhausted, overwhelmed, and traumatized from your stint as a wooden doll in Drosselmeyer's house, and from what has happened to your kingdom. You feel like a failure, and you want something to give you hope and make you feel better."

He's glaring at me, the tips of his ears flushed red. "Is that so?"

"You showed me your weakness today, and I comforted you. So you decided you want someone to pet your hair. You want someone around who will be strong when you're weak. That's the only reason you confessed your love."

His lip curls. "So I am a careless, apathetic male who abandoned you tonight, a weak coward who only craves your strength. I'm a confused, traumatized victim, and a pompous king who doesn't deign to share space with you."

I hesitate, fists clenched, blood heating my face. "I—I don't know. Maybe."

"Maybe." He takes a step toward me. "Or maybe I'm the Prince who, after speaking with his people, as a leader should do, tried to go to his own tent and found himself seeking yours instead. Maybe I'm someone who needs to be close to you—who will always crave your nearness, no matter which of us is being the strong one on a given day."

He's right in front of me now, his green eyes ensnaring mine. "Maybe I'm the male who has finally caved to his desire to fuck you, even if you'll never agree to anything further between us. Maybe you're trying to wound me because you're afraid, like I was. Afraid of the connection we have."

His voice takes on a thread of sweet desperation. "I am sorry for the things I've said to you since we met, Louisa. No matter what pain and confusion I felt, I had no right to cut into your heart with my words. I understand if you cannot forgive it. But I am asking one more time if you could love me, if you think you could choose me. If you do not, and you cannot, I will leave you alone. I won't make any more confessions, or disturb you on this topic again."

"It's not that I want to reject you," I whisper, shame coloring my cheeks. "But you're right—I am afraid. Afraid this isn't true, that you'll come to yourself and realize I wasn't the person you wanted. And I'm afraid of myself. I'm scared that one day I'll grow bored and weary, and I'll find someone to amuse myself with, and I'll hurt you. That's the last thing I want to do."

"Loving someone is baring your heart to pain." He cups my shoulders, rubbing them gently. "I understand that, and I accept it. If you choose me, and then later you tire of me, I will not hold you back from seeking your joy. But let me assure you, the Chosen bond provides the keenest pleasure known to my kind. I don't believe you'd find anyone else satisfying once you've experienced it with me. That's what I've heard, anyway." He gives me a slow half-smile.

I suck in a quavering breath.

"You wanted me, tempted me," he whispers. "You have me. Now it's your decision. Choice is freedom."

Those three words flame through my heart, a sudden, violent truth.

By choosing him, I'm not stepping into a cage.

I'm leaving one.

Because he is everything. He is all the longing I felt for years, all the things I was searching for. I found pieces of what I craved in so many different people—but with him it's all there. And all of it is mine.

Out of every person in both of our realms, he wants me. The beauty of that knowledge is something that could never be painted, or tasted. It can only be felt.

"I do, and I can," I whisper, looking up at him with a shy wonder I've never felt with anyone. "I love you, and I choose you."

He closes his eyes briefly, inky lashes brushing his cheeks. Inhales slowly, while his fingers tighten on my shoulders. "Say it again."

"I love you, Lirannon, and I choose you."

"I choose you too," he whispers. "My Louisa."

Our lips meet, a trembling brush, a soft contact.

"It's funny," I murmur against his mouth. "All this time, I've been trying to seduce you—and now, I—I don't know what to do. Sex has always been a game to me, Lir—a diversion. But with you, it's different. I know it, I feel it. It means something. And that's fucking terrifying."

He laughs a little. "I'm terrified, too."

"You are?"

"Immensely." He kisses me again, lightly, quickly—once, twice, three times. Small tantalizing kisses that twist the breath in my lungs and tremble in my belly. The familiar fire ignites inside me—lust flaring at my core, twisting through my body—but it's brighter, richer, more intense, because it's blended with the searing truth of my real feelings for him.

"Lir." His name on my lips is a fierce demand, and he obeys.

He seizes me. Hauls me against himself. My body thrums with frenzied heat—I think I might burn through my clothes.

I back away from him, fumbling with toggles and buttons, fighting my way out of all the layers of clothing I just put on, until I'm bare before him. I feel as if I've clawed away my skin and flesh as well, leaving my heart naked, thumping, and vulnerable.

He undresses more slowly, devouring me with his eyes like he did that night in Fin's house, when I lay on the couch and played with myself in front of him.

"Lie down," he says thickly. "And spread yourself for me."

I want his touch so badly I'm shaking. But I obey, crawling onto the bed and laying down on my back, legs open.

Lir approaches, all of his perfect body revealed. The paneled abs, the mounded pectorals, the toned arms, bulging with muscle. Every bit of him belongs to me.

He crawls between my legs and sinks his face into my sex with a relieved moan.

I didn't expect it, and I vent a breathless, blissful squeal, gathering fistfuls of the blanket while he devours me open-mouthed, his tongue lashing between the lips of my sex, plunging into my body. He nibbles my clit, and I buck, my hips yearning up off the bed.

"Inside, inside, please," I pant. "Please, Lir. No games, I need your cock inside me." I'm clutching his black hair, using it to drag him up along my body. He yields slowly, kissing and licking the roundness of my stomach, pressing his mouth into the softness of my breasts. He sucks a nipple gently, lets it pop free.

I'm done waiting.

I renew my grip on his hair and jerk his head down so I can kiss him. And while I'm kissing him, I lock my legs around his waist and I reach between us, positioning the hot tip of his cock over my entrance. Lifting my hips, I take all of him inside me.

Lir breaks our kiss with a harsh groan that rattles through his body. His skin breaks into goosebumps, and I smile.

Cupping his backside with both hands, I push him deeper in. The sensation of him sinking into me is exquisite. He's thick, hard, and satin-smooth, hot as fever and just as dizzying. In the haze of sensation, I can't remember what anyone else's cock felt like—only his.

My Chosen.

"I want you to ride me, Louisa," he whispers. "I want to see the way your beautiful body moves."

He's rolling over, taking me with him. Landing on his back, with me astride his hips, his cock still firmly lodged in my pussy. He stares at me with a wondering sort of smile, splaying his fingers over my breasts and squeezing them, then smoothing his palms over my generous bottom, indulging in every rich curve.

"You are so beautiful," he breathes.

I drape myself over him, leaning down to taste his perfect lips. "I have never seen a man as beautiful as you."

Then I straighten, my hands planted on his chest, and I begin to fuck him. I ride him just like he wanted, my breasts bouncing, all of me devoted to the movement. When I look down at where we're joined, I feel as if my pussy should be glowing—it feels incandescent, pulsing with a building heat, a crescendo of maddening pleasure.

Lir's cock is even harder now. His body is straining, his breath quick and shallow, his green eyes wide, black hair tumbled over his brow as he watches my pussy lips slide up and down on his shaft.

I want to make him come like this. But he isn't moaning yet, and I'm determined to elicit the sounds I need.

I rise high on my knees, letting his slick cock pop out of me.

"Louisa," he whimpers, and my pussy flutters.

"That's it," I murmur to him. "Good boy, cry for me just like that."

Kneeling between his legs, I slide my lips over his cock and go all the way down, just once. Then I pull off completely.

His dick bobs in the air, and a broken sob cracks from his throat. "Louisa... Louisa..."

I touch him with one finger, teasing delicately along the underside of his shaft.

Another male moan, thin and desperate, while his chest heaves. I coax his dick with my finger again, making it jerk, wrenching another moan from him.

"You're toying with me," he says hoarsely. "But you forget who I am, Louisa." He rises on his elbows, his green eyes snapping. "I'm the King of Faerie."

My skin bursts into chills. It's the first time he has called himself that.

He's rising while I stare, mesmerized... the tables turned, the predator becoming the prey...

He pounces on me. Rolls me over onto my stomach and slides his fingers through my wetness, moving them back up to slather my clit with my arousal. I nearly come on his fingers, thighs trembling. My pussy is quivering, spasming, craving fullness.

When he rams his cock inside me, I'm gone. I fly out of my body and I soar into the clear night sky, into a void of bursting stars that spatter my skin with scintillating light.

He's driving into me, groaning and grunting helplessly with every thrust—every sound I've wanted to hear from him. He's fucking me, fucking me hard—the King of Faerie buried in my heat, driving himself wild inside me.

When he comes, I feel the heavy pulse of his orgasm, and his warmth filling me up.

Once his curse breaks, I will make him pump me full of his release every day. There will never be another man for me; no cock but his. My body knows it, screams it, shatters around him again as he keeps thrusting.

When my second orgasm hits, Lir bellows in shock, and I scream.

My world is whited out in a blaze of sublime ecstasy.

It's like rising on the crest of a wave that never ends, that just keeps climbing, and glittering, and arching higher and higher in the bright glare of the sun.

And then it's over, and I manage to inhale. I forgot to breathe while it was happening—that erotic, divine, insane peak we just achieved together.

Slowly, shakily Lir draws himself out of the suction of my pussy and keels over on his stomach beside me, huffing through the blissful aftermath.

"Was that—" I whisper.

He nods. "The Chosen bond."

"Oh fuck."

"Indeed."

"I love it. And I love you, and I will love doing this forever. Especially when your curse is broken. Which should be today, yes?"

"Today." He closes his eyes briefly, his palm sliding over my skin as if he loves the feel of it, as if he can't get enough of me. "It will be dawn soon, and we'll have to leave. You should rest until then."

"We could sleep a little," I suggest, wriggling closer to him. "And then we could—do this again."

"I love that plan." He brushes back my hair with his fingers and kisses my forehead.

But then he frowns and sits up, tilting his head as if to catch a sound.

"What is it?" I sit up as well—a difficult feat since the climaxes have turned my muscles to jelly.

"I'm not sure." He rises from the bed and takes a step toward the tent flap, still listening.

His handsome face pales, his features stiffening with sudden alarm. "Louisa, get up. Get dressed."

"What? Why?"

"They're coming. The Unseelie."

"You can hear them?" I gasp, hastily pulling on my clothes.

"Yes. The thunder of hooves, the stamp of beast-mounts, the tramp of booted feet—all of it blended, shaking the ground. Some distance away still, but coming nearer." He hitches his pants into place, fastening the buttons.

Our tent flap swings open while I'm buckling my belt, and Orain appears in the gap, apprehension written across her dark features. "The winged patrols have raised the alarm, my lord. They've clashed with Unseelie in the air, and the ones who survived the encounter say the Unseelie army is on the move, coming this way. No doubt they plan to destroy us and take control of the Pool."

"We will fight with you," says the Prince.

"Your pardon, Majesty, but in this cursed state you cannot help us. We need you to ride for the Pool. We will send an escort with you, a dozen warriors—"

"No," says Lir. "No escort. Louisa and I made it this far on our own—we can finish this. And you need every fighter here."

I should be flattered he's so confident in our ability to do this together, but terror is constricting my lungs. I focus on hauling in deep breaths as we don our capes, as I snatch Fin's satchel of spells, as I follow the Prince out of the tent. Quickly we mount two of the white reindeer.

"Stars speed you, my King," Orain calls as we gallop away.

I've never ridden a reindeer before, but it's similar enough to riding a horse that I'm not too out of my depth. The saddle is a little higher and narrower than I'm used to, and my stag seems restive, but so far he's heeding my direction.

Lir and I urge our mounts through the awakening camp. It must look to the roused Seelie warriors as if their newly returned king is fleeing the battle. I can only hope Orain and the others will explain the situation. I want to shout to them all, "We'll return as fast as we can!" But I have no idea how soon that will be.

We clear the camp and race for open ground—no blue crystals here, but snow over grassy earth.

"It will be a long ride," Lir shouts, twisting to look back at me. "But we can make it. A straight shot to the Pool, and then—"

His face changes, transformed by dread as he stares at something above and behind me.

I turn to look back.

Outlined against the darkness, an inkier black against the night, soar a dozen winged Unseelie. And with a cry of triumph, they dive.

25
CLARA

I'm so sore I can barely stand. The orgy has been going on for hours.

About half the time, Fin was only pretending to fuck me, but sometimes he had to actually be inside me, since others at the orgy kept prowling around, wanting a turn.

Fortunately for us, the Rat King didn't seem to care whether Fin shared or not. He was too busy enjoying himself with several different partners.

During those hours, I came until I couldn't come anymore. I'm lying on the floor, nearly insensate, my body shifting slightly as Fin thrusts slowly, gently as he can. He's still fully clothed and cloaked, and no one has mentioned it. Some of the Unseelie appear to prefer cloaks or garments too, even during revels, so he's not the only one who didn't undress.

Fin lowers himself down, his chest against my back. "It's time, dearest. Can you stand?"

"Yes," I murmur.

"Good. Stay down until I tell you to get up. I'm going to glamor you."

He rises with an exaggerated yawn, tucking himself back into his pants, glancing around the room. I feel the trickle of tingling magic along my ears, over my body. "All right, love. Up you get."

I rise quickly, glancing down at myself. I have furred legs like a doe, and tiny green spikes jut from the flesh of my arms. Purple drapery covers my breasts and genitals.

Fin and I meander toward the exit, threading through the dwindling crowd of Unseelie. Some of them are still lazily fucking, while others are nibbling sweets or downing goblets of wine. A surprising number of the Court are snoring on the floor, while others are spinning dazedly, lost to the music in their minds. I suspect Finias had something to do with the general sleepiness of the group. Even the Rat King is snoring on his throne, draped in naked bodies.

"A most dreadfully delightful evening," Finias says to the guards on our way out, giving them a brief salute. They show no sign of hearing him. And they don't stop us, either.

The way out of the lair seems horrendously long, a maze of twisting corridors and upward slopes and sharp turns. It's all I can do to walk slowly and casually beside Finias. I link my arm with his, petting his shoulder and smirking like a female of the Unseelie Court might do.

Finally, at the end of a hallway, I can see the ragged hole up ahead—the one that leads outside.

We've made it.

I squeeze Fin's arm.

We're nearly there. I can see trees and the pale peach glow of the dawn sky. I can feel the fresh cold air on my face.

And then an eight-legged shape scuttles across the opening, blocking our path. Magda, the spider woman.

"Leaving so soon, Sugarplum?" she asks.

"The party is over. I've done my work well." He smiles at her. "Thank you for your kind words on my behalf."

"Yes, I did vouch for you." The spider woman crosses her arms over her chest. "But you see, later in the evening I spoke to the Rat King again, quietly. And I told him where I believe your true allegiance lies. He thought it best to use you for the party and then—keep you on hand for further amusement. After all, precious—you do taste so damn delicious."

She's moving nearer, leg after leg, in that horrible way spiders have.

"And who is this?" She exhales sharply, and a puff of white dust flies into my face. I sneeze, and when I glance down, my glamour is gone, and I'm dressed in the black ribbons of a concubine again. "Trying to steal the Rat King's property?"

"She doesn't belong to him," Fin bites out. "She's mine."

"Yours? How fascinating."

"Move aside, Magda," Fin says. "You have no idea what I'm capable of."

"You can't be capable of much, I'll wager, after you spent so much magic impressing the Rat King tonight. Yes, we allowed you to drain yourself on purpose, so you would be weak. As helpless as you are stupid." She laughs, thin and poisonous.

Finias chuckles. "I was drained, yes, and exhausted, too. But my energy recharges much faster than most, and you kindly allowed me the time I needed."

A flicker of alarm enters Magda's eyes.

"And now, dearest," says Fin. "If you would hold onto me, please, and stay quite close."

I wrap my arms around his body, pressing my cheek to his chest—and the world explodes around us.

The first pulse of rainbow light from Fin's hands shatters the entrance to the cave system, cracking it wide open to the dawning sun. Magda disintegrates on the spot, reduced to black dust on the wind.

"Perfect. I need sunlight for this spell," Fin says casually. "Switch to my back side, would you, love?"

He's turning to face the tunnels we came through, from which echo the shouts of the Rat King's oncoming soldiers. I duck behind him while he faces them. Another burst of iridescent magic rockets from his hands, traveling in a vibrant, humming wave down the underground corridors, destroying every rat-soldier it strikes.

He blasts them again and again, while we back away from the lair toward the treeline.

"We're going to fly in a minute, sweetheart," he says. "Be ready."

But I catch movement out of the corner of my eye. More soldiers, pouring out of a side exit—a hidden tunnel nearby. Some of them are carrying crossbows. One creates a ball of black lightning with his hands and flings it toward us.

"Fin, to the right!" I scream.

"Fuck," he hisses. He fires his own pulse that collides with the incoming spell. It fizzles out, and he casts another light-wave to disintegrate the soldiers.

"More on the left," I warn him. "Conjure me a weapon, so I can fight!"

"I can't. I can only conjure clothing, sweets, lights, a few other items—nothing metal—"

"What about that trick you did with the chair in your house? It disappeared and then reappeared somewhere else! Do that with one of the rat-soldiers' weapons! Or with us!"

"It doesn't work like that! There's a very limited range to that ability, and I can't move something as large as our bodies."

"Give me something, Fin," I persist. "If you can conjure boots and belts you can make me *something*—how about a whip?"

"Brilliant woman," he says, and the next instant a long leather whip, sheathed in a pink glow, appears in my hands.

He sends off a volley of his striped candy darts, then several swarms of the burning rainbow orbs he used the night his house was attacked.

A group of rat-soldiers slip through his guard on the left, so I lash out with my whip, striking the leader in the face. But the rat behind him stops and unslings a crossbow from his back.

"Fin!" I scream, and he whirls just in time to demolish the whole cluster of rats.

The soldiers keep coming, flooding out of the lair, shooting spells and crossbow bolts until I'm sure the entire underground maze must be empty. Fin must have slaughtered hundreds by now. His forehead is filmed with sweat, and he's panting heavily.

He rallies for another concussive blast of magic, wiping out the next wave of the Rat King's forces. When no one else appears, he nods wearily.

"We have to go," he says. "I think I got everyone with magic and crossbows for now, so they can't shoot us down. Come."

He vanishes his cloak, and his wings flutter to life. The next second I'm caught up in strong arms, borne upward in a rush toward the bright sky, toward freedom.

The second after that, a strip of writhing shadow coils around Fin's throat.

He chokes, his golden eyes going wide.

More shadows slash his wings like dark blades, shredding the gauzy blue.

I'm shrieking, trying to free his neck from the shadowy noose, but I can't feel the shadows, can't grip them.

More shadows curl around us, binding our legs together, dragging us back down. We crash to the earth, me on top of Fin, and I hear bones snap somewhere deep inside him.

I want to scream, but the sound won't come.

The first shadow withdraws from Fin's neck, leaving a scarlet line across his throat. Blood slides slowly from the cut. He chokes, more blood bubbling from the corner of his mouth. Pieces of his beautiful wings drift down around us like flakes of blue snow.

The Rat King is standing in the broken mouth of his lair, leaning on his scepter.

Fin's eyes are closed. Not dead—not yet—but perilously close to it.

An incandescent fury roars through my blood.

I'm still clutching my whip, and it's still glowing pink. Like my sweet Fin's hair. In fact, the angrier I get, the brighter the weapon seems to glow.

On impulse, I drag the whip through the shadows wrapped around my legs. They vanish with a hiss.

I climb to my feet, not caring that I'm dressed in nothing but black ribbons. The icy morning breeze tosses my hair as I stand over Fin, gripping my glowing whip.

"You want him?" I shout at the Rat King. "Come and get him, if you dare."

With an angry growl he takes a step forward, planting his scepter with a thud upon the ground. His shadows flood toward me, crawling along the earth, slithering through the air.

Seething, my teeth gritted and bared, I slash the shadows to pieces, one after another. Every tentacle of darkness he sends toward Fin, I destroy. Days of travel have hardened me, made me stronger. My whip snakes out, over and over, destroying the dark magic until the Rat King screeches with rage.

"Archers!" he cries out.

"The Sugarplum Faerie took out most of them, Majesty," calls one of the soldiers.

"Find some more," snarls the Rat King. "The rest of you, go get me that human woman!"

They're coming for me, a fresh flood of guards. I view the scene as if I'm soaring above it all, looking down at myself—a lone figure braced over the body of her lover, while enemies pour across the meadow toward her—lethal, inexorable.

When the first rat-soldier reaches me, I brandish the whip, slashing off his muzzle. I slice the next one's head clean in half, split another one open at the belt. I wield my weapon like I wield a brush, painting lines of searing pink and splashes of crimson blood on the canvas of the snowy ground.

I scream, and I slash, and with Fin's pale, unconscious face held in my mind, my whip glows more violently. I'm no longer the girl in the corner, the one who watches. I'm not the prey in the forest or the girl in the cage.

Because of Fin, I've surpassed everything I used to be, and I've become something else. A force of destruction.

I don't know how long I fight—only that my arm is weakening, muscles softened and shaky. Parts of bodies are piled up around me. I have killed more living things than I ever thought possible.

The stream of soldiers coming out of the lair is thinner now, a mere trickle. The Rat King is stomping and screaming his impotent rage. He snatches a huge sword from a nearby soldier, and holding it in two paws, he barrels toward me.

I take one step to meet him. Lift my trembling arm.

And pitch forward onto the stack of steaming bodies.

Before my consciousness fades, I see shadows unfurling around me.

Darkness, burying me alive.

26
LOUISA

We've been riding hard for four hours, pursued by the Unseelie.

Whenever they dive toward us, I throw something from Fin's satchel—anything to distract or repel them. I tried the mayhem spell—its burst of cacophonous light and sound confused them temporarily, but they soon caught up again. I've used deflection spells, glare bombs, high wind, hailstorm, and probably two dozen others. Some missed, or had no effect. One of them took down two Unseelie in a knot of lightning and screams.

Yet still the remaining Unseelie pursue us.

Fortunately the three Unseelie who were carrying ranged weapons appear to be out of bolts and darts now. I spent several of Fin's candies protecting Lir and myself from those projectiles. If I ever see Fin again, I'll have to thank him for leaving me his bag of tricks.

I don't think the Unseelie know who we are. But the fact that we're racing away from the battle, clearly bent on some important mission, is enough for them to keep pursuing us.

Or perhaps one of them did catch a glimpse of Lir's face, and recognized him. Fin told me once that some Fae can see in the dark—not just the enhanced sight most Fae have, but true night vision.

No dawn came today, only a lowering sky of dark gray clouds. Snow is falling thickly, whisked past my cheeks by the wind of our speed.

One of the Unseelie darts nearer, skimming along beside me, matching his pace to my stag's. His skin is gray, mottled with blue and purple splotches, and his arms form the top of his batwings, which end in three long, clawed fingers. His lean body is naked except for a scanty loincloth. One of his batlike ears is tattered, and his wing bears a scorch mark. Both wounds are my work.

"Give up, human," he hisses. "Yield to our pleasure and your doom."

I take a handful of candy from Fin's bag and throw it at the Unseelie. He laughs, catching one in midair. "What are these? Sweets? Are they poisoned? You've run out of tricks and you're trying to poison me now, little human?"

"I'm very tired of being called 'little human,'" I snap.

Lir falls back to my side. "Begone, devil."

"Well, if it isn't the long-lost Prince," sneers the Unseelie.

So they do know him after all. Fuck.

"Are you sure you recognize me?" Lir says grimly. "Come a bit closer. Take a good look."

"But I daren't come closer! I'm so scared of your rapier." The Unseelie recoils in mock terror. "You know, I've heard you're a being of immense power and stunning magic, Lord Prince. Yet I've seen nothing from you but a little swordplay. Could it be that you are currently powerless?"

Lir clenches his jaw and doesn't answer.

"So it's true! The Prince of Seelie, too shy to claim the title of King, is entirely impotent. He's at our mercy!" he calls to the others, who jeer in response.

"See here, you two," says the bat-winged Unseelie. "We've had good fun. Now it's time for you to yield. You're out of spells, girl, or you would have thrown another one at me by now. Give up, and we'll make your death quick. For the girl, not for you, Highness," he says, looking at Lir. "You, we'll take back to the Rat King."

A female Unseelie with a human head on a vulture's neck swoops down, keeping abreast of Lir's mount. The tips of her breasts protrude through her mottled gray-and-black feathers.

I glance up. Four Unseelie are descending rapidly from above. Behind us, four more are skimming along the ground, rapidly closing the distance.

"Louisa!" Lir's tone is harsh desperation blended with violent hope.

I follow his gaze ahead, to a belt of trees taller than any I've ever seen. Their trunks shoot straight up, smooth and bare, all the way to the underbelly of the winter sky, where their leafy crowns mingle with the clouds. They're set close together, a wall of trunks so tightly arranged I can't see what lies beyond them.

This must be the place. This ring of ancient trees must encircle the Unending Pool.

"Go!" I scream, kicking my stag with my heels. It's the animal's life at stake as well as mine. Whether he understands that or not, he responds with a fresh burst of speed.

Lir is roaring to his mount as well, urging him to gallop faster. We streak across the open space, closing with the line of trees slowly, slowly—

The Unseelie screech, flapping hard to catch up with us. One of them dives, trying to pluck Lir out of his saddle, but he slashes expertly with the rapier and it wheels away, screaming, blood spraying from a damaged leg.

Claws dig into my shoulder, and I shriek, clamping my thighs around my stag's body just in time to avoid being plucked off my mount. I brandish my dagger at the vulture-Fae, and she squawks when my blow glances off her wing.

Again the Unseelie dive, taking turns zooming in to attack us, while we try to ride faster and fight at the same time. I'm riding abreast of Lir again, sticking close to him so it's harder for two of the Unseelie to attack us at once without their wings becoming tangled.

"If they get me, promise you'll keep going," I shout to Lir.

"Not likely," he says.

"You have a responsibility to your people. If you can ride faster and get ahead of me, do it!"

"Not a fucking chance."

"Fine. Bastard."

"I love you too."

With a tearful laugh, I hunch close to my stag's neck, keeping my body low and tight, urging him on. I feel like apologizing to the stag for my weight—I'm probably much heavier than lithe, toned Lir—yet somehow we pull ahead. Which makes Lir's stag unhappy, apparently, because he finds a reserve of energy somewhere and launches himself forward, straining as if we're in a race.

My shoulder burns where the Unseelie vulture seized it. She's diving in again—the rough edge of her wing scrapes my cheek.

Another Unseelie soars above Lir, then drops, his wings flung straight up and his legs apart. He lands on the stag's back, right behind Lir, and I scream. I rake my hand through Fin's satchel and come up with just two items—a piece of candy and an orb.

I fling the orb, and it explodes into orange dust against the Unseelie's arm.

He begins to melt, acid steaming through his clothes and flesh.

"Push him off, Lir, push him off!" I scream.

Lir twists, grips the Fae's collar, and flings him off the stag. The Unseelie collapses into the snow, shrieking as more of his body is eaten away by the acid.

"Sweetheart," calls Lir, his face stricken. "Don't help me that way again."

"Noted." I'm trembling with the thought of what could have happened to Lir and the stag if he hadn't thrown the Unseelie off in time. And what if my aim had been off and I'd hit Lir with the acid? I have to be more careful.

A quick glance over my shoulder shows the rest of the Unseelie charging us again, deadly intent in their eyes.

But when I face front again, the treeline is right before us.

We charge into the narrow space between two trunks, slowing down a little to thread our way through. It's a thicker belt of trees than I realized, but at the pace we're going, we navigate it quickly, breaking out into a field of blue grass studded with smooth, upright rocks, man-sized, white as bone and chiseled with countless runes. The snow is still falling, but each flake evanesces the moment it touches the rocks or the grass.

In the distance, beyond that great field with its standing stones, lies a sheet of water, mirrorlike, reflecting the gray sky above.

The Unending Pool is utterly still and glassy smooth. I can't see its farther edge; it seems to melt into gray mist, no horizon to be seen. Magic shivers in the air, tangible even to a human like me.

The Unseelie seem to have fallen back for the moment. They couldn't fly through the belt of trees, and they will have to fly impossibly high in order to find a way over the treetops.

"This is good," I say to Lir. "We have a chance now. Keep riding hard, and we'll—"

"Louisa." The wooden rasp in his tone startles me. "Louisa, I—"

His body spasms, limbs stiffening. His jaw works oddly, and his skin color has altered.

He's reverting to Nutcracker form.

"No," I gasp. "No, it's too soon, isn't it?"

"Something—about this place," he chokes.

"We'll pause for a moment. I'll give you some blood..."

"No!" He leans into the gallop. "Won't risk—draining you. If we stop—they'll catch you. Kill you. Louisa—"

He groans, and the sound changes halfway through, a deep wooden creak that makes me want to scream. But he's still his right size, still gripping the reins and riding.

Just a little farther. A little farther now...

Behind us, cries of fury and the whip of great wings tell me that our Unseelie pursuers have surmounted the ring of ancient trees. They got over it much faster than I expected. Shit.

I have nothing left. The remaining candy is a musical one, and that won't help us. All I have is my dagger.

Lir can only cling woodenly to his stag's back, and I'm not sure how long he'll be able to stay in the saddle. I shout to my mount and his, urging them forward, pelting at top speed toward the Pool.

But the Unseelie can see where we're headed. They must have figured out by now that Lir reaching the Pool is a very bad thing for them.

They descend on us in a tornado of wings and talons.

I'm torn from my saddle, flung free, spinning in midair. I crash to the ground and hear the crack of a rib and the snap of a wrist bone.

Screams shear from my throat as I'm picked up and thrown again.

"Lir!" I shriek, flailing with my sword. My other hand is useless, my broken wrist shooting fire along my nerves. I think a claw caught my forehead or scalp, because blood is running into my right eye.

The Unseelie are high, high above me, among the gently falling snowflakes. They're tossing Lir in the air, throwing him for each other to catch, crowing and howling their triumph. He's stiff, unresponsive, his limbs locked in place as they torment him.

But halfway between two of them, his body changes.

He shrinks down to the size of the Nutcracker.

The claws of the Unseelie who was supposed to catch him snap shut on thin air.

And the Nutcracker doll falls.

Agony floods my body as I wrench myself upright and hobble forward. I discard my dagger and reach out with both hands.

The Nutcracker drops into them.

I curl him against my chest. Teeth set, blood streaming down my face, anguish searing through my ankle and wrist, I limp toward the Unending Pool.

"I can fucking do this," I spit through the blood. "I can—fucking—do this—"

Claws sink into the flesh of my back. But the Unseelie behind me doesn't have a good grip—I rip free of the hold, screaming as skin tears. The shadows of the Unseelie fall over me, darkening, descending. Tottering, half-blind, dizzy with pain, I give one last great lunge, and I throw the Nutcracker doll into the Unending Pool.

There's a soft plop as he sinks into its gleaming surface.

I collapse face-first on the blue grass, the soft blades tickling my nostrils with each ragged inhale. My vision is blurring, but I blink hard, trying to clear it. Even with one side of my face pressed into the grass, I can see the surface of the Pool, rippling slightly where I threw the Nutcracker in.

What is supposed to happen?

Did it even work?

The Unseelie aren't attacking me—they're hovering warily, watching, just like I am.

A single, huge, shuddering ripple pulses from the Pool.

Then another.

With a concussive force like a sun exploding, Lir bursts out of the water.

He's immense—more than ten times his usual height, his naked body streaming silver liquid. His black hair is longer now, tossing around his pointed ears. Titanic silver wings burst from his back—like bat-wings but reflective, shiny as mirrors.

On his upper arm there's a deep groove, a permanent valley carved where the splinter broke off the Nutcracker.

With giant fingers Lir catches a handful of the Unseelie and crushes them into pulp. The others flee, shrieking, while our reindeer gallop away into the trees.

Lir bends, laying his enormous hand, palm up, on the grass beside me.

"Come, Louisa." His voice booms around me, immense and deep as the sea.

Disbelief clashes with wonder in my brain as I crawl into his palm. He curls his fingers around me carefully, heat and magic flowing from him into my body, easing my pain, knitting my bones and flesh back together.

Giant Lir walks out of the pool, crosses the meadow in a few strides, and parts the belt of trees easily, like a man might brush aside a branch and let it spring back into place once he passed.

"I need to change form," Lir says in his booming, echoing voice. "Are you healed?"

I nod, unsure if someone as huge as him would hear my tiny reply.

He sets me down gingerly. Then his body alters, shifting, rippling in silver waves—forming silver scales. His wings remain the same, but the rest of him morphs into a gigantic silver dragon. And the dragon, too, has a deep scar on its foreleg.

I would be terrified, except the dragon's green eyes are familiar. I know them—they've sparkled ragefully at me during arguments, stared at me with gloomy disdain, burned into mine with a passion beyond anything I dreamed of possessing.

Instead of being terrified, I'm exhilarated.

Because this is the beginning of the end for the forces of the Rat King.

27
CLARA

I'm not sure how many days have passed since Fin and I woke up in a foul-smelling, ink-black cell. He's wearing a collar that locks away his magic, and my whip was taken away. His conjured clothes have long since disappeared, so he's naked, and I'm wearing only my ribbons. But his wounds have healed, and his shredded wings have repaired themselves. I only know this by touch, because there is no light in this place, only darkness.

By now my sister, Lir, and the others must have passed through the Ravine. If they made it through alive, they should reach the Unending Pool soon, if they haven't already. If the last loyal Seelie fighters can hold off the Rat King's forces, and if Lir can get into the Pool, his curse will be broken. He'll reclaim his power, and he'll be able to drive the Rat King back to his own kingdom.

So many "if's." I chew over them endlessly in my head, hope giving way to despair and despair yielding to hope in an endless cycle.

There's a stinking pit in our cell, intended to be the toilet. I nearly fell into it when we were first put here, as I was exploring the room on my hands and knees, feeling around in the dark.

Since then, Fin and I have stayed far from it unless we need to relieve ourselves.

Even after days of imprisonment, his body and breath still smell delightful, but I'm not so lucky. What I wouldn't give to be able to wash my body and clean my teeth!

Now and then we're given two cups of oily water and fed a grainy gruel with strange, chewy lumps that I try not to think about. Fin insists I eat some of his share. As a faerie, he can survive on much less food.

"Do you think the Rat King has forgotten about us?" I curl against Fin's chest, stroking my fingers down his arm.

"Not after you and I decimated his army."

"Mostly you."

"You as well, dearest. You made the Rat King respect you enough as a warrior that he put you down here, instead of shutting you in with the other concubines, in one of those Inescapable Cages. I wish I could have seen you fight for me." He traces the round edge of my ear.

"If we ever get out of here, I'll paint the scene for you," I promise. "In fact, I'll paint the whole story. I have the scenes already planned out, with the colors I'll use and everything."

"Of course you do." He chuckles quietly, a warm affection in the sound.

I find his mouth, molding my lips to his, shifting my body nearer. Sex with him has been the one delight of our confinement. I don't know why they put us in a cell together, but I'm glad of it.

"The Rat King is going to do something especially awful to us, isn't he?" I whisper.

"I'm afraid so."

"I wish I knew when."

"Would that make things any easier?"

"No." I wrap one leg over his hip, urging my center closer to the hardness prodding my belly. Fin's body twitches as I grasp his cock, guiding it into my heat.

"You're soaked," he whispers, his hand sliding over my breast.

"I'm always wet for you."

He hums low in his throat, gliding deeper into me. But a clang down the hall distracts both of us.

"It's not time for the food yet, is it?" I whisper.

"No." Fin slides out of me. "I think they're coming for someone again."

We've heard other prisoners screaming as they're dragged out of their cells and taken up to the higher levels of the lair.

This time, the heavy tread of two pairs of boots halts outside our door. A sickly-green faerie light floats along beside the Unseelie guards, spilling some of its doleful radiance into our cell.

"The Rat King summons you to a festive dinner," says one of the guards. The other snorts a laugh.

"Are we to be the main course, then?" asks Fin, a strained lightness in his tone.

"Not this time," answers the guard. "You're the entertainment."

The Unseelie female with the bird in her chest bathes me, shaves me, scents me, sweeps my hair into a fancy coiffure, and dresses me in a few silky green scraps linked together by thin green ropes. Then I'm gagged, manacled, and led to the Rat King's throne, where I sit between his feet—not on his lap, thankfully. Not yet.

That's when I see Fin, chained between two pillars. He's been washed and oiled until he gleams, but instead of clothing, scarlet ropes crisscross his toned body in an elaborate pattern, making the bulge of his muscles even more pronounced. The knotwork seems to highlight his pectorals and genitals. His wings are undamaged, thank god—they shiver at his back, a telltale sign of his agitation.

A dozen Unseelie Fae circle him, eager grins, ravenous eyes, and slavering tongues, taunting him, but not touching him.

The crowd in the throne room is much thinner, and the Rat King's concubines are nowhere to be seen, but there's a feast table burdened with all kinds of food, some of which looks very edible. My stomach growls, and I flinch, hoping the Rat King didn't hear it.

"I present to you the traitor, the Seelie they call Sugarplum," bellows the Rat King. "He is the one responsible for the slaughter of so many of my people. First we will feast. And then, he will provide dessert."

A raucous cheer rises from the Court.

"One of my best spellworkers has prepared a little treat for our guest, to give him the inclination and the stamina to serve us all," says the Rat King. "And when he is drained and begging for death, I will take his human in front of him, before I kill them both."

More cheers, but I barely hear them. My mind is stuttering, refusing to accept the horror that awaits Finias tonight.

His head hangs forward, his pink hair tumbling over his brow. Every muscle in his straining arms and chest gleams in the amber light, and he's so beautiful I think my heart will break because I can't save him, I can't help him. I can't even speak to him.

The feast begins with a clatter of plates and a whine of dolorous music. Servants bring a heavily laden tray to the Rat King, and he props it across his thighs. He's eating right behind my head—now and then I can feel droplets of his saliva on the back of my neck.

Despite how grotesque the Rat King is and despite my torturous anxiety about the events to follow, my rebellious stomach keeps growling. I think if the Rat King told me to suck his cock in exchange for a plate of decent food, I might be tempted to try it. Though its girth would likely break me. That's what he plans to do later—wreck me in front of Fin, as the final torment.

Amid the roar of the feasting Unseelie, a bang echoes along the corridor outside the cavern, like the closing of a very large door.

"What was that?" growls the Rat King. "You, and you—go and check."

Two of his soldiers hurry to obey.

A few moments later, I notice something moving near the throne room entrance. Two toy soldiers with white rat's heads, marching jerkily across the floor. Miniature versions of the two guards who just left.

I hold my breath.

Following the tiny rat-soldiers, three metal orbs roll into the room. With a click and a whirr, they open.

The air in the chamber shudders, a visible ripple that turns everything wavy and watery, and carried on that watery air is a voice, somber and firm, speaking words I don't understand—a long chain of words that vibrate with power.

It's Drosselmeyer's voice.

The Rat King lunges for his scepter, but he's too slow—he has the tray of food on his lap and I'm already moving. I fling my whole body at the scepter, catching it between my bound hands and rolling with it off the dais, down the steps. Pain bursts through my elbows, my knees;

I'll have bruises, but I don't care. I clutch the scepter as the spell continues, resounding throughout the room.

The Unseelie are moving in slow motion now, as if they're caught in a giant vat of thick, gooey, invisible molasses.

Drosselmeyer strides into the chamber, his coat flowing behind him, brass spectacles gleaming, clockwork rings glinting on his fingers. He intones another spell, layering it over the first. One by one the Unseelie begin to shrink, and to change. Smaller they grow, and harder, and brightly colored, made of wood and paint and ball joints. They topple onto the seats of their chairs or tumble to the floor, reduced to a child's playthings.

The Rat King is the last to go. He's fighting his way through the thickness of the magic, clawing toward me, toward the scepter. But it's too late. I watch him shrivel down to the size of my palm, to a wooden figure of a three-headed rat in a purple robe. He's the tiniest toy in the room.

I struggle to my feet—a difficult matter with my hands bound, but I'm still clutching the scepter, and I press the butt end of it against the floor to pull myself up. Then, with that same end of the scepter, I smash the Rat King toy. I strike it again and again, smashing, screaming, until the heads and limbs have broken off and the body is reduced to splinters. I keep pounding and crushing him until I become conscious of

Drosselmeyer's thin, dark-clad figure standing quietly nearby.

Panting, I look up at him.

"It has taken me a long time to track you down, Clara." Advancing, he extracts a pair of tiny tools from the cuff of his coat and unlocks my manacles. "And once I found you, I didn't think I would be able to get into this place. But it turned out to be poorly defended."

"Thanks to Finias," I say, nodding toward him.

But the chains between the columns hang empty.

On the floor lies a doll, a slim male faerie with cloth wings. The collar he was wearing around his neck has slipped off and lies beside him, no larger than a woman's ring.

"No," I breathe. "No, no, no—you cursed him?"

"I cursed every Fae in the entire complex," says Drosselmeyer coolly.

"He's one of the good ones." Tears fill my eyes as I rush to the Finias doll and drop to my knees beside him.

"There are no good ones."

"You're wrong," I snap. "You have to reverse this. Please. I could do it with my blood, but it won't last. Please just fix him."

"I can't do that. Come with me, Clara. We need to find your sister and go home."

"No." I rise from the floor, holding Finias against my chest. "This faerie and his cousin Lir, the prince you cursed—they saved our lives. They are our friends. And you—you left us. You saw the rat-soldiers approaching, and you fled."

"I was unprepared to battle the darkest of the Unseelie," Drosselmeyer says. "When I saw the Rat King's soldiers in the forest, I knew he must have conquered the Seelie part of the realm. I knew there would be more soldiers and monsters flooding the forest, and I knew I couldn't fight them all. Your sister took my most powerful bombs with her when the two of you went through the portal—I had to return to my workshop and contrive a different solution. I designed a way to expand the effect of the curses I usually use. Instead of one Fae at a time, I can now curse many. Necessity is the impetus behind brilliance." He smiles, clearly pleased with himself. "Never fear, my dear, I always intended to come back for you and your sister."

"By the time you returned with your bombs and curses, we might have been *dead*," I retort. "Leaving us was cowardice on your part—admit it."

Drosselmeyer's eyes narrow. "So you think I should have charged to your defense immediately, at great risk to myself, after you betrayed me? Two girls I barely knew, whom I took into my home for your father's sake, and you turned against me the first chance you got. You didn't ask me about my work, or stop to think that perhaps, just perhaps, I might have a good reason for what I was doing."

"A good reason?" I vent a hard laugh. "What possible 'good reason' could there be for capturing the Fae and cursing them? Enslaving them?"

"They are wicked, all of them," he seethes. "Seelie and Unseelie alike—wild and cruel, careless and murderous. Your father used to hunt them with me, when we were young. Your father and I met at boarding school, you see, and we discovered that we had both witnessed the savagery of the Fae. My two little sisters were stolen away and replaced with pixie changelings, who then tore out the throats of my parents. Your father watched a pair of Seelie Fae lure his mother, his father, and his older brother into a dance circle in the forest. The Fae plied them with drugged wine and raped them over and over while they were dazed and pliant. Stories of Fae cruelty and cunning abound in our world, Clara. And these are the creatures you would defend?"

"They aren't all like that," I say. "Finias isn't—he wouldn't—" But I pause, because I don't truly know what Finias is capable of, or what he may have done in the past. I only know the person he is now.

"Wrong has been done," I continue. "But that doesn't mean you have the right to capture and enslave Fae who may or may not be as cruel and wicked as you think. Did you try to select Fae who were evil, or did you simply hunt and capture any who happened to be around when you stepped through the portal?"

For the first time, Drosselmeyer looks uncertain, perhaps even guilty. He doesn't meet my eyes when he says, "I began by seeking revenge on the cruel ones. Those are the stone statues in my gallery—the first Fae I hunted down. But my methods evolved, and as my curse-casting skills improved, I suppose my goals changed as well."

"You liked hunting them," I say softly. "You enjoyed the thrill of it, the triumph. Like some men enjoy hunting beasts. And then you realized you could use them in your house. They could serve you."

"Financing my work has occasionally been difficult," he admits. "Especially when my buyers don't see the value of certain pet projects of mine. To fund those, I needed to save money elsewhere. With the automatons, I could avoid the cost of keeping servants. The ones I didn't need as servants became part of the dollhouse— very popular with my clients."

"And what of Lir?" I ask. "The Seelie Prince you captured? Why did you take him?"

Drosselmeyer pinches his lips together and shakes his head. "Vanity, I suppose? I happened to open a portal near the gardens where he was reading. He had sent his guards away so he could have privacy. I'd seen him before during my hunting trips—captured a few of his best warriors, in fact. But finding him in that spot, alone and unprepared—it was the best kind of luck. I shot him with a bolt that stunned him instantly and negated his magic for a short time. Then I took him with me and stripped him of all his power. I, Drosselmeyer, a human scientist—I captured the future King of the Seelie Court. *I bound the most powerful being in Faerie.* It was my crowning achievement. So yes—when you freed him, I was angry. Disappointed. Vindictive, perhaps."

It's probably the nearest he'll get to acknowledging any cowardice or vengeful intent on his part. I let my tone soften a little, because whatever his faults may be, he did come looking for us. "And how did you find me?"

"I did a spell to track you, using samples from your hairbrush and Louisa's." He pulls up his sleeve, showing a strange, shifting map delineated in thread-thin black lines on his forearm. "The map will vanish once I've found you both. See, there is Louisa. Wait—" He frowns, peering at the lines. "That's very odd. Just moments ago she was here, near the Ravine—and now she's moving dreadfully fast in this direction."

Hope flutters in my chest. "She was with Lir, helping him break his curse at the Unending Pool. Maybe they've done that, and they're heading this way."

"Then we should go." Alarm blooms in Drosselmeyer's eyes. "The Fae Prince will be looking for revenge on me." He unslings a weapon from his back—something like a hand cannon. "I have a few of those stun-bolts that temporarily remove a Fae's magic, but I doubt he'll let me get close enough to use them this time. The portal is in the corridor just outside this room. Come, Clara. Quickly."

"So you'd have me flee with you, and you'd leave Louisa here, with the Fae folk whom you claim are so dreadful?" I glower at him. "No. I'm not a child you can command; I'm a grown woman. I won't go with you. In fact, I don't plan to leave at all."

Drosselmeyer hisses his frustration through his teeth, casting a frantic glance at the map on his arm. "This isn't you, Clara. They've bewitched you somehow. Your father always said you were the careful, reasonable one—he said except for your artistic affinities, you had the best sense. Louisa is foolish and flighty, but you—"

"I'm strong," I cut in quietly. "Stronger than I ever realized, with more freedom than I've ever had. I'm not bewitched, but I won't go back. I'm staying here, with him." I touch the tiny carved face of the Finias doll. "If you won't lift his curse, I'll travel to the Unending Pool myself and free him. He is someone I need, someone who cares about all of me, including the parts I don't let anyone else see. He's someone I love."

I lift pleading eyes to Drosselmeyer. "You've loved people. You know how it feels to lose them. Human or Fae, Seelie or Unseelie—we are all guilty of something. And there are members of each race who have done wicked, wretched things. That doesn't mean we condemn them all. It doesn't mean we keep hating and punishing everyone of that race for wrongs committed long ago. The Fae wronged you deeply, and you've wronged them, too—but it must end."

"So you want me to return your lover to you," says Drosselmeyer grimly. "And these others?" He gestures to the Unseelie Court, miniaturized and scattered about the room. "What about them? I suppose you want them to remain cursed, since they're your enemies? Do you not see your own hypocrisy?"

"They are the aggressors here," I counter. "And they've committed unspeakable horror against the Seelie, with no sign of remorse. So we'll leave them like this, until the rightful King can decide their fate."

Drosselmeyer is wavering, but he's not convinced yet. I scan the room, searching for inspiration, for a final bit of leverage to sway him.

The Rat King's scepter is lying on the floor. Holding Fin in one hand, I pick it up. "I know you enjoy Fae artifacts and weapons. This belonged to the Rat King, and it's imbued with shadow magic. You could probably learn to use it. If you free Fin, and you promise to stay and speak to Lir and Louisa, you can have it."

I bite my lip, waiting. I've appealed to his morals, his compassion, and his collector's nature. The choice is up to him.

After a moment, the bolt-gun he's holding drops to the floor with a clang.

"I'm tired," Drosselmeyer says simply. "Weary of all this. Let it be done. I'll restore your friend, and if the Prince kills me when he arrives, so be it."

"He won't kill you," I say. "I'll make sure of it. Perhaps you can trade your life for the assurance that you'll dispel the curse from the Seelie prisoners and concubines in this lair, and from all the cursed Fae in your house. The Prince has friends among your captives. And you can begin by freeing Finias."

"I suppose if I want leniency, cursing the Prince's cousin isn't the way to begin," Drosselmeyer says. He glances toward the throne room entrance again. I can sense his fear, his urge to simply flee back through the portal and abandon us all.

I approach him, holding out the Sugarplum Faerie doll. "You're doing the right thing, you know. If you run away from this, you'll never have peace. But we all have a chance to sort things out and settle them, right now. Please."

"Very well." Drosselmeyer speaks a quick string of words.

The Finias doll expands, growing right out of my hands. He's still oiled, naked, and clad in the scarlet ropes. He falls to his knees, gasping, his wings shivering

Drosselmeyer hooks an eyebrow at me. "I can see the appeal."

I ignore him and help Finias to his feet. "Are you all right?"

He sniffs and shakes himself. "I've never experienced anything like that. Ah, Drosselmeyer. We meet again. I do believe you tried to trap me once."

Drosselmeyer peers at Fin's face, and then his eyes widen. "I believe I did. You're very quick."

"Clara, dearest," says Fin, eyeing my godfather. "I suppose you've made some sort of deal, so I can't kill him?"

"That's correct."

"Pity." He cracks his neck, the ropes on his body vanishing. A gauzy shirt, a purple vest, and a pair of trousers appear in their place. "Much better."

"Lir and Louisa are headed this way," I tell him. "We should go out and meet them. They're moving oddly fast, in a very straight line—I have no idea how they're traveling so quickly."

Finias looks as if he's trying to hide a smirk.

"What?" I frown at him. "What is it?"

"It's so much more fun as a surprise, sweetness," he tells me. "But first, if you'll permit me, I'd like to conjure you some clothes. Well, I wouldn't *like* to, because you look absolutely fetching in those scraps—but maybe you'd prefer to greet the King of Faerie in something with a bit more coverage?"

"Please, yes."

Fin envelops me in an outfit that closely matches his own, except it's much tighter, and shows ample cleavage. I give him a half-reproachful smirk, and he winks at me.

We hurry out of the lair, and I inwardly determine never to enter it again. Drosselmeyer keeps glancing nervously at the magical map on his arm, until the dot representing Louisa is nearly on top of us.

"Where are they?" I exclaim, perplexed, glancing around. "They should be right here."

"Dearest heart," says Fin, a laugh in his voice. "Look up."

When I look up, I'm nearly blinded by the flash of light on metal. Something enormous is descending from the sky, right toward us.

"Fin!" I squeal, clutching his arm.

"It's all right." He chuckles. "It's Lir. His curse is broken."

"Lir?" I squint, shading my eyes, as the shape descends.

It's a dragon.

A great silver dragon, with mirrorlike scales, a long neck, immense wings, and a sleek snout. And my sister is riding on its back.

"Lir is a dragon?" I gasp.

"It's one of several forms he can take, as the King and High Protector of the Seelie," says

Fin. He practically skips forward, shouting, "Welcome back, cousin!" He smacks the side of the dragon's neck and the beast rumbles in response.

Louisa slides down the dragon's shoulder, flushed and windblown. Her clothes are bloodied and torn, but she looks whole.

"We came as soon as we could," she says, throwing her arms around me. "We had to burn up all the Rat King's armies in the Ravine, of course, and finish off another part of the army that was attacking the Seelie, but the minute that was done Lir scried where you were, and we headed this way. Oh god, Clara, I've been so worried! I'm so glad you're both all right?"

I open my mouth to answer, but a rippling snarl interrupts me. The Lir-dragon is crawling toward Drosselmeyer, its jaws leaking smoke.

"No, don't kill him, Lir!" I cry. "He defeated the rest of the Rat King's forces, everyone remaining inside the lair. He saved us. And he has agreed to free all his captives, if you'll spare his life."

The dragon's shape contorts, shivering and shrinking until Lir stands before Drosselmeyer— the Lir I've come to know, his usual height and size. He's completely naked, but Finias clears his throat and conjures a kingly velvet robe around him, one with glittering embroidery, an immense feathered collar, and a ridiculously long train.

Lir glances down at the robe and shoots a glare at his cousin.

"Sorry." Finias winces, then grins. "Thought you needed a bit of finery while you pronounce judgment."

"Drosselmeyer," says Lir.

There's such dreadful intensity in that word, such a wealth of suppressed power. I'm not surprised when Drosselmeyer drops to his knees.

"You've caused me a world of trouble," Lir continues. "Explain to me why I should spare you."

28
LOUISA

I believe Lir always intended to spare Drosselmeyer in exchange for the return of the captive Fae. But he makes the inventor grovel for it awhile, and honestly I love him for that.

Once the bargain is finally struck, Drosselmeyer and Fin go back into the Rat King's lair so Drosselmeyer can dispel the curse on the Seelie prisoners and concubines. Lir and I walk through part of the lair, marveling at all the Unseelie lying there, reduced to harmless toys.

"The most powerful sorcerer your world has ever seen, I think," murmurs Lir, picking up a shard of the former Rat King. "A pity his magic is limited to curses."

"While we're speaking of magic and powers—you never told me about your different forms. A giant? A dragon?"

He smiles, a dimple popping into one cheek. I've never seen him smile so widely. "I thought that part of my abilities should be a surprise."

"I nearly *died* of that surprise."

"You did not." Laughing, he pulls me in for a kiss.

"What other forms can you take?"

He looks at me quizzically. "You're thinking about this for sex, aren't you?"

"Maybe." I flutter my lashes at him. "You have to admit, this ability of yours will keep things interesting. How does it work if you come in your giant form? Is there a river of cum?"

Lir blushes right to the tips of his ears. "Hush, you!" He catches me up in his arms and carries me out of the lair, while I giggle and squirm. Once we're outside, he sets me down.

"I have to deal with several matters," he says, sobering. "My people will need me after this time of turmoil, and so will the prisoners Drosselmeyer frees. But after that, sweetheart, you and I—we are going to do everything you can imagine."

There's a sultry heat in his eyes, a wicked promise in his words. I thrill with excitement and pull him in for a hard kiss.

When we separate, Clara is watching us, smiling. "So you two have settled things?"

"I'm staying," I tell her exuberantly. "Please say you are, too!"

"Fuck yes," she says, and then flushes scarlet, her face shining with soft joy. "Wherever Fin goes, I go."

"I'd say it's the other way around, dearest." Fin saunters out of the lair, carrying a glowing pink whip. "After all, I'm the one who followed you here."

Clara leaps forward, collecting the whip eagerly. "Oh, you found it!"

"I can track items I've conjured," he says with a wink. "Thought you might care to have it back."

"Conjured," she says, her face falling. "Does that mean it won't last?"

"I think we can find a way to make it permanent."

"Oh good." She looks at me, lifting the whip. "My new weapon!"

"You'll have to tell me everything," I begin, but at that moment Drosselmeyer's portal appears on the turf, looking exactly as it did the day we first stepped through it. He must have decided to move it from the smelly underground tunnel to the open air. A good choice.

Drosselmeyer exits the lair himself a moment later.

"It will take me a little time to set them all free," he says. "I'll return shortly."

"If you don't, I know where to find you," Lir replies darkly. "There are other paths between our two worlds."

With a nod, Drosselmeyer steps through the portal.

He's gone for a long time. But at last an impossibly tall Fae woman with doe ears and white curly hair steps through the portal, bending over so she doesn't strike her head on the arch. She moves with the graceful caution of a warrior, and she grips an ax with a head carved of icy crystal.

"Andil," exclaims Lir, and he strides forward to embrace her.

This is the dear friend he mentioned weeks ago, when we stood in Drosselmeyer's weapon room.

"My wife," says Andil. "Is she all right?"

The sliver of jealousy that was beginning to work its way into my heart melts away, and I feel guilty for yielding to it. This beautiful creature has a wife. Someone she loves, whom she hasn't seen in months.

"Our realm has endured great upheaval, and much death," says Lir. "But we will find your wife."

Andil nods. "Thank you, my King. It is King now, yes?"

"As soon as our people are returned, the ceremony will take place."

"That will be a glad day." With a smooth bow, she glides past him, taking up a position nearby.

One after another, more Fae come through the portal—Seelie and Unseelie alike. They appear vaguely confused, and though they all have some recollection of their existence in Drosselmeyer's house, some are more shocked than others to find out how much time has passed since they were cursed.

Finally the stream of Fae ends and Drosselmeyer himself steps through the portal. He's carrying some of mine and Clara's luggage. After depositing it on the grass, he goes back through, only to return with our trunk. Clara must be glad to see that—some of her favorite paintings are still wedged in the bottom, wrapped carefully for travel.

Lir speaks to me under his breath. "Say your farewells, you and Clara, before I banish him from Faerie forever."

I don't chide him for the dramatic words. The pain he and his people have been through because of Drosselmeyer is incalculable. There's nothing I can say to make light of it or cheer his heart. Drosselmeyer not only stole years from the cursed; he incited the Rat King's war by kidnapping the Seelie Prince. All the ravages, the loss of life, the hideous torment and the ruinous dark magic—it all began when Drosselmeyer saw his chance to capture the Prince, and took it.

Lir stalks away without another word, and I let him go. But Fin stays, watching as Clara and I hug Drosselmeyer, a little awkwardly. We barely know the man, but it seems right to acknowledge how drastically our short acquaintance with him has changed our lives.

I exchange glances with Clara, and somehow I know she's thinking the same thing I am.

"I think," Clara says, "you should keep our inheritance, Godfather. After all, Louisa and I won't need it. We're both marrying rich, beautiful Fae men."

"Who says I'm rich?" Fin cocks an eyebrow.

Clara flushes. "Oh, it doesn't matter if you aren't! I'm sorry, I wasn't thinking—I just assumed—"

"You assumed someone as powerful and gorgeous as I am must have found a way to amass a significant amount of wealth." Fin winks. "And you'd be right."

"I agree with my sister," I tell Drosselmeyer. "We have no use for our father's fortune anymore. Take the money, hire some human servants, and create everything you've wanted to make. Except weapons. No more weapons."

"No weapons," he agrees.

"Can *I* make weapons?" Fin asks. "Because it seems I have a talent for it. That whip I conjured for Clara is the first weapon I've ever made, infused with love, passion, and rage. I'd like to see what else I can do."

"In the interest of defending our lands, perhaps," says Lir, striding up. He gives Drosselmeyer a stiff nod. "You've freed everyone."

It's both a statement and a question. Drosselmeyer bows his head briefly, respectfully. "All your subjects have been returned, and all the Unseelie I trapped as well. Those whom I turned to stone during my first years of hunting could not be restored, but everyone else has passed through."

"Then you may go," Lir answers coldly. "I don't expect we'll see you again."

"No," says Drosselmeyer. "You won't. As we agreed, I will shatter the portal upon my return, and close this chapter of my life."

He steps up to the circle, one foot propped on its edge as he turns back for a final wave. He's wearing a suit with many buttons and collars, like the day we first met him. And he's holding the Rat King's scepter, the reward Clara promised him. Hopefully he'll use it in a kinder way than it was used here in Faerie.

"I'm going to paint him like that," Clara whispers. She waves to him.

With a nod, Drosselmeyer steps through the portal.

And vanishes from our lives.

Moments later, the vines that make up the portal ring shudder, then disintegrate into brittle fragments of root and twig.

Turning away from the debris, I slip my arms around Lir's waist. "It's over," I tell him. "You did it. You freed your people."

"I did none of it alone," he says with a sigh, rubbing his hands along my upper arms. "And the work is not yet done. Now you and I must stabilize our kingdom."

Lir is crowned the next day, in a hall of white marble and gold columns and shimmering light. Chills race over my skin multiple times during the ceremony, especially when he seats himself on the throne and a shudder of glorious power runs through the entire realm of Faerie.

At the end of the ceremony, Lir announces that I'm to be his queen, once the land is settled and purged of the final remnants of the Unseelie forces. The few dozen weary, hollow-eyed Fae who are present at the ceremony somehow muster the enthusiasm to cheer for me as I step onto the dais beside Lir. There's no throne for me yet, but there will be soon.

Lir doesn't imprison or kill the cursed Unseelie from the Rat King's lair. He loads the cursed toys into carts and sends them across the border, into the Unseelie kingdom.

"The Rat King is gone, and his armies are decimated," he says. "Let the Unseelie deal with their own as they see fit. Finias tells me not everyone in the Court of Dread wanted this war. Most are pleased with their own land and don't care to conquer others. We should not punish them for the deeds of their ruler and his followers."

It's a new attitude for him—less prejudiced, more accepting. Even though I voiced those same thoughts to him days ago, I find myself not entirely pleased to see his new-found mercy in practice. I can't help thinking of what the Rat King and his Court did to Clara and Finias—and what they *almost* did, before Drosselmeyer showed up. If it were solely up to me, I would not have been so kind.

But the decision is Lir's, and I yield to it. In the future we'll share such choices—he'll push and I'll pull, or the other way around, until we reach a compromise. When I'm impulsive or uncaring, he can be the voice of reason and compassion; when he's anxious, angry, or indignant, I can point out the humor in the situation, ease his tension, and help him focus on our true goals.

And through all of it, we get to have sex. Sex whenever we want, in any place we like, as many times as we want, in any form he chooses to take. I can't imagine ever wanting or needing anyone besides him.

All those others I seduced and kissed and fucked—they each had a taste of what I wanted—freedom, pleasure, love, and power. But if they were a taste, Lir is the meal—satisfying all by himself. Exactly the person I need.

29
CLARA

It's been weeks since Lir's coronation as King of the Court of Delight. Weeks during which Lir and Fin have been gone more often than not, clearing out the monsters that invaded because of the Rat King. The noxious magic the rat-soldiers leaked into the land has cleared, too, and the Seelie kingdom, so quiet and perilous during our travels, has come alive with Fae of all kinds. They crept out of hiding—tall Fae and pixies half my height, hairy fenodyree and mossy gnomes, delicate Racers and fluttering sprites, white deer and flocks of golden birds.

Louisa and I have been staying in the royal city—the most beautiful city I've ever seen. Colonnades draped with winter roses, mirrorlike pools in groves of ice-glazed trees, houses decorated with intricate engravings and exquisite molding, shops covered in ivy, frosted by the breath of winter. There are quaint markets and elegant halls, graceful architecture and cottages so cozy I want to curl up in them and never come out.

Lir gave me a whole hallway in the palace and asked me to paint the history of what happened with Drosselmeyer, himself, and the Rat King; so whenever I'm not wandering the streets with Louisa, exclaiming over everything we see, I'm perched on a stool in the gallery, with my paints laid out around me. The servants have standing orders from Fin to disturb me every two hours so I drink something, and they're also mandated to put me to bed if I'm still working at midnight.

I'm putting the finishing touches on the scene where Drosselmeyer enters the throne room of the Rat King, when Louisa dances into the hallway with a platter of tiny iced cakes in her hand.

"Here." She shoves the platter in front of my nose. "Eat something. Sister's orders."

"Hm." I lean closer to the painting, trying to see if I've got the shading on Drosselmeyer's coat just right.

"Your eyes are tired from being in here for the past two days," Louisa says. "You're coming with me. I've got something to show you."

"Very well." I slide off my stool with a sigh and begin packing away the paints.

My maid, a pixie with brown skin and fiery hair, comes running from the end of the hall. "No, no, Lady Clara, I'll do that."

"But I don't mind. I'm used to it."

"Lady Clara." She gives me a firm look. "This is my job. I'm well-paid to serve you, but you let me do precious little. It's very boring. Please allow me to do this, or I'll go mad. I'll be sure to put everything away exactly as you like it."

"Well, in that case…" I laugh, relinquishing the supplies to her capable hands.

I turn to my sister, but she's frozen, staring at a painting I finished a few days ago—one of her, bleeding and battered, flinging the Nutcracker doll into the Unending Pool.

"You captured it so well," she says quietly. "And you weren't even there."

"You described it vividly." I pluck a cake from the platter she's holding. "You have an artistic sense, too, you know."

"I appreciate art, yes—I see it, but I could never make it. Not like you do. Not like this." She whirls to face me, and I catch one of the cakes as it flies off the platter. "I'm sorry, Clara. I've thought those words, but I haven't said them aloud. I'm sorry for the way I've treated you. For a long time you were the only one who saw me, the only one who listened, and I took advantage of that. I cut you down in little ways, because I felt so small and empty myself. It was wicked of me."

"You're forgiven. And I judged you harshly for your seductions, for taking comfort and pleasure in different people so often. It was wrong of me. We were really just surviving, both of us, in our own ways. Surviving until we could finally come alive. I don't know why I'm crying…" I laugh through a sniffle.

"Do you ever miss it?" Her eyes are brimming with tears too. "Do you miss home, and Papa?"

"I feel guilty that I don't," I whisper.

"So do I." She releases a long sigh, as if the admission is a relief. "I loved him, but it was exhausting, living in a house with so much fear, and so many rules."

"I wish he could have let himself work less, worry less, and live more."

"I know." She grips the platter in one hand, wiping away tears with the back of her wrist. "Enough sentiment! Let's eat sweets and walk in this beautiful city."

We fetch our coats and leave the palace together. Louisa leads me down a sloped street paved in colorful stones, toward the river and the market.

"Think of it, Clara—a lifetime in Faerie, and you get to paint it all. Everything." Her excited breath puffs in the cold air. She does a spin and nearly crashes into a baker's cart. The gnome wheeling it shakes his head at both of us, and we hurry on, stifling giggles.

"And I'm going to be Queen," Louisa continues, more soberly. "I know what you're probably thinking—I'm flighty, and volatile—I make bad decisions and I can be cruel sometimes—"

"Stop." I catch her hand, turning her to face me. "Louisa, I'm happy for you. And I think you'll be just the right sort of queen for Faerie. They don't need someone perfect—a little wickedness might just help you understand your subjects better."

Relief floods her gaze. "I hope so. And Lir is good for me, Clara—he balances me. We balance each other."

I squeeze her hand, then release it as we continue walking.

"And it's not just being Queen," she continues. "Lir wants me as one of his advisors regarding border defense. He says I'm naturally good at strategy and fighting. I'm going to train, Clara, and maybe someday I'll be a captain."

"A captain who loves parties and gowns and sweets." I hook an eyebrow at her.

"And why not?"

"Why not indeed."

"And you," she says gaily, "you and Fin will be so happy too, with the new spells-and-sweets shop, right here in the city—" She stops abruptly, her eyes going wide. "Fuck. I spoiled the surprise."

My stomach does a double-flip. "A shop? For spells and sweets?"

"*And* art. There's a studio space, and a gallery, and living quarters above it all. Fin already put the painting you made him right in the front hall. Stop me before I tell you anything else."

"And Fin," I say, breathless. "Is Fin back?"

My sister takes my hand, squeezing it gently. "He and Lir are waiting for us at the shop. Their dangerous work is done—they won't be leaving again, not for a long time. Or if they do leave, they'll take us along."

My heart swells, warm and bright. "Why are we still standing here?"

I start to run, and she yells after me, laughing, "Clara, you don't know the way!"

I let her pass me, and we race together through the streets until she pulls me to a stop before a large building.

The house is a rambling, multistoried, multicolored thing, pink stone and sage-green roof tiles, bluish ivy powdered with snow, and a yellow front door. It seems to smile at us as we stand there, panting, red-cheeked, and wind-blown.

Before either of us can move to go inside, Finias bursts out of the yellow door, his entire face aglow. I run to him, and he catches me up in his arms—the tightest grip, his face buried against my neck.

"Dearest," he whispers fiercely.

"I missed you," I whisper back.

Something snuffles against my cheek—a tiny adorable face, white-furred and pink-nosed. There's a weasel-cat clinging to Fin's back, peeping over his shoulder at me.

"When I went to fetch my things from the old place, I found Kriss nosing around," Fin says apologetically. "She seemed to want to come along. Do you mind?"

"Of course not!" I hold out my hand, and the little creature gives my fingers a tentative lick with its tiny pink tongue before pattering onto my palm.

As I'm scooping the weasel-cat into my hands, I see Lir lounging in the doorway of the house, his eyes fixed hungrily on my sister. Louisa paces demurely toward him, a little flounce in her step, while his whole body stiffens as if he's trying not to pounce on her.

When she reaches him, she tips her face up, and he leans down. The moment their lips touch, every bit of tension seems to flow out of him, and he relaxes into the kiss, his eyes closing, the sharp tips of his ears flushing pink.

She is his Chosen, and Fin is mine.

We are new to this world, but we've already seen it at its worst. We've endured. We've made mistakes and hurt each other, but we have also become, and overcome.

And we are not afraid. Because a love so imperfectly flawless is all the magic we need to dispel fear.

For bonus chapters from Lir's and Fin's points of view, purchase the hardcover edition of this book or buy the Wicked Darlings Bonus Content volume that collects all the bonus chapters in the series, available on Amazon.

MORE BOOKS by REBECCA F. KENNEY

The WICKED DARLINGS Fae retellings series
A Court of Sugar and Spice
A Court of Hearts and Hunger
A City of Emeralds and Envy
A Prison of Ink and Ice

The MYTHIC HOLIDAYS series
(standalones in theWicked Darlings universe)
A Hunt So Wild and Cruel
A Heart So Cold and Wicked
A Heist for Filthy Rivals

The DARK RULERS adult fantasy romance series
Bride to the Fiend Prince
Captive of the Pirate King
Prize of the Warlord
The Warlord's Treasure
Healer to the Ash King
Pawn of the Cruel Princess
Jailer to the Death God
Slayer of the Pirate Lord

The BELOVED VILLAINS series
The Sea Witch (Little Mermaid retelling with male Sea Witch)
The Maleficent Faerie (Sleeping Beauty retelling with male Maleficent)
The Nameless Trickster (Rumpelstiltskin retelling)
The Midnight King (Cinderella retelling)

THE VAMPIRES WILL SAVE YOU trilogy
The Vampires Will Save You
The Chimera Will Claim You
The Monster Will Rescue You

The MERCILESS DRAGONS series
Serpents of Sky and Flame
Warriors of Wind and Ash
Storm of Blood and Shadow
Wings of Frost and Fury

The GILDED MONSTERS classic retellings series
Beautiful Villain (retelling of "The Great Gatsby")
Charming Devil (retelling of "The Picture of Dorian Gray")
Ruthless Devotion (retelling of "Wuthering Heights")
Cruel Angel (retelling of "The Phantom of the Opera")

The IMMORTAL WARRIORS adult fantasy romance series
Jack Frost
The Gargoyle Protector
Wendy, Darling (Neverland Fae Book 1)
Captain Pan (Neverland Fae Book 2)
Hades: God of the Dead
Apollo: God of the Sun

Related Content: *The Horseman of Sleepy Hollow*

The INFERNAL CONTESTS demon romance books
Interior Design for Demons
Infernal Trials for Humans

Printed in Dunstable, United Kingdom